ALSO BY GRANT GINDER

This Is How It Starts

DRIVER'S EDUCATION

Grant Ginder

Simon & Schuster

New York London Toronto Sydney New Delhi

Simon & Schuster
1230 Avenue of the Americas
New York, NY 10020

First Simon & Schuster hardcover edition January 2013

SIMON & SCHUSTER and colophon are registered trademarks of Simon & Schuster, Inc.

For information about special discounts for bulk purchases, please contact Simon & Schuster Special Sales at 1-866-506-1949 or business@simonandschuster.com.

The Simon & Schuster Speakers Bureau can bring authors to your live event. For more information or to book an event contact the Simon & Schuster Speakers Bureau at 1-866-248-3049 or visit our website at www.simonspeakers.com.

Designed by Nancy Singer

Manufactured in the United States of America

10 9 8 7 6 5 4 3 2 1

Library of Congress Cataloging-in-Publication Data
Ginder, Grant.
Driver's education / Grant Ginder.—1st Simon & Schuster ed.
    p. cm.
I. Title.
PS3607.I4567D75 2013
813'.6—dc232011048981

ISBN 978-1-4391-8735-7
ISBN 978-1-4391-8737-1 (ebook)

For my grandmother, Jacqueline, who taught me to shift into neutral and coast down hills

A well-thought-out story doesn't need to resemble real life.
Life itself tries with all its might to resemble
a well-crafted story.

—*Isaac Babel*

DRIVER'S EDUCATION

WHAT YOU SHOULD KNOW BEFORE

I'm editing scenes from someone else's life when my granddad calls and begs that I bring Lucy to him. That I drive her across the country and collect the endings to all his stories.

"I've lost them, Finn," he says.

I tell him, "That's impossible. You know them all. You've told them to me a thousand times."

He says, "I've forgotten. I'm forgetting."

He's a big man, my granddad, not necessarily in size or proportion, but in other ways, like the manner in which he lives. The trouble in which he finds himself. The magic that he conjures and the spectacular things he believes.

Outside, down on Seventh Avenue, a siren's whirling lights lasso parked cars in ropes of red and blue and white.

"And what's this about Lucy?"

"She's in Chinatown with a man named Yip," he whispers, his voice just clouds of smoke.

"A man named *what?*"

He rattles off an address and I scramble to find a pen, to scratch it on the back of a hamburger wrapper I've got folded on my desk. And it's like he must have his lips pressed against the receiver because honestly it sounds like he's sitting right next to me.

It's after midnight on Wednesday—the first few minutes of what will become an interminable June. And it's hot. It's so damned *hot*. The sort of hot where stripping your clothes off isn't enough; where the only thing you can imagine doing is peeling away your sweat-slicked skin. Letting your organs breathe.

"Granddad?" Aside from the editing bay where I sit, the rest of the office is dark. I fumble for a second before I press pause, managing to stop all the faces on all hundred screens in front of me. "Does Dad know you're calling?"

"I've mailed you a map." His voice grows strained, as though his throat is a hose being twisted, but then he coughs once and he breathes easy. "They're all there. My endings."

"But how will I know where to find them?"

"You will."

"And if I don't?"

"Then," he says, "you'll come up with better ones."

It's been a year and a half since the first stroke. A year and a half since it became clear that the only option for him was to move from here—New York—to San Francisco, in order to live with my father, the Screenwriter.

"But Lucy—"

"She'll get stuck when you shift her from second to third. And her rearview mirror won't do you much good."

Then there's a second cough. "Finn—Finn, do this for me."

I stand up from my chair and the high-definition faces project their smiles, their frowns, their puzzled gazes against my damp T-shirt.

I say, "But, ha. Really. What's this all about?"

His tenor grows, exploding against the walls of the room: *"I need to drive her."*

HOW TO MAP YOUR MEMORIES

Finn

The Arthur Kill is a spit of ocean just below Manhattan's southernmost tip. The Dutch are the guys who named it—"kill" comes from *kille*, which means "riverbed" or "water channel"; "Arthur" comes from *achter*, which means, basically, "back"—though nowadays most people just refer to it as the Staten Island Sound.

In the mornings it's green, the Kill. And in the evenings, when the rest of the bay goes red and gold and silver, it stays brown, the color of weak coffee. It's dredged every now and then, its depth sucked down to about thirty-five feet and its width shrunk to around six hundred so it can maintain its utility as a commercial shipping passage for the barges that slug their way into Port Newark.

It's short—maybe ten miles long—with the port at its head. It snakes down, running almost parallel to Interstate 95, past Elizabethport and Linden, under the Outerbridge Crossing. Alongside New Jersey's steaming industrial sites, its spewing plants, the Chemical Coast.

Before the Kill reaches Raritan Bay, before it spills into the Atlantic, it pools along the southwestern coast of Staten Island, in the low salt marshes near Rossville. There, in those shallow wetlands, you'll find streams made of sewage and hills built on garbage, plastic bottles capping their peaks. You'll find old bikes, rusted tires, kitchen tables, and broken forts; half-eaten things, things that haven't been eaten at all. Condom wrappers and dolls. Buildings, tops of skyscrapers. Leftovers from a closed landfill that, until about a decade ago, was dumped with an unfair ratio of the city's waste, including a huge portion of the September 11 mess.

And then, situated deeper among the plastic and the concrete and the miscellaneous wreckage are the ships—the so many ships—of the Witte Marine Scrapyard, the only boat cemetery I can think of, and definitely the only one I've ever seen.

It opened in 1964, and at one point it had more than four hundred dead and dying craft; J. Arnold Witte, the man who opened the yard, acquired broken and decommissioned vessels faster than he could break them up. Now there are just under two hundred. For the most part the ships are only something of their former selves, wiped blank by time and rain and salt. Their skeletal frames and decayed, rotting beams form these half-submerged labyrinths. Portholes ripped into windows ripped into gaping wide scars. Still, you can find rows of steam tugs that have run aground, their hulls emptied of water and their wooden cabins bare and sun faded. You can find ferries, and car floats, an assortment of different barges that you can still make out. There are remnants of famous crafts, like the New York City Fire Department's *Abram S. Hewitt*, which was the last coal-burning fireboat in the FDNY's armada; there are afterthoughts of ships that were barely given names. They're all there—every species of ship from every decade of the twentieth century—rotting, waiting, biding their lost time.

The water in the shallows isn't green and it isn't brown—it's grey, basically damp ash. It swirls and settles like snow in the city, dirtying the base of the marsh's reeds. It carries with it the rust and the paint of the boats—generations sinking on top of one another.

My friend Randal and I go there on a Sunday. Specifically: the Sunday after the phone call, when my granddad instructed me to bring Lucy to him, to deliver his memories. After I've finally received his sacred map.

Or: the exact same Sunday Randal loses his millionth job and he agrees, without much argument, to leave and drive alongside me.

"We have to do this for the old man," I say. "I owe him."

"Right. But I guess the question is, what do I owe you?"

"I don't know. Something, probably." Then: "Can't you just come with me, though?"

He cocks his head, raps his fist against a ship's rusted berth. "Yeah," he says. "Yeah, sure. I mean, what else am I doing."

We spend three hours at the graveyard, picking through the ruins, calling out names in those cavernous empty hulls. I film it all with a new camera I ended up blowing the better part of my savings on: a Sony 4.15MP Handycam that's got spectacular 150x digital zoom capabilities and a 3.2-inch LCD screen. But then, after I've captured each shot a hundred times over, we feel like we've been sinking too deep. It's become too much, we say. Too much death. And too much nothing. Especially right now, when all we feel is life.

So we return to Manhattan, to the piers along Hudson River Park, where we can make our plans while we watch buoyant ships, hearty and full, play games on the water.

We spy on them with a cheap pair of binoculars that I bought from some nameless store in Times Square. We pass the binoculars back and forth between each other. And when it isn't our turn we suck on the heads of gummi bears and drink piss-warm white wine that we've got swathed in a wet brown paper bag. We look out across the pilings of the piers that no longer exist and we read aloud the names, reciting the berthing ports tattooed in chipped paint along the hulls of the boats.

There are barges, crusted in iron, from Newark; there are long, flat container ships from Seoul that look like they've had their stomachs sliced out; there are bulk carriers from Denmark and tankers from Panama and coasters from up north, in Boston. There are stubborn tugboats. But unlike the ones in the graveyard, these still have their proud barrel chests that patrol the water's open spaces. There are schooners, their sails open and white like so many sharp teeth, from Newfoundland; there are catamarans from Long Beach and single hulls from Athens and these tiny sabots, the kind you can rent down at Chelsea Piers, which look like snowflakes out in the river. And then there are the fishing boats, the trawlers and the seiners and the line vessels delivering their slick, wide-eyed bounties to the Fulton Fish Market over at Hunts Point.

We watch all of them as their bows cut canyons between the two banks of the river, as nervous aluminum skiffs jump the hurdles in the bigger ships' wakes. We are on the pier at the end of West 10th Street, and I'm lying in the grass on my stomach, propping myself up on my elbows while the sun burns my shoulders, causing more and more freckles to explode and align in new constellations on my pale back. Randal drinks wine and sits with his legs crossed in front of him like some skinny Jewish pretzel, and when a clipper ship from London struts out in front of us with its masts blowing upward, he takes the binoculars from me.

On the grass in front of me, I've got my granddad's roadmap, its corners weighed down with so many bright bears.

Randal lifts the binoculars to his face, toggling the focus left, then right.

I met him about a year and a half ago at an Israeli restaurant where he was a bartender. It was on Chrystie Street, on the Lower East Side, not far from where I was living then; it had low black ceilings and dark walls and it was always, always empty. I went the first time because my boss Karen—one of the editors for a reality television show that you've definitely heard of but whose name I won't mention here for professional reasons—was in love with one of the waiters. They ended up moving to Toronto together, and then three months later she bought a dog—a big one—and the waiter came out as gay, so now she's back. Back as my boss, back writing reality fictions. But we didn't know that any of that would ever happen on that night when I met Randal, when he poured me free kosher red wine. As we watched them (or, just Karen, I guess) flirt.

I kept going back to that place on Chrystie to get free wine. Randal eventually got fired from that job, just like he got fired from the rest of them, because he had been too charitable, not just to me but to everyone, pouring glasses that were much too full. Because, really, that's just how he was.

He's still got the binoculars glued to his face and he bites at a piece of dead skin that dangles from his chapped lower lip. The clipper ship stalls. It whips its sails furiously in the wind: the white heads of a Hydra out on the Hudson. He keeps watching it as my elbows sink deeper into the grass and as the freckles on my back multiply and as tiny globes of sweat orbit his curls, sitting on top of his head like tight dark clouds.

"All those ships. Think of all those goddamned sinking ships we just saw. These ones are going to end up doing the same thing." He swats at the camcorder. "Get that thing out of my face, would you?"

I should say this: I'm still not totally sure why he's agreed to go with me—or, at least why he hasn't put up some sort of a fight. I told myself a half hour ago that it was because he views us as I view us: more or less this indestructible pair. A Han Solo/Chewbacca thing. A Batman and Robin. A Rick Blaine/Louis Renault. But there are, if I'm being honest, some other (more realistic?) theories I've also been tossing around.

Like, for example:

#1: Gainful Employment: The job he lost last night (he'd been a waiter at a place where waiters wear cowboy hats) was the last in an epic series of dabblings. He's been a bartender, a locksmith, a janitor at a school for the deaf. He's answered phones and opened doors and sorted mail. He's sold peaches on the corner of Fifty-seventh and First, has collected and traded and often forged the autographs of almost-famous people. And each time he's lost one of those gigs, you get the sense that the orbit he's been following has been jolted. You get the sense that whatever makes shit happen for Randal Baker has hit pause. Or:

#2: A Girl: She lived in Hoboken and they dated for a year until two months ago when, suddenly, they stopped.

I never met her, and I never will, because she's out of the picture now. I've never even been allowed to say her name—I can tell you that much. I know what it is, obviously, but I've never been allowed to say it. I'll start sometimes, for the fun of it. I'll get the first letter, and then first syllable to buzz on my lips, but he'll stop me, usually, by smacking me. He'll say, *Damn it, Finn, what'd I tell you?*

So, the point being: I don't know all that much about her. He's told me stories, though they've never really been enough. I'll ask him—beg, really—to tell me more. He'll try. He'll have a few hesitant starts, but each time he'll stop. He'll sigh. He'll pull at some blades of grass.

I'll ask, "Can I see a picture?"

He'll tie the grass into knots and walk away.

And so. I'll be left with these countless iterations of her. These imagined variations. The Girl as Bardot-ian bombshell—all blond, all tits, voice composed of nothing but gravel and sex. The Girl as Holly Golightly-ish flirt—saying what she feels but never what she means. The Girl as Hayworth—strong-minded, disagreeable, always going to restaurants and ordering something that's not on the menu. The Girl as Phoebe Cates—always getting out of a pool. Just always getting out of a pool.

Basically, whatever it takes for a girl, for This Girl, to have insinuated herself into the vast mythology of Randal Baker. Or to have turned him into something of a romantic, which I think is just about the worst thing a girl can do to a boy.

Or maybe it's just me who is being the romantic. Maybe the real reason it's been so criminally easy to convince him to come along is that—

Theory #3: He's Just That Sort of Person. The type of guy who, if Karen and I saw him in casting footage for the Very Popular Reality Show, we'd define him by a-total-going-along-with-it-ness. A passive quality that has the potential to become suddenly and explosively active. Not a joiner and not a doer—but the person who allows both to exist.

"We'll leave on Tuesday," I say. "After I talk to Karen."

Randal has been looking over my shoulder, stealing glances at the map. "So, okay. Pittsburgh first, it looks like."

"And then Columbus."

"And then Chicago."

"And then—"

"Oh, God, what is that? They all look the same. Is that *Nebraska*?"

I position the camera in my lap with its lens tilted upward, toward the boats and the river and the sky and the lower half of Randal's ear. I take the binoculars from him and I give him back the wine, and after he slugs from it long and thirstily he starts fumbling in the pockets of his khakis. He bites his upper lip and frowns till there's this crevice between his eyes, until finally he claws out a bent cigarette and a BIC lighter with a fish on it.

"Can you say that again?"

He turns his back to me, to the wind, and when he hunches over to light the cigarette I lift the camcorder and zoom in; his spine looks like so many speed bumps.

"Say what?" He exhales and the smoke rushes south. "Say what aga— Finn, Christ. Come on."

So instead I film south toward the Hudson's mouth and the upper bay; toward the boats coming, merging, coughing steam, growling; toward the Statue of Liberty and the northern tip of Staten Island; toward the graveyard, the infinite blueness tricked out in ash.

I leap up. My knees are stained and matted with weeds and they feel light, full of helium. I step from the grass to the pier's pavement, treading lightly as my feet grow warm, then hot against the concrete. I rest my arms against a green guardrail and watch as the light wanes, as its reflection on the Hudson dulls from gold to rust. Everything smells like salt and oil.

Randal follows me, cursing as he hopscotches barefoot across the concrete.

There's the fluid, liquid sigh of traffic behind us on the West Side Highway. I begin picking at a spot where the railing's green paint has chipped. I tear off a large sheet of acrylic from the iron bars, turning it on its side so it looks like a cutout of Florida.

Randal stubs his cigarette against the railing, kicking off the ash, which lands on his toes.

"All right," he says. "Let's see it then."

"See what?"

"The map."

I use my fingernails to peel off another sheet—rectangular, almost perfectly so. I tell myself it's North Dakota, or South Dakota, or Wyoming, or any of those other states that have unmemorable, half-assed shapes. In front of us two kayakers paddle in figure eights.

When I lift the paper it smells ancient and important, like newsprint. The edges are brittle, its creases sharp and yellow. There are lines drawn on it—mostly illegible scribbles in black and blue and red and grey. There are cities and towns circled, places my granddad has been; there are roads, and counties, and—in the case of Florida—an entire state crossed out. Artifacts from his unbounded memories.

And then, in the margins, there are new notes: instructions he's written expressly for me. Like: *In Chicago—Never look the Gangster in the eye.*

I drop North Dakota to the grass and turn to look out at the water. The clipper ship has tacked so the wind is at its rear, pushing its sails out in wide grinning crescents.

We are walking east on Jane Street and the sun floods the thin alleys between low buildings and the reflection, all the reflections, glow white and angelic on the camera's LCD screen. The bricks of the walk-ups around us change from orange to red to brown. A woman with a stroller slows behind us, and we step aside to let her pass.

I lean against a low green wall and bite at the dulled tip of my thumb. I smell like sweat and wine and just-chopped grass.

I rub something from my eye with the bottom hem of my shirt.

He says: "So, you must've considered the possibility by now."

"What possibility?" I can feel the uneven mortar play tic-tac-toe on my back and I wipe at my face again.

"The possibility that maybe he's . . . And that's why he wants to see the car. Just . . . I don't know. So he can drive it one more time before he—or something."

"I see what you're saying—"

"It was just a thought."

"But, ha, it's not the case."

I think about the map. I think about all its lines, printed and scribbled. There are so many of them, the roads. So many ways in which they tie themselves into knots, entwine themselves like the legs of guilty lovers.

"But hypothetically, what if it is."

"Then," I say, "we'll be the ones who save him."

DAD, YOU'RE KILLING ME

Colin

"Dad," I say.

"Colin?"

"You're killing me."

He hacks. First, the dry exasperations of a *k*. But then, something else. Something that submerges and bubbles below the surface: a cough swimming in motor oil.

We sit in the kitchen of a house that I can no longer afford. Four broad windows reach out over the bay, where currents swell beneath the Golden Gate. The sun, flooding in from the east, turns the water to rusted silver. When his coughing subsides, I hand him a napkin so he can wipe his mouth. He folds it unevenly and struggles to slip it into the breast pocket of his blue oxford—the same shirt he wore yesterday, and the day before that. The shirt I wash each evening. The shirt I iron for him every morning after helping him from his bed, before combing his threadbare hair. The only shirt that—now—he'll agree to wear.

"I'd say it's the other way around," he tells me.

I press my mug away from me and I begin spreading butter across two pieces of toast.

"What I'm saying," I say, "is that when you ask me every morning when the last time I sold a script was—that's killing me."

I slice away the bread's burnt crust and hand both pieces to him. He watches them on the chipped plate in front of him, a look of anticipation and then defeat slipping across his face. *But it's toast, Dad. What do you expect it to do? Sing? Dance? Restore your expired youth?*

He holds a finger, curved into an arthritic claw, against the side of his nose. "I ask you that every morning?" He sounds as if his cheeks are stuffed with marbles.

I open the *San Francisco Chronicle* and leaf through the pages until I find the crossword. When he arrived last year, he would beat me at these things; it'd take me two hours to get through one puzzle, whereas he'd finish it in thirty minutes or less.

"Show the doctors that," he'd say. "And then ask them if I need to be living with my son. Ask them if I shouldn't be back at home in New York, where I belong."

I'd tell him, "But, Dad. It's not your head; it's your heart."

Now, though, I'm not sure. He still completes the puzzles—in fact, often faster than he did before. But now once he's growled *Done,* once he's thrust the torn newsprint beneath my nose so I can survey his handiwork, I'll notice mistakes. Missed clues. Answers that don't fit. Three letters shoved into one cramped box.

19 down. Three letters. *Washington bigwig, abbr.:* ASSHOLE
7 down. Five letters. *Grateful:* FOR WHAT
1 across. Four letters. _____ *Boleyn:* LUCY

At first I would circle the flubs in black ink and hand the puzzle back to him. I'd say, *Molière wasn't a Confederate general, Dad.* He'd shake his head defiantly, toast crumbs tossed from the corners of his mouth. *And the clue calls for three letters, second letter E.* He still wouldn't listen, though. He'd hold the point of his pen against the table and lift a single eyebrow in my direction. He'd keep it raised until I'd say, finally, *Yeah, all right. I can see it. Molière at Appomattox. Why not!*

Now I just let him have them.

He still has his finger pressed to the side of his nose, but now he's tapping it slowly. He knits his brows together as he looks at me from across the table, his eyes grazing over the dirtied rims of empty cups, the stacks of my half-finished scripts.

I say, finally, "It was called *The Family Room*. It premiered in nineteen eighty-three. Yes, that's more than twenty years ago. Yes, it starred two very famous people who have since died. Yes, you remember correctly, it was nominated for four awards, but not the Oscar. And yes, you remember even *more* correctly: it won precisely none of them."

He stops his nose tapping. "It's funny—"

"That you never saw that particular movie?"

He nods.

"Yes, I know. Ha, ha, a real hoot. Hilarious every morning!"

I ask him if he's finished with his toast. He looks down at the un-eaten slices and the despair returns to his face: first in the folds where his neck meets his chin, then, climbing upward, to his sagging jowls, his stretched ears, his pocked crown. *You've disappointed me, toast.*

I take the plate and shovel the mess into the trash. I return to fix the collar of his shirt, ignoring him as he mutters to himself, to the table, to the piles of paper: "Nineteen eighty-three was a long time ago."

The call came two Februaries ago in the early afternoon: 1:30 PST/4:30 EST. I had finished my lunch and was cleaning the windows when Finn phoned, repeating all his cries in threes.

"Oh Dad, oh Dad, oh Dad."

"Something's happened, something's happened, something's happened."

"If I hadn't missed the train—I'm sorry, I'm sorry, I'm sorry."

I said, "Finn?"

"Oh, Dad. Oh, Dad, we're at the hospital."

"Stop," I'd instructed him. "Slow down. Explain to me—exactly—what's happened."

He'd arrived in Westchester an hour earlier, he told me. He'd missed the 1:34 train and thus had been forced to wait for the 2:11. He'd come up from the city to visit my father—his grandfather—who was still living in Sleepy Hollow, in the house where I grew up. The two of them had planned to meet at the Tarrytown station, where my father would pick him up in that goddamned car. They'd eat lunch. My father would pour my son some Lowland scotch and offer him cheap cigars. They'd pull from their collections of finely woven stories; they'd trade them with each other, sewing them into imaginary shapes.

But when Finn arrived, my father wasn't there. He waited for an additional half hour. He scanned the parking lot for Lucy's rusted yellow frame, ducking between minivans and sedans, hoping she was hiding somewhere between their hoods. He began to think: maybe his grandfather had gotten tired of waiting and left—Finn was, after all, late. Or maybe she'd broken down again? Maybe he'd been forced to call a mechanic? Or maybe he'd remembered the plans incorrectly? Maybe he was meant to take the bus?

He told me that this had happened before.

My father—he's not all that patient. And he does have a tendency to forget.

Still, though, it wasn't until Finn knocked on the front door and my father didn't answer that he became nervous. That he was hit with the suspicion that something was wrong.

By nine o'clock I've led him into the den, where he'll stare at the television for the next six hours while I work. He'll watch shows I've never seen him watch before, shows that I didn't realize were still on the air. *Bonanza, Charlie's Angels, Diff'rent Strokes.* He'll manage to find every infomercial for every product that should have never been conceived: sleeping bags for cats; plates that double as cheese graters; a set of twelve *katana* samurai swords.

My office sits directly above the den, on the west side of the house, and is cut in the same square shape. The room's blue carpet curls up in each of the four corners, where there are small holes in the floorboards; the frayed empty spaces allow the television's strangled voices to seep upward, to ping-pong off the surfaces of my desk, the sagging bookshelves, my ribs. I try closing my eyes before I turn on the computer's screen.

The truth is, I used to be so good at this. Twenty years ago, blank white sheets used to be wide-open highways, clean, paved roads; conduits to thrilling and accessible places away from myself. I used to fly down them with terrifying certainty, taking the banks and curves at breakneck speeds, never shifting down to fourth; never clamping my heel against the brake; never noticing the wheeze of a tank that's out of gas.

After the near success of *The Family Room,* the calls from studios, producers, and directors found their way to me at a wondrous and alarming rate. *Anything,* they'd tell me. *Just write anything, and we'll get it on the screen.*

And maybe it was the openness of it all, that blank-check promise of success that gummed me up. As the phone rang and the projects accumulated, filling the empty corners of the house, I fumbled and dropped the keys beneath the seat—unable to find the damn things again. The pages became something else: roadblocks. Detours in flashing lights, half the bulbs gone dead. Robust, angry trucks jackknifed on tight mountain roads. I'd spend months constructing two lines of dialogue, convincing myself I'd been productive if I managed to change two strokes of punctuation. I'd paint scenes with no sense of space, races with no sense of time.

Trash bins became bonfires, piled high with half-used sheets.

In the evenings, I'd call the producers and the agents, situated high in their glass Rubik's Cubes along Wilshire Boulevard. I'd pant into the phone, feigning a sense of excited exhaustion, as if I'd come in from running a marathon, as if I hadn't spent the day recumbent on the floor of my office, picking at the corners of the carpet, watching the way shadows chased themselves on the ceiling. *Just a little more time,* I'd beg them. *I need just a little more time.* They stopped calling back.

I worked odd jobs, and sometimes I still do. These low-glam assignments sent my way by folks who're too young to have heard the news. A one-episode script for a sitcom that failed after a few seasons. Four commercials for an acne cream. A set of jokes for the People's Choice Awards. But no screenplays.

You're right about that, Dad.

It wasn't, though, for lack of trying. I spent years taking stabs at other genres, forms of storytelling either more marketable or obscure: romance, mystery, comedy, French art house. I'd start each of these projects with a sincere and earnest belief in my genius; a sense that, finally, my feet were lifting off the ground; that, finally, I'd managed to kick-start the engine. But then I'd turn back. I'd look upon the draft's first pages. I'd read, *Why don't we get out of these wet clothes?*

I listen to the synthetic cries of his infomercials as I leaf through these drafts, set at angles on my desk; I run a finger along their yellowed edges.

What Happens at the Water Cooler . . . ; The Empty Garage; The Vintage of Love; Punching Horses; Congress! The Musical; Only Swallows Cry at Night; Bottoms Up; The Grass Is Always Greener; The Apples in the Attic; Two Days After Yesterday; The Sand Is Full of Grains; Her Dangerous Heart; The Ventilator; The Vaporizer; The Blender; Punching Horses, Again; Longing Is a Breadless Toaster; Palm Fronds at Dusk; Bottoms Down; Kappa Kappa Killer; Don't-Post-It; Windmills Only Turn Once.

No. No, it was *Palm Fronds at* Dawn.

I arrived at Phelps Memorial Hospital the day after Finn called. I was groggy from the overnight flight, the skin beneath my eyes ringed and purple—but still, he looked worse. His cheeks were flushed red, and his hair—auburn, the color of my father's, the color of mine—was matted with something: sweat. He'd pulled a plastic chair to the side of my father's bed and he lay there, his head resting on the mattress next to his feet, his thin hands folded on top of each other, propping up his chin. There were four empty cups of orange Jell-O stacked at his feet.

My father had had a stroke, is what Finn had told me when he called, and what the doctors at Phelps Memorial reiterated. Technically speaking: a thrombotic stroke, caused by a blood clot in one of his arteries, blocking the flow of blood to his brain. When my father didn't answer the door, Finn had unlocked it with a key he'd been given. There was a kettle of water that was boiling over on the stove, drops hitting the range with an exaggerated hiss. Once he'd switched off the burner, he called my father's name out in the kitchen. And then in the foyer, in the living room, in the garage, under Lucy. He opened closets, pushed aside moth-ridden coats drooping from their hangers. He said, in that voice he's got that's somewhere between a laugh and a whimper, *All right, Granddad. Now I'm starting to get worried.*

Where he found him was in the bathroom. The bathroom Mom used to use, across from their bedroom. He was sitting on the toilet with its lid closed, his pants still up but his belt unbuckled. Finn put a hand on his shoulder and shook him gently, but he couldn't lift his chin: he'd raise it to about ninety degrees, so he was gazing at Finn's belly, but then— then his head would fall again, thudding against his concave chest.

"I tried again," Finn would later tell me. "And again, and again! I said, 'It's me, Granddad, it's Finn.' But his eyes were droopy. Like sleepy cartoon eyes. He just sort of looked past me."

I wish I could say I reacted to Finn's call in a way that'd make my father proud. That, after I heard the news, there was the initial icing of my veins, followed by a flow of heated panic. That once I'd found my wits again there was—obviously, and obligatorily—a sense of guilt. Guilt that I hadn't been there; guilt that I hadn't prevented my son from being propelled to that age where death becomes routine. Despite everything that my father had done to me, guilt that when his chin was lifted in my mom's bathroom, it was my son's face he saw with his half-closed eyes. All of that.

Once I'd cradled the phone, I choked on my own throat till I induced tears; I paced the kitchen; I glanced in the mirror, verified that I looked distressed. But if I'm being honest, all that hit me was a slow-burning envy. The sort of twisted jealousy you feel when something awful happens to someone else, something that should've happened to you. That wrench you feel in your gut when someone recounts a particularly harrowing car accident; schadenfreude in reverse. The sudden knowledge that once my father's gone, once he's dust, I won't be able to recount to friends, in hurried sobs, about the Time I Found Him There.

In the hospital, I had stepped out into the bleached hallway so Finn could continue sleeping, and I asked the attending doctor, "So, how bad are we talking?"

"Bad, but not disastrous," she told me. Doctors are wonderfully inadvertent liars.

"You'll forgive me, but I really don't know the difference."

The doctor looked too young, too frazzled. I wanted to comb her hair and wash her face. To say, *If you're telling me all this, at least try to look presentable.*

"He's lost function in his brain stem and portions of his cerebellum."

"Again—I'm sorry, but I don't—"

She pulled at her hair, which wasn't blond, but also wasn't brown—some unwashed tone in between. She wrapped it around one finger, like I'd seen my son do while he worked.

"He's lost some basic muscle functions, particularly on the left side. He'll have trouble walking, swallowing, maybe writing. And talking. Definitely talking."

"Well," I told her. "Ha. Well, there's a silver lining."

She continued pulling her hair, a little more aggressively than before.

I turned my feet inward, as if I were preparing for this girl to chastise me. To throw me out of the hospital and leave my father to my son. I said into my shoulder, "Maybe that was a little too soon."

She only let go of her hair when she shrugged—*He's your fucking father.* She reached into the pockets of her white coat—the sort of pockets that initially you don't notice, but when you do they seem infinite—and she handed me a set of blue brochures. Pictures of old people, falling apart people, their children steadying their walkers. Everyone smiling.

"We have a wonderful stroke clinic here at the hospital." She nodded at the brochures.

I looked through the thin window in the door that separated me from my father, me from Finn. Finn still slept, though now he was dreaming. Reflexively, a foot kicked out, scattering the Jell-O cups in four different directions.

"And he'll learn to speak again?" I asked.

"Really, Mr. McPhee. Look into it."

"Coooooooooollllllllliiiiiiiiiiiin!!!!!!!!!"

When he calls my name, I hear it in two places: first, through the floorboards, in those spaces where the carpet's peeled away; his voice hits my feet and reverberates through my shins. Then, through the open door of my office, after it's traveled through the house's diagonal corridors, picking up dust and other bits of life.

He calls again, this time louder, both voices hitting me almost at once: "COOOOOOOOLLLLLLLLLLLLIIIIIIIIIIIIIN!"

I drop to my hands and knees and crawl to the northeast corner of the room, where the hole in the floor is the largest. "Jesus, Dad." I have my mouth pressed against the floor. It tastes new, but also very old: industrial musk. "WHAT?"

"IT'S STARTING, COOOOOOOOLLLLLLIIIIIIIIIIN!!!!"

I scramble to my feet and arch my back, feeling the hinged pop of my spine cracking. There's a single round window in this room, cut in quarters by four wood beams. Outside, there are two clouds, one to the west of the bridge, and one to the east; they cast shadows onto the bay. At my desk I check the time: 12:27. I've been slumped here, folded over myself for three and a half hours. I've pulled up a fresh page on the computer, but I've yet to write a goddamned word.

Downstairs, in the den, the blinds have been pulled shut, the light pushing through them in aggravated spits. I carry in two highball glasses of Lowland scotch. If he had his choice he'd start drinking at eight; I insist he wait till after noon.

I find him sprawled in the middle of the couch, his loose skin spreading out, blending into the beige leather. As he's sunk down within the cushion, the belt he has to wear has crept up his torso. It sits uselessly now. It hangs from his chest, where it's bunched his oxford, the collar now clinging to his ears, like a hood. His white hairless stomach lifts, falls, exposed.

"Dad." I flip on the lights, raise open the blinds. "Let's get you up. Let's fix this thing."

"I'm fine. We'll miss it."

"Knock it off, we've got two minutes."

I crouch before him, planting my heels on either side of his feet. I try to remember what the nurses told me: Slip both hands upward, under the belt. Lift, don't lean. Use your legs, not your back. His head to your chest as you pull upward; hoisting sloshing buckets of water from a well.

"Press into me, Dad."

"I told you I'm fine."

"You're not making this any easier."

People always say that the old have a distinct scent. Cough drops, I've heard. Or vitamins. Also cucumbers. And as his chin dissolves into my chest, as his arms hang limply to the middle of his thighs, I wish that was the case. That he smelled like an accumulation of all those things, instead of like me. Just like me.

"Okay," I say. "Now—set your hands on my waist."

He presses his lips together and then curls them inward toward his teeth; they vanish into each other, lineless pockets of skin. He mumbles, but without making any sounds.

"Dad, please—just put your hands on my waist so you can steady yourself."

"We're missing the start of it," he says.

"We won't miss anything."

His hands don't move. They continue to hang, but now with added weight and defiant girth. He won't look at me.

"Fine," I tell him. "Try not to fall."

I pull the shirt down first, releasing it from his neck, adjusting its collar so it sits squarely on his breastbone, buttoning the flaps over his exposed flesh. Then, the belt: I twist the canvas as I lower it to his waist. He yelps as it pulls against his skin; I go tense.

"Shit. Shit, I'm sorry, Dad. Just one more pull."

When I've lowered him back to the sofa, and when I've taken my place next to him, he says, "We've missed it."

"We haven't missed anything. It's twelve thirty-one."

"Then." He lifts a chin toward the television, where there's an infomercial for a pillow that changes temperature as you sleep. "Then the television is broken."

"It's not broken. It's just on the wrong station. Let me change it."

I find the remote control wedged between two cushions. I scan upward, pass network television, basic cable, basic premium, the various stations I can't afford but have bought since his arrival, for his entertainment; I climb to channels that are higher than I believed channels existed. I stop when I see the girls: padded knees and stickered helmets. Painted roller skates.

Watching Derby Death Match 2000: I'd say that it's one of the more beguiling rituals we've accidentally adopted over the past fifteen months. I can't remember how it started. Did I, during one of my panicked fits to entertain him, think that girls in skates, bludgeoning one another into a pulp of tits and ass, might serve as some sort of balm? Or was it him? When he could still operate the controller, before the damned thing became some tormented maze, was it then that he stumbled upon channel 378? When he called me down anxiously and said, *Colin, look. Look at this.*

The two teams competing today are the ShEvil Dead and the Wrecking Belles. On the screen, the rosters: names like Angel Maker and Astronaughty; Edith Shred and Sugar Pusher. The pivots and the blockers align themselves in packs—slender, beautiful, wicked—while the two jammers square off behind them. Then, once the referee has blown his whistle, and once the first pivot has been slammed to the track, we begin our separate game.

"That one," he says. "The lady who just fell—she has the cheekbones."

"Windigo Jones? Her nose sits too high on her forehead." I lean forward. "The Wrecking Belles jammer, though. She's about her height."

"She wasn't that tall."

"The helmet adds a few inches."

As the girls fall down, we speed up:

"That one."

"Or that one."

"Or that one."

But the fact is none of them look like Mom.

He entered Phelps Memorial's stroke recovery clinic forty-eight hours after Finn found him. He stayed there for two weeks before it was suggested, or encouraged—by doctors, nurses, therapists, administrative assistants, men in plain clothes on the streets—that he either move into a home or, alternatively, to San Francisco to live with me.

Neither of us could afford a home—so. Well—yes. So.

I remained in Westchester for the entirety of his rehabilitation: I stayed at a Howard Johnson Inn a half mile from the grounds. Each afternoon, when Finn had completed his vague work in the city, he'd take the 5:27 Metro-North to Tarrytown. We'd eat burgers, or chicken fingers, or—once—fish sticks at one of those nameless restaurants that populate the strip malls along the lower Hudson.

As we folded ketchup-stained wax wrappers in our fists, he'd say, "If I hadn't missed my train, I would've gotten there sooner."

I'd tell him, "Oh, Finn. These things just happen."

And he'd answer with, "But still."

Then, if it wasn't snowing—or even if it was—we'd walk to see him.

The recovery center itself was brief and unimpressive: a two-story wing tagged onto the hospital's administrative hub. An afterthought, if anything, whose thin grey corridors played stage to the choreographed movements of halted walkers and slippered, shuffling feet. It faced directly west, so the individual rooms were flooded with too much light in the afternoons—or, in the mornings, none at all.

His rehabilitation therapist was a blond woman named Christie, who had a soft, Judy Garland disposition couched within a runner's sinewy build. She was tireless in her efforts; she'd point to his left hand and say, *Now, move these three fingers, good, good,* while I wanted to scream, *Oh, come on, just* lift *the damned things.* She instructed him in these movements—shifting in bed, sitting up, swinging his legs to one side—and, when he couldn't accomplish a task on his own, she'd place a hand on the small of his back, guide him through it.

She taught Finn and me how to handle him and bear his weight.

"This is called a guard belt," she said one day, unraveling a strap of milky-grey canvas three inches wide. "Fasten it above his belt line. The top of the belt should hit the bottom of his rib cage."

"What's the purpose?"

"It'll give you something to hang on to."

"And he'll need to wear it—"

"Always."

He was perched on the bed, facing us, and we talked about him as if he weren't there.

"When you lift him, rope your arms under his and take hold of the belt's back strap," Christie said. "Give him a count, then pull him up and into you."

We watched as she performed. As she raised him—him, weighing nothing at all—from the bed and into her arms.

"Have him rest against you as you both catch your breath."

His head lodged and snuggled between her breasts as she spoke. The corners of his mouth twitched up in a smile.

I told her, "Christie, maybe show us how you did that again."

Finn bit and tore at his nails. He said, "I'm just afraid I'm going to break him."

"Where are you going?" he asks when the match has ended; the Wrecking Belles have taken it by twelve.

"Just upstairs, Dad. To work."

"What if the television stops working again?"

I look toward the screen. Purple-haired girls are sweaty, high-fiving, hitting helmets as the production credits roll.

"It's not broken," I say.

"And you'll just be upstairs?"

"Just upstairs."

Here's another change: when he first came here—when he was still able to complete a crossword puzzle, when he was still indignant and irritated by California—he wasn't like this. The idea that his survival hinged on my aid infuriated him. He wouldn't call for me when he should have: more than once, I found him sprawled in a pile of limbs on the floor, his hand gripped desperately around some table leg or chair or lamp as he tried to lift himself. And when I did help him, I could feel the reluctance in his muscles each time I'd lift him, how they'd tighten and strain, and resist my pull.

He's still stubborn like all hell. But now, as his mind has fogged over, he's started to panic whenever he's alone. Doors aren't doors to other rooms, they're doors to some total disappearance. It started about six months ago: I had left to run an errand, maybe, or to take a walk, to remember there's something beyond this house, only to return and find him trembling, sweaty.

"Where the hell were you?" he shouted.

"Jesus, Dad." I lowered him to a chair. "Out. Walking."

"To where? TO CHINA?"

"What? No." I brought him some water. "Would you just— Christ, would you just calm down?"

I started, then, to leave the portable phone in his lap whenever I left the room, the house.

"Who am I supposed to call?" he asked.

"I don't know," I told him. "Finn?"

So, he did. Often. Twelve times before noon, according to one phone bill. But he dialed other places too: numbers that no longer existed, people who'd long since died. Occasionally, strangers. He'd press the receiver to his ear, holding his breath as they repeated *Hello,* as they said, *Who is this?* Then, when he'd run out of people to call, when he'd exhausted his catalog of numbers, he'd listen in on my conversations. I'd be pleading with a producer, with an agent, and there it would be—his smothered cough. "Dad," I'd say. And then: "Excuse me, I'll have to call you back."

After that pattern repeated itself enough times, after I'd lost enough jobs, failed at enough pitches, I bought him a mobile phone. One of those hulking devices designed specifically for people who're too old to operate them: numbers the size of half dollars; screens as big as picture frames. A red button in the dead center of the keypad that reads EMERGENCY.

"It's not for me, obviously," I'd told the young salesgirl at the electronics store. "I mean, ha ha, have you ever seen anything so big? It's for my dad. Can't get the guy to stop listening in on my calls, ha ha. Old people, though. What're you going to do?"

She'd asked, "Would you like your receipt?"

On the way to my office, I make it through the kitchen and to the first creaky stair before he yells, "Colin?"

"I'm still here."

The blank page on the computer is still taunting me, flashing about its plainness, its unwrittenness. Downstairs, through the holes in the floor, I hear him coughing again. Hesitantly, almost as if the keyboard in front of me is painful to touch, as if it'll reach out and claw my fingers if I get too close, I begin to write.

HOW TO MAKE LIFE BEAUTIFUL

Finn

It's 7:30 on Monday morning and I'm doing 360s in my swivel chair at work. I still have my granddad's map in my pocket.

After I stop spinning, I shove a pen into my mouth and chew, leaving tiny craters in the black plastic. I've had a nagging difficulty sleeping during the past year, ever since my granddad moved in with my dad. It's not that I've been plagued with horrible dreams, I don't think. Like the sort of nightmares involving death and forgetting and disease? It's more the fact that I've been having no dreams at all. I've only seen the back of my eyelids before I fall asleep, and I'll see them and only them again as I awake: I see exactly nothing in between. These periods of nothingness will last sometimes for five minutes, sometimes for two hours—but always, always it's the absence of something, as opposed to the presence of it, that jolts me back to consciousness again.

The phone on my desk rings. I look at the number displayed on the caller ID screen, and I see that it isn't my granddad or Karen, who always calls when she has some extremely urgent crisis that she needs my help fixing, so I let it go. I just watch it till it shuts itself up.

The headquarters of the network that airs the reality program on which I work is located in Times Square. But our offices—the show's writing and production offices—are farther south near Thirtieth Street, carved out of the fifteenth floor of a building along the west side of Seventh Avenue. It's a crowded section of the city if for no other reason than it acts as a corridor to more desirable places. We're south of Penn Station, but too north to be considered part of Chelsea proper. We experience all the annoyances generated by the mobs in Times Square and Herald Square, though none of the fleeting benefits of being positioned in either of the two. (Street food! An abundance of take-out coffee places! So many nine-story candy megashops!) We're in an infertile urban valley, we say, because occasionally we'll say things like that, a valley whose arid grounds are stampeded by tourists and salesmen and lawyers and God-knows-who-else every single day.

And like I said: the show itself is very famous, or at least used to be, though—again—for professional reasons I'll refrain from mentioning its name now. Just know that each season chronicles the lives of a handful of youngish adults (youngish being qualified as eighteen to twenty-four, though casting will make exceptions to this rule, particularly if someone is thought to have television potential) for roughly six months while they live, together, in a very expensive house in a very expensive city.

I was hired two years ago—when I was twenty-one and when I had first moved to New York—as a production assistant for this particular show, and then was promoted to the position of assistant story editor once Karen returned from Toronto, after she bought her large dog, after the gay Israeli waiter had finally come out of the closet. Most people argue that having a story editor guide the action of a reality show makes that reality inherently untrue, which I'll concede is a solid (but totally unoriginal) point. What you've got to understand is that we are more interested in massaging the order in which certain events happen as opposed to creating new events entirely.

But sometimes, ha, sometimes we do that too.

Because as Karen describes it to me: Reality is a perfectly fine concept, but in our line of work it's entertainment that's crucial. And you can't expect—you can't just hope—that beginnings, middles, ends, that sympathetic characters and goals, conflicts, and resolutions; that soul-lifting, heart-wrenching *entertainment* will somehow magically mold itself from hundreds of hours of footage of *reality*. Particularly, I think, when that footage is of youngish adults.

And so anyway that's what we do; we are diviners. We sift through hundreds and hundreds and hundreds of hours of footage, deciding what is interesting, what isn't, who makes things works, who doesn't. We work backward to link together sequences of events and plot twists; we massage and rub and pull and stretch; we cut, zoom, pan, and recut our narratives. We do all these things until we turn reality into what everyone wants it to be, until we turn it into something sculpted and spectacular.

I enjoy it and I'm good at it, I'd like to think. During these mornings, when I come to work early, or during nights when I stay at work late, I'll sit at our editing bays, surrounded by logged tapes and the vacant cubicles of our empty office. I'll sit alone with the overhead lights off and I'll watch them, the tapes, so many times over again.

I'll slow down the footage of the cast members; I'll speed it up. I can tell you who looks the prettiest when she cries, or the most terrifying when he laughs. I can tell you whose smile is real, and whose is fake, and what percent of the time. I can tell you that when he's nervous, or uncomfortable, he'll start grinding his teeth. I can tell you that she peels away her cuticles when there's something or nothing to do. I can tell you which sort of men find her lack of beauty appealing.

I can tell you about the sort of devastating melancholy that seizes them when they realize they can no longer surprise one another.

But there's something in it, honestly. Something in turning ordinary people into these exceptional and exciting creatures. It is, I think, the very basic illusion that if I can move one piece, or shift one talk, or misplace one mistake, then I, me, Finn, can create something fascinating and wonderful and wholly unique.

So I'll splice arguments together sequentially, how they are supposed to happen, from fight to discussion to reconciliation. And then I'll switch the order—I'll turn reconciliations into catalysts for fights, sobbing admissions into causes for looped laughter. I'll succumb to some of my own youngish adult impulses and edit footage involving first kisses together with bouts of drunken vomiting. I'll run footage of dialogue in reverse. I'll slip in sound bites from other conversations into scenes where such bites don't belong: five minutes of seven people telling one another to *answer the phone* and nothing else; five minutes of seven people telling one another *I hate you,* telling one another *leave me alone,* telling one another *I love you. I love you, I love you, I love you.*

Then, as the morning grows late and as the cubicles around me become less vacant and as the city becomes more crowded, I'll erase it all and start over again.

By noon—this noon and every noon—I'm tired, but not tired enough to sleep. My eyes are crossed and the pull of the building's air-conditioning has left them scratchy and dry. I go to see Karen.

The glass door to her office is open, but I knock anyway, and she says, *Yes, Finn, come in.* It faces west, her office. But we are only on the fifteenth floor and we are surrounded by buildings that are much taller, much grander than ours, and so the view to the river is blocked; each day Karen stares into a medical services company and—much farther below—the pocked roof of a T.G.I. Friday's.

She hides each day behind three wide computer screens and at least a thousand pictures of Hugo, that goddamn dog. There's always seemed something a little insincere about them. Almost as if their joint purpose is to remind her that she loves him. That despite what she wants to believe Hugo isn't the reason the Israeli waiter has decided he likes boys. There are these moments when I imagine her alone in her glass office, sitting Indian style on the rough blue carpet with the frames piled high in her lap. They reach past her shoulders, past her small ears, until they press their flat faces against the ceiling. She'll hug them. She'll press her wet face against their soft wood corners. She'll say, *It's not your fault,* without really knowing whom she's speaking to.

Or I don't know. Maybe she doesn't do any of that. Maybe she really does love that goddamn dog. Though I don't know what's to love, really. He's basically just brown, and he has indigestion problems, and he often smells like salmon.

"Have you ever been to Pittsburgh?" I walk past her desk and stand at the window and watch a million people perform medical services at a million grey desks.

"Yes." Her eyes stay fixed on the three screens. On two of them: paused raw footage from the show, profiles of The Boy and The Girl, strong aristocratic noses leading their faces as they walked away from each other. On the other: rotating still shots of Hugo. Hugo in the bath. Hugo at the beach. Hugo reclined on a shag carpet, legs spread like Mata Hari.

"What's it like?"

"It's awful."

"How awful?"

She clicks something and the footage crawls forward at a fourth of its original speed, the space between The Girl and The Boy stretching.

"Better than Cleveland but worse than Philadelphia." Then: "This isn't working. This shot isn't working."

Her eyes have rings around them, but they aren't sunken and dark. They are flushed in white, skin pale and thin. We all have this look. All of us who've come to realize that our lives are best lived through the lives of others.

I say, "I've never been to Cleveland," and I pull up a chair next to her.

She toggles the footage and plays it again. They are arguing about something, something that someone has said to someone else that is true, but not entirely.

"There," Karen says, pausing the footage. She pushes phantom hair from her forehead. She cut it short and spiked it when she returned from Toronto. "I don't know what the problem is—but it's *there*."

I pull my chair closer. I bring my face next to hers. I say, "I'm going to have to go away for a while."

"This needs to be fixed. We need the ratings." Then: "Oh?"

I say again, "I'm going to have to go away for a while."

I roll the chair away from her and I sit with my hands folded in my lap and so does she and we both look at each other.

Outside Karen's office, at one of the editing bays, someone keeps playing a clip of one of the youngish adults laughing, hyperventilating.

"I'm guessing, then, that it's happening?" she says.

"Explain what you mean when you say *it's happening*."

Karen pulls at her hair. She says, *I'm sorry,* which I'm already tired of hearing, even though I haven't heard it yet. Whoever is editing has stopped working on the laughing clip and has moved on to splicing together a thirty-second conversation about someone vomiting from a roof, topless, or pantless, which is played both forward and backward, English turning into gibberish and then back into English again.

She stands. She rests a hand lightly on top of my head, walking around me to the window. She looks out through tears in the skyline toward slits of atmosphere. Blue streaked with cirrus clouds, white afterthoughts stretching the length of Manhattan.

"How much time do you have?"

"To do what?"

"Before he . . ." She trails off. She starts again. This time saying, "I just assumed that, possibly, something had happened with your grandfather. Because of . . . That maybe he had . . ."

"He's fine," I say, suddenly aware that I might be shouting. "He's just asked me to do him a favor." Then: "And I owe him. I mean, you *know* I owe him."

"I don't know if that's necessarily true."

She picks up one of the 3 million pictures of Hugo. She traces the edge of the frame with her forefinger, the nail bitten down to the raw pink flesh.

She says, "Well, again. I'm sorry."

"Maybe you should stop saying that?"

She sets the frame on a small glass table beside the window. "I don't know what to do with that clip."

"Let me look at it."

"I don't think you know what you're doing."

"But you taught me everything I know."

"I'm not talking about the clip."

"I think," I tell her, "I liked your hair better when it was long."

I spin in the chair till I'm facing the three computer screens. Karen has paused the footage at this moment where The Girl has her top lip sucked against her teeth. Her forehead has three thin creases. I toggle the controls, moving the scene forward, then backward. Lips sucked in, then pushed out; creases, then no creases, then creases again.

I can tell that she's taken a step toward me; her shadow eclipses the screens, I can smell the turkey, the mustard she ate for lunch. I can feel her hands resting slightly over the dome of my head, wanting to touch it, but not. Afraid she'll break something.

She just says: *Finn.*

I scratch at the space between my eyes. I run the tapes again. What bothers Karen, what she can't articulate, is this: at the moment of highest intensity, when you'd expect there to be a slap, or a kiss, or something wonderfully offensive, The Girl turns the other way. That's it—she just turns the other way. I think that, too often, it's the decency of people that always confuses us.

Karen keeps talking. "Have you ever noticed how the people on the street, on Seventh Avenue, move faster than the clouds? Maybe it makes sense, but I don't think it should. People moving faster than clouds. There's just something that seems so wrong about that, you know? Just so disrespectful. They should have the decency to move at the same pace, at the very least."

"You should air the footage backward," I say, finally.

"Sorry?"

"That's really all you have to do. Just—watch. Play the footage backward, and use that in the final cut." I show her: The Girl turns toward The Boy; the creases in her forehead smooth themselves into clean flesh; her lips relax. They look at each other.

She says, "I worry about you, sometimes."

"What do you mean?"

"I worry that I've taught you too much." Then, as she finally touches me. As she pokes me softly in the nose: "I worry that you've watched too much reality TV."

WHAT I REMEMBER

1956: The Avalon

By Colin A. McPhee

The Avalon Cinema was on Saw Mill Road, an eight-minute bike ride from the house in which I was raised. The night that it opened, the theater rented two spotlights from a company called Ducky Joe's that was based in the Bronx—but those globes only spent twenty-five minutes tracing circles in the sky. For the rest of the eight hours they were on loan, they beamed straight into the theater's lobby. Blinking, searching.

"There has been a break-in," the lobby manager announced to the crowds who were huddled in frozen pockets outside the theater's glass and gold doors. His voice trailed to the rear of the pack, and as it did it collected whispers of gossip from the other onlookers. This was a town with a population well under ten thousand people, and General Eisenhower was sailing easily into his second term as president; crimes were small and inconsequential and received disproportionate amounts of thrill and fanfare. People stood on their toes to get a better look. Fathers placed sons on their shoulders.

It was a boy, a woman relayed to those surrounding her. At one moment he'd been standing near the front of the audience that had gathered near the glass doors ten minutes before they opened, his hands placed in his pockets as the excited and anonymous moviegoers enveloped the space around him. No one had recognized him, though it's questionable if anyone tried. He was ten, or maybe twelve, or maybe eight, but it was said that he already had the lean ropy look of a runner, a jumper. This was all easy to see, even though he wore a sweater that was one size two big (it was blue, but also it could've been yellow). He had half-weary eyes and skin crusted with film from the city.

The boy hadn't looked nervous, or maybe he had, as the crowd doubled, then tripled, and then quadrupled. He'd looked up at the silver and green neon sign—THE AVALON—that crowned the theater's marquee, and he replaced strands of his stringed hair that fell in front of his face while regarding his reflection in the theater's glass and metal doors. At one point, he'd tried to reach out and run a finger along the gold engravings that adorned the doors' frames, but the lobby manager— who stood guard in front of the theater before it officially opened—had slapped his hand away. So the boy went back to combing his hair with his fingers.

"And he was alone?" someone asked.

Completely alone—or maybe not completely alone? It was difficult to tell. There had been other boys around him, but they didn't have his look. They'd appeared better fed, more filled out. They wore V-neck sweaters and wool caps and their skin was scrubbed clean. They'd stood at deliberate distances from him: the sort of preconceptualized space that boys imagine will prevent Them from turning into Him.

Because this was the Avalon's grand opening, there were vendors from the theater who stalked the crowd as we waited to get in. They wore striped caps and carried trays that wielded Coke and candy, popcorn with butter that clung to the evening's fog, wormed its way into our noses. A man bought some for his wife and daughter and they ate it in greedy handfuls.

The same woman who'd been speaking explained that the boy had bought some too—popcorn, that is. Or maybe it was a box of something else—chocolates, Flicks. He hadn't eaten it, though, and that was the strange thing. He'd held it to his chest very piously, as if it were some sort of offering. As if he were paying his tithe before kneeling for communion.

The woman said, "And then, suddenly, he was gone."

"Gone?" someone else asked.

"*Gone.*" The woman nodded.

A mother who was listening to the story tightened her coat across her chest, pulling each lapel to the opposite shoulder. "Where did he go?" she asked.

The woman explained that it all happened so fast—or, not so fast, but *at once*—which is what the people standing in front of her had heard. The lobby manager (a man whose name we gleaned was Earl) had opened the doors at 7:30 with great pomp and aplomb, telling the crowd of hundreds that they were to be canonized as part of Sleepy Hollow lore, or Sleepy Hollow history, or the Annals of Cinema, or the Epics of Film, or all of the above, depending on whom in the crowd you asked.

But then, right as Earl had finished his speech, a girl from the crowd, an almost-pretty young thing with cropped dark hair, gasped and pointed.

She yelled, "What the—"

The crowd gazed past Earl and into the lobby's center, where the boy had suddenly materialized under the glows and shadows of the theater's lights and pillars. He was still holding his popcorn, and he ate the kernels casually, nonchalantly, as he stared back at the crowd. He scuffed his heels against the red carpet as he leaned against a pillar as thick as a sycamore. The manager tugged at the tails of his coat; his eyes narrowed and he shouted to his staff, "Get that boy!"

The two ushers stormed into the lobby and reached for the boy's heels, his hips, his shoulders, his head, but whenever they caught hold of him he'd vanish at once (as it happens, on that evening everything was *at once*). It was a tired and half-witted bout, and when it was over they'd be left with nothing more than locks of his greased hair.

"But how'd he get in there?" someone asked the woman.

"No one knows."

"And where is he now?" the mother asked.

"In there, somewhere," she said, pointing past the heads milling in front of us to the theater's entrance.

A father whispered up to a son, who was sitting on his shoulders, "I bet he snuck in through the back door. Always sneak in through the back door."

When the snow started, they let us in. They hadn't found the boy, but Earl, the lobby manager, told us that in all likelihood he'd disappeared—crawled back to wherever it was he'd come from.

The picture shown at the Avalon that night was *The Tender Trap*, with Frank Sinatra and Debbie Reynolds; it was the first picture ever shown at the Avalon, and also the first picture I had ever seen. People shifted uncomfortably at first, afraid of where the boy lurked, of what intruder stalked beneath their seats. I sat still, though. I was nestled between my parents, my knees pulled to my chest, as the projection flickered and filled the screen. I held my breath as Edward R. Murrow introduced the prologue, a short science fiction piece called *From the Earth to the Moon*. I kept it held through the footage of the rocket blasting away from earth, through the prologue's conclusion and the film's actual beginning, Sinatra cycling through Lola Albright, Carolyn Jones, Jarma Lewis.

"Breathe, Colin," my mother pressed her lips to my ear and whispered.

But I couldn't—or, I must have, but nothing more than quick gasps, and only when I absolutely had to. I was afraid that if I made any larger action—my chest rising as my lungs filled with air, or falling as I exhaled—something awful would happen. The screen would tear down its center and the lights would suddenly turn on. I had the vague sense that I was witnessing some sort of magic—or not magic, but some kind of wonderful trickery—and I had the churning fear that if I made any sudden movement the veil would be yanked away and I'd see how the parts were put together, how the gears turned into themselves. How it was made.

"Really, sweetheart," she said again. "You're going to pass out."

I didn't, though. I wheezed my way through it. Conscious. And when the curtain fell and Earl the Lobby Manager stepped onstage to thank us, the first audience, I looked away from the screen and into my mother's lap.

As my family and the audience filed out of the theater, I saw the boy—though, to this day, I'm absolutely positive that I was the only one who did. Somehow he'd succeeded at hiding, undetected, in the second-to-last row of seats in the orchestra section. His hair wasn't long, or greasy, but cropped short, hugging the space around his ears. His cheeks were darkened, freckled with dirt like the woman said, but he still wore the V-neck sweater that was standard in the town. He was my age—eight—and he looked at me curiously as I paused, his eyebrows arching as feet shuffled past him.

I almost said something then, a standard greeting: *Hello, how goes it, were you able to breathe?* But my father pressed a hand to the small of my back. He took my wrist and told me to keep walking. I watched the boy as he shrank away between two seats and my mother kissed me on the top of my head.

As we drove home that evening, I sat in our Buick's backseat and recreated each of the film's scenes in my mind. Charlie meeting Julie Gillis at that fateful audition. Joe pouring out his love for Sylvia. I didn't realize the permanence of the thing, I gather now. I thought the trickery was a one-time deal: that once an ending was happy, once the good guy had won, once we'd all gotten up and left, the trickery would dissipate swiftly. A picture wasn't a picture, but instead something more fragile: a sand castle caught in a wave's backwash. So as we wove through Westchester's empty streets I schemed: I found ways to burn those images into my mind, to file them away in slots where they could be archived, retrieved, relived.

"Well I loved it," my mother said. But then, she would've—she'd never met a movie she didn't like.

"I mostly did," my father answered. I can still picture him saying it—the way the streetlamps cut through the fog and bounced off the sly tilt of his smile.

"What wasn't to like?"

"How about the ending?"

My mother twisted in her seat so she faced him completely. "But he married her! They got married!" she said, touching his wrist. "Charlie and Julie!"

My father said, "But who wants a girl like that?"

She laughed, first quietly and then with great heart. She kept her fingers pressed lightly to his wrist. Said, "Oh, Ali."

When we returned home that evening, they danced alone, without music, in a darkened living room, which they often did, while I lay on my bed, projecting scenes of rockets blasting away from earth on the ceiling with my mind.

We went to the Avalon to see a movie on every Friday of 1956, and each time there were two constants: my father never liked the endings, and I always saw the boy.

First: a note regarding my father and endings. From what I can gather, and from what I can remember, the man had never liked them. They were either too short or too long; the protagonist was either too brave or not brave enough; he either deserved the girl or he didn't; whoever was telling the story had always gotten it terribly and irrevocably wrong.

This revisionist streak ran deep in my father from as early as I can remember. Before she'd given up on God completely in November of that same year, my mother would wearily insist that my father read Bible stories to me each evening—and the frustration was there, too. Eve ate the apple, causing her and Adam to be banished from Eden—but not before Adam fried up the serpent for dinner, using its skin to fashion a pair of scaled loafers. Noah populated his ark with two of every species of God's creation, and as he poured down rain for forty days and forty nights, Noah taught them all to do circus tricks. Dogs jumped through hoops; elephants tiptoed on their hind legs; bears wore skirts and danced to polka music.

Moses split the Red Sea and then promptly invited the Jews to go body surfing on the ensuing walls of waves.

"Ali," my mother would say, her head slipped through the door of my room. "Knock that off. Tell him the truth." I'd pull the sheets up to my chin.

My father would answer, "If we're going to bore him with all this nonsense, he may as well learn something from it."

Nothing changed when we began frequenting the Avalon. Endings were always rewritten, always reconceived. In *Giant*, after Bick tells Jett that he's not even worth hitting, he should've taken the wine in the man's cellar, instead of demolishing the shelves and the bottles they held. In *Lust for Life*, when art and passion and agony eventually cause van Gogh to commit suicide—*My God*, my father would say, *if painting makes you that mad, why not throw in the towel and open up a hardware store?* In *Casablanca*, my father would've hatched a plan so he could have it both ways. In *The Ten Commandments*, he took issue with at least three of those stone-chiseled rules.

At the time, I relished in my father's imagination—the way he could retie knots that already seemed so perfectly fastened. I'd listen to his version of stories, and then I'd rescript them, recast them, reshoot them in my mind; I'd project them onto the same ceiling in my room. But then, this was when I was eight years old. Well before I knew the difference between a storyteller and a liar. Well before I knew on which side of that delineation my father fell.

And now, the boy: sometimes he'd be ducking into one of the theater's dark enclaves—the rounded space, for example, behind a five-foot-tall urn that stood to the left of the theater's grand staircase. I'd see his eyes dart from around the urn's concave edges, scanning the lobby for ushers, for Earl. His fingers would click along the porcelain as he surveyed the room. And from where I stood, between the thighs of my mother and my father at the concession stand, I could almost hear the dull tapping. I'd release my mother's hand, and as my father searched his pockets for cash I'd creep over to the urn, biting my upper lip as I peeked behind it. Always, though—always the boy would be gone.

Other times I'd see him in the actual theater. He'd be sitting calmly, in plain sight, his chin resting on the seat in front of him. Sometimes he'd be near the back of the orchestra; sometimes he'd be near the front of the balcony. He'd look halfway calm—or, at the very least calmer than he appeared when I spotted him in the lobby: his hands wouldn't fidget, and his gaze was stoic and focused. Still, even in those quieter moments, there was something wild about him—something unwritten, untamed. I'd look forward to where he sat near the screen, or I'd crane my neck back so I could spy him in the balcony, and I'd catch the whiteness of his eyes, which seemed too bright. Impossibly white. Technicolor white.

He was always alone.

From what I can recall, it was only when the house lights dimmed that he seemed fully at ease, when he seemed to inhabit his own skin completely. As the rest of the audience dissolved in the theater's enfolding darkness, as I held my breath and my chest burned, he became some breed of fantastic: you could feel him on the back of your neck, in the spot where your shoulder blades pinch together. His presence was so striking that when the show stopped and the curtain fell and I began breathing normally again, I'd instantly turn to look at him—but whatever had felt so remarkable in the dark would've ceased by then. He'd be by himself and shrunken, lodged awkwardly between normal and mysterious.

We grew together that year, the boy and I. On the first Friday of March I came to the theater with Band-Aids on both my elbows and a gash under my left eye—war wounds from a particularly bad run-in with a bicycle. Under the Avalon's meteoric neon sign, I noted that he bore the same scrapes and cuts. At the end of April, when the weather had finally turned warm enough for my mother to allow me to wear shorts in the evening, the boy arrived at the theater with the same grass stains on both his knees. That summer, as my hair grew long and the sun teased out the blond from the russet—so did it for his. On Thursdays I'd bruise myself, intentionally, to see if his skin would bloom with the same purples and greens—always, it did.

The whole thing was at once comforting and beguiling—comforting in the fact that there existed this version of myself who seemed to inhabit a world that I was desperate to understand, beguiling in that we dealt in each other's secrets even though we'd never spoken. Until November.

What happened that month was this: my mother stopped coming to the movies.

At first it was a simple thing not meriting explanation. On the first

Friday of the month, I waited in our family's Buick, which was parked in the driveway. It was windy, and the sycamore that stood over the garage rained down yellow, orange, red. My parents were taking longer than usual to join me, and as I worried that we might miss the seven o'clock showing, my father emerged from the front door, alone.

Once he'd sat down in the driver's seat and shut the door, I asked, "Where's Mom?"

"She's not coming tonight." He started the car and said, "You want to sit up front?"

I told him no, I didn't.

At the Avalon, we orbited around each other gracelessly, terribly unbalanced. A triangle with two points; dual parts of a trilogy. I was either standing too near to him or too far away. At the concession stand, my father ordered three boxes of popcorn, only to send the third one back. Two people behind us, the boy looked on.

We left a seat between us. It wasn't a decision that was discussed or plotted. Rather, it simply happened, with a tacit sense of necessity. Just how in the car the seat next to my father's was hers, so was the case with the middle seat at the Avalon. Still, I remember how my father looked at me from across the vacant space seconds before the lights dimmed. I remember the dullness in his eyes, the awkward way he shifted his body as he tried to lay a hand on my shoulder, how he couldn't quite reach his elbow around the high-backed seats.

The next week, my mother was absent again. And the week after that, and the week after that. She'd already seen *High Society*, my father told me, one day while I was at school and he was at work. Or she wouldn't be able to stomach *A Kiss Before Dying*, as she'd never been a fan of Joanne Woodward. She'd suddenly and inexplicably taken up bridge. My father did this, though: he wove up elaborate excuses to tell me, to tell himself, and neither of us ever believed them.

On the fourth Friday of November, the picture was *The Invasion of the Body Snatchers,* and while I assume my father was displeased with the ending, neither of us spoke about it afterward. Before we left the theater, while my father talked to Earl, I excused myself to the bathroom—where, incidentally, I saw the boy. Except for the two of us it was empty, and when I entered he stood before a sink, rubbing soap into his hands. In the mirror he watched me as I passed behind him to the urinal, as I unzipped my pants and stood awkwardly on my feet's outside edges. He ran the water hot until steam began pooling in the sink's basin.

"Where's your mother been?" The question came as I was buttoning my pants, and when I heard it I stumbled backward. His voice was exactly like mine, but also different. It held the same tenor, and the question lifted at the end in a familiar, self-conscious way—yet something was off, unsettling. As if it were coming out of one speaker instead of both.

"Busy," I told him. "And she sees a lot of movies on her own."

I pushed hair away from my forehead and so did the boy.

"No," he told me. "She doesn't."

The faucet he was using still choked out scalding water. As I began soaping my hands at the sink adjacent to his, he did the same.

"And you'd know, I guess, right?"

"Cool it," the boy said. "You would too."

There was a silence, then, in which we both heard the perturbed buzzing of the bathroom's lights, in which the popcorn exploding behind the concession stand sounded like mines combusting in a field.

"My dad's waiting outside." I shut off the faucet and began drying my hands, spending too long on the spaces between my fingers.

The boy said, "You know what happens to her, don't you?"

I punched him and both our noses bled.

HOW TO TAKE THINGS APART SO YOU CAN PUT THEM BACK TOGETHER

Finn

Randal and I agreed to meet this afternoon on Thirtieth Street, under the languid shadow of my office. Since last night the temperature has gone from miserably hot to stifling to suffocating: streets and subways are plugged with sweat, the stench of 8 million people plus us. I'm wearing this black ROCK AND ROLL HALL OF FAME T-shirt that Karen got for me when she visited an aunt in Cleveland, on her way back from Toronto. I zoom in on Randal, who has a Coke can pressed to his face.

"It's hot," he says. "It's just so fucking hot."

"You'll be all right."

He adjusts his backpack on his thin shoulders and then moves the sweating can to his left cheek. We've both got packs. And we've stuffed them full with items we've deemed essential. Toothbrushes. Camera batteries. Doritos. Two sets of underwear. In Randal's case: three individually wrapped sporks.

"You just—you never know."

I fix the cap to the lens. In my back pocket: the hamburger wrapper where I've written down the address.

I say, "We should definitely get going."

We catch the M train at Bryant Park and ride it south to Houston and Second Avenue. It's hotter downtown: there are fewer patches of cool ground where the sun's been hidden by skyscrapers, more open sky, more bricks baking in the heat, more halal meat charring on stands erected along the sidewalks. On Houston we walk east, toward the river. We pass the Sara D. Roosevelt Park on Chrystie Street, where a group of teenagers in flaccid jeans are smoking Swisher Sweets and listening to a hip-hop song, the one that everyone's already heard 3 million times this summer.

"That song," Randal says. "That fucking song."

At Allen we turn right and we walk by places we know. Places like Lolita Bar and Rockwood Music Hall and Congee Village. And then, farther south, there are wholesale kitchen supply stores, pushing blenders and cutting blocks and things whose names I don't know. The storefronts have signs written in English, rarely with small Chinese characters scrawled under them in bright red. I film a food processor. Randal asks why, and I tell him I've always wanted one.

He says nothing, he just tightens the straps on his backpack and nods as we move farther south.

And then we're below Broome and we go right on Canal and the Chinese begins to overtake the English on the storefronts and the streets get more crowded. We pass under lower Manhattan's concrete mixing bowl, where the off-ramp for the Manhattan Bridge plunges into Bowery and Chrystie and Canal. Periodically Randal asks me to slow down so he can peel his sweat-soaked shirt off his sticky skin.

"What time does this place close?" he asks.

"Seven?" I say. "Maybe eight? I don't know. It's a meat market. When do meat markets close?"

We keep going.

On Canal near Mott there are the jewelry shops—thousands and thousands of them. In their windows are displays of mock red velvet necks draped in spectacular golden lotuses. There are rings with squares of jade or pearl globes and pink-beaded necklaces and jeweled statues of fat happy Buddhas. There are watches, handbags, DVDs of movies that haven't hit theaters yet, and all the men who are selling them tell us and 1 million tourists that they have *a special deal for us, a special deal only for us*!

Then, down Mott, the greengrocers: boxes stacked thousands of miles high with dried peanuts and shriveled mushrooms that look very illegal. Stands hawking apples and oranges and pears, but also exotic, fascinating-sounding fruits like rambutans and mangosteens and pomelos. And fishmongers—so many fucking fishmongers. Tubs of raw grey shrimp, jagged bouquets of detached crab claws, whole fish shoved into buckets, their gaping mouths and black eyes the only things to stick out through the ice.

Randal sees the George Meat Market International first. It's on the east side of Mott, past Pell Street and the Peking Duck House and Hop Kee and Wo Hop: a long white shop that spans a quarter of the block and has slabs of God-knows-what dangling from the ceiling and in open-air cases on the sidewalk. A sign hanging from the store's awning advertises REAL AUTHENTIC CHINESE BUTCHERS. We walk slowly along the troughs of pork and beef and chicken. We count flies and dodge past tourists and screaming women with canvas shopping bags, stopping in front of a set of pigs' feet that are attached to strings that hang from the white awning. I feel Randal grab my bare arm, and he whispers some awful joke, like, "Man, these guys will have a tough time getting *a foot in the door,* wouldn't you think?" before he pokes one of the hooves, sending it rocking.

It feels as though we're standing in the middle of a convection oven, the hot air cracking like whips around us, our T-shirts sticking to our backs in wet zebra lines, and it's uncomfortable, which is probably why we can't stop laughing. We poke the foot, make it tap dance, do the can-can—things that are wholly inappropriate and borderline disrespectful. And it's at that point that one of the butchers—this massive guy with a thick brow and arms the size of palm-tree trunks—ducks out from within the market to tell us, in so many words, that if we push that pig's hoof one more time, he'll give us something to laugh about.

"You coming here you need something?"

There's a brief moment when we have to unscramble his words, and then: "Yes. Yes, we need some help. We're looking for a man named Yip."

"You find Yip?"

"Yes, we find Yip."

He cranes his neck back and looks past the customers—the excited rabid women, the tourists in baseball caps, with cameras dangling from their necks—and then back toward the shop. "Yip at this time very busy. Yip a busy man."

"He's expecting me," I say. "He knows my granddad. They talked."

He looks at Randal, and then at me, and then back at Randal again. "You wait here," he says. Growls.

The street and the stalls outside the shop are getting more crowded with pedestrians contending for space. Randal leans into me and asks, *Who is this guy again?* and I tell him the truth, which is that I don't know, that I have no clue how he knows my grandfather or how he's come to play Lucy's keeper.

"But—they've spoken, right? As in, recently?"

"I think?" Then, because I can tell his eyes are boring into my skull and I want to throw pigs' feet at his head, "Yes."

"Finn—"

It's for an exhausting few minutes that we stand there, dodging women and their bags and the various chopped-up appendages hanging on all sides of us. We see the brute with the cleaver first, motioning wildly, waving his knife as he speaks to a man who's half his height but twice his width, a man who we surmise is Yip.

They bark back and forth at each other as they approach, but the brute slinks back when they're about two feet from us. Calling Yip stout would be generous, I think, because the guy is straight-up fat. Fat and bald with a broad creased face that funnels downward, ending in three slick grey hairs that hang from a cleaved chin. He takes me in his arms immediately, squeezing me around the waist till I have no breath left, till all I can smell is the raw pork on his glowing head. Around us, the *click click click* of tourists' cameras.

"Can you think!" he shouts, and rocks me back and forth. "Can you think last time I seeing this one?" He buries his head in my chest but turns his face toward Randal. "The last time I seeing this one he so small!" He finally releases me. "Can you imagine? He so small and pink

I holding him like this!" Yip holds both hands in front of him as if he intends to cup water out of a fountain. "I holding him like little piglet! So tiny! And he moving like this!" He flails his arms and his legs in these waves. "He looking up at me and he dancing like this!"

I look to Randal, who is now smiling and nodding earnestly, completely infected with Yip's enthusiasm, and then I look back to Yip, to this bald man who is now holding both my hands in his blood-caked paws. "You no remembering me!" he says. And then, before I can say no: "Is fine! I expecting you no remembering me! I expecting this because the last time I seeing you you so pink and tiny and dancing like this!"

He shakes his limbs again and more cameras click. When he stops, he points at the camcorder hanging from my shoulder, points at the bright red light next to the lens. "What, bub! Whoa! I am being on the *Candid Camera*? I am being television star?"

I ask, "You want to be a television star, Yip?"

"Yip is having been made for the television! How I telling so many people this! How I telling them that Yip is having been made for television!"

And so I keep filming.

"You looking so confused! He looking so confused! You want the story how the way I know your *ye ye*? Yes, yes you want story how the way I know your *ye ye*." He turns around, faces the shop, starts walking into it, still holding on to one of my hands. "You follow me, you follow Yip."

The interior of the George Meat Market International is populated by more carcasses of slaughtered beasts than people. I lose my grip on Yip quickly. He sweeps through them adeptly, these hanging pieces of flesh; his head is inches lower than the longest duck or the broadest rib cage. We lose him for a second behind some massive cow leg, and then he reappears, materializing on the other side of an army of plucked, humiliated chickens. We try to keep up with him, Randal and I, as we trace his path through the flesh, but it's basically pointless: we end up getting sideswiped by some short loins or tangled up in rounds, and then he just vanishes again. The only reason we're able to find him in the end is that he shouts, very loudly, for everyone to hear, *I always moving very very fast! I always losing people! But you come, you come here!* He's standing in front of a steel door with chipped blue paint, and he ushers us into a room that, at least from the looks of it, used to be a meat locker.

The place has been turned into a makeshift office. On the wall: a framed picture of Yip with a Chinese movie star I'm pretty sure I recognize. In front of it, two mismatched chairs and a single wooden desk, upon which sprawls an orange cat, ragged and ancient, with only one front leg.

"Sit! Sit!" he tells us, pulling out both the chairs. He perches, authoritatively, on the desk. He reaches into one of the drawers and offers us both unfiltered cigarettes, which we both take, and which makes me hack. He motions for Randal to close the door.

"My God," he says in unaccented English after he gets the thing lit. "It's exhausting, isn't it?"

The smoke rises, forming clouds that blanket the ceiling. I cough some more.

"Pardon?"

He nods to the door, to the circus of sightseers that festers outside. Smoke seeps out of his nostrils, a dragon. "Just this—this whole routine. *So tiny and dancing like this!* Christ almighty." Yip waves the cigarette in wide dismissive loops. He motions, again, to the tourists. "But which one of them wants to buy things they can't pronounce from a guy who's lived in Long Island City since he was eight? A guy who talks like he's Tony Fucking Soprano? I'll tell you who—not a goddamned one of them.

"Chen at Global Seafood, over on Broome—he's the asshole who came up with the shtick first. *They want authenticity,* he said. *They come from Kansas and Iowa with their cameras and they want authenticity.* This! Coming from a Szechuan Jew from Astoria!" Then: "They came, though. Can you believe it? They bought the gag, and they came. Now Chen's got tourists lined up around the block, paying to take a picture with him and a goddamned plucked *duck.* And let me tell you something about tourists, kid—they don't haggle over the price of mushrooms. They don't bitch about the shrimp not being big enough. They buy shit, and they get out of your hair. So, here we have it: *authenticity.*"

The cat makes a noise, something asthmatic and irritated.

Yip tells us, "Just ignore Mrs. Dalloway."

"Is she—all right?"

"Mrs. Dalloway? She's fine. Better than fine, unfortunately. Damn thing is fifty years old. I've had her since I was fifteen."

"That's impossible."

"You're calling me a liar?"

"No. Or, maybe? No, I'm not. It's just—"

"Lighten up, kid, I'm kidding. But yes, a cat that's fifty. No one can figure it out. No vet, no medicine man. She just—she just won't *die*. She can't breathe to save her life, and in ninety-two her front leg got chopped off in a ground beef portioner. But still."

Randal eyes her, suspiciously. He's always hated cats—psychotically, almost. As in, I completely understand the age-old delineation between cat and dog people, but he's expanded the dichotomy to a point that's either frightening or impressive or both. With cutting accuracy, he'll detail certain cats' physical similarities to serial killers, to genocidal murderers. A Russian blue as Slobodan Milosevic. A Maine coon as Charles Manson. And now this one—this one who just won't die.

Mrs. Dalloway's tail twitches and Randal holds his breath.

I hack again from the unfiltered smoke. I say, "Yeah, I mean. That's nuts." And then, because I have nothing else to add, about immortal cats or otherwise: "Yip, my granddad mentioned you know him?"

He stubs his cigarette out on the desk, next to a row of burned circles. "Alistair McPhee," he says. "I can't tell you how long I've known that man." Then, more somberly: "I'm sorry to hear he's sick."

"Oh, I don't think he's sick. I just think—"

But he continues: "He called me about a week ago, you know. Had to repeat his name three times for me to understand him through the coughing. Finally, when I figured out it was Alistair, that old sonofabitch, I said, 'Whoa, bub, keep both your lungs, eh?' But listening to him—I got sad. Ended up crying, as a matter of fact." He lights another cigarette. "You wouldn't believe that, would you? A guy like me, crying?" Smoke sits as a swamp between his lip and nose. "Don't be fooled. I may look tough, but I'm a sentimentalist when it comes down to it. Anyway,

I stopped crying about as soon as I started. When I cry it tastes like blood—they don't tell you that about working at a butcher. You're around this much blood, everything starts tasting like it—even your tears."

I take a deeper drag on the cigarette, and then Randal asks him to explain how he knows my grandfather.

He ashes his smoke into a jade ashtray.

"Before working at the George Meat Market International I was working at Franky's Automotive Repair Shop on Delancey Street. I was putting cars together and now I'm taking animals apart. Franky, he was an asshole. I'm talking grade-A, award-winning, sphincter-clenching asshole. He'd charge a guy two hundred dollars for a tune-up and all he'd do is loosen a few screws so the poor bastard would have to come back a week later. Sonofabitch eventually fired me because he found out I was tightening too many screws." He drags slowly on his cigarette again.

"Anyway. Before I got canned your *ye ye*—your granddad—he comes in with his car. God, I can still remember it. It was Saturday, in winter, and before I left for the shop my wife starts screeching, *Aiiiiii-ya, Yip, don't forget fish for Chu Xi!* Every year it's the same thing—don't forget the fish for Chu Xi.

"So there I am, and all I can think is: *For the love of all that is holy do not forget the fish for Chu Xi.* My wife, you've got to understand—she's terrifying. Huge hands and a back stronger than an ox's. One year, I forgot the fish for Chu Xi, and she went and broke my nose. Look." He points to his nose. "So, right, I know my place. I go and promise her that I won't forget the fish and I leave before she can throw anything at me, and I figure, fuck, it's just going to be that kind of day." He extinguishes the cigarette, lights another one, number three. Mrs. Dalloway yawns.

"But then—*then.* I see your *ye ye* and his car. All beautiful and golden. He's driving it into the shop and I say to Franky, *Franky, how can something that looks so beautiful sound so rotten.* And Franky—I told you what a scheming asshole he is—Franky says, *Yip make the car quiet and charge him triple.* And then he leaves.

"So—it's just me and your *ye ye* in the shop. He tells me that his car is making too much noise and I'm thinking, *Bub, there's not a person south of Thirty-Fourth who doesn't agree with you.*

"But the car—I know I keep going back to this—but the car really was something spectacular. It needed some work, okay. But what spectacular thing doesn't need some work? I remember I told him this—just how beautiful I thought it was—and for whatever reason, that did it. Your *ye ye*—he just starts crying.

"I was going to put a hand on his shoulder but my hands were covered in grease. Grease, blood—Christ, it's been thirty years since I've actually seen the skin on my palms. So what I did was I said, *Bub, talk to me.* Then he looks at my ring and he says, *Tell me about your wife.* I tell him, *Bub, you don't want to know.* I tell him, *Just this morning she nearly whupped my ass into remembering to buy fish for Chu Xi!* I tell him, *Bub, she's got the biggest hands and the strongest back you've ever seen.* And then I showed him my nose.

"I'll always remember this: your *ye ye,* he says to me, *You must love her. You must always love her.*"

"And what'd you say?"

Yip shrugs. He says, "I told him the truth, which is I've never loved anyone so much, and I'm terrified of ever loving anyone else. Then I say, *All right, bub, let's fix that car.*"

He pauses for a moment while he ignites cigarette number four.

"So what was wrong with it?" Randal asks. "Why was it rattling?"

"The check valve was loose."

"That's all?" I say.

He nods. "And then when I fix it—this is great—when I fix it he says to me, *Let's take her out for a spin!* I look at him and say, *Bub, you're crazy. You don't know Franky—he'll whup me harder than my wife whups me for forgetting the fish for Chu Xi.*

"And you know what he told me? He told me, *Franky's not here.*"

"So what happened?" I ask.

"I went, damn it!" He shouts and slams an open palm against the desk and laughs hugely, raucously. "I went, goddamn it! And Franky—the sonofabitch he never knew it! Your *ye ye* helped me find fish for Chu

Xi. He drove me to the best place to get fish in the Bronx and the whole time I'm saying, *Bub, you're crazy!*"

Outside, beyond the door of the meat locker, there is haggling and yelling and a sort of general pandemonium that leaves Yip unfazed.

"We drove every weekend after that. We drove to Brooklyn, and Queens. We drove to Long Island, all the way to Montauk. We saw things that were so beautiful you couldn't help but cry. We drove south— to Philadelphia. Farther."

"To Baltimore?" Randal asks.

"Yes."

"To Washington, D.C.?"

"Yes!"

"To Richmond?"

"Yes! Yes, yes, yes! To all of those places!" He pauses then, reaching for his fifth cigarette, but he stops himself. "And that's why I cried all that blood when I found out he was sick.

"He called me a year ago, you know," he says, "before he took off for San Francisco. Your *ye ye* called me two days before he left and said, *Yip, you need to come and pick her up.* I told him, *Bub, you're crazy. We're driving her to Boston.* But he just said, *Come pick her up, Yip.*

"And—I'm sure he told you this—but that was when we made our bet."

I think back to the conversation I had with my granddad a few nights ago, the way his voice sounded pushed and desperate. There was the map, the one he'd sent me. And also, he'd mentioned his endings. But, "No. No bet."

Yip pulls at the half beard that hangs from his chin. He says, "Your *ye ye*, he told me he'd never be back for the car, and I disagreed. So, he said, *Yip, if I'm ever back for this car I'll take that goddamned cat off your hands.*"

There's still that soundtrack of haggling and customers wrestling with their discontent and the occasional thud of a cleaver blade coming down on flesh.

Wedged in the corner of Randal's eye: a hint of soul-folding terror as the cat on the desk stretches its three legs and yawns, showing us a collection of broken teeth.

"And then on Tuesday he calls to tell me you're coming! Right out of the blue. He says, *Yip, give him the keys and have him bring her to me.* I tell him he's crazy. I tell him if he wants her out there, I'll drive her myself. But—no. He said again, *Yip, give him the keys.* So I told him, *You got it, bub: one car, and one cat.*"

"But technically, he's not the one who's picking up the car."

Yip ignites his cigarette, lifts an eyebrow. He whirls it again in that same dismissive way: *Anyway.*

I start: "Yip—"

Randal finishes: "—we're not taking that fucking cat."

He looks at both of us, making a tepee with his hands and setting his chin atop the point formed by his thick fingers. Mrs. Dalloway licks her front paw, gets bored with it, sticks the whole thing in her decaying mouth and chews.

He states simply, "No cat, no car."

"But my granddad—"

"Is a man who'd honor the terms of a bet."

"But don't you want to see her die?" Randal says. "Alive for fifty years! Don't you think it'd be something amazing when she dies?"

Yip's fingers press into the creases of his chin until there are two, then four, then eight. No—no, Yip does not want to see Mrs. Dalloway die. For reasons that are practical and unsentimental, Yip has no interest in seeing Mrs. Dalloway die. Mrs. Dalloway missed her chance for a performative death about thirty-eight years ago. Now the whole idea of it is just taking up space.

"Those are the terms."

In a voice that's above a whisper but below a squawk, Randal says to me, "This is some motherfucking *hardball.*"

I tell him, "Open your backpack."

"You have got to be kidding me." Then: "*You* open *your* goddamned backpack."

"No really, yours is bigger."

This is true: Randal's pack is massive, the sort of multistrapped, countless-buckled contraption reserved typically for mountaineers and mothers of triplets. Reluctantly and theatrically, he unzips its largest pouch.

Yip pets Mrs. Dalloway once on her orange skull as I reach across the table for her. When my hand is inches away, she flops on her back. She reaches her front paw out to me, as if to say, *Oh, God, just get this over with, it's not as if it matters, really*. Before I nestle her into Randal's backpack, she regards both of us. Bored.

"All right," I tell him. "We're ready."

He leads us out of George Meat Market International, through the maze of hanging meat, past the brute with the cleaver, out onto Mott Street, where the light has dulled and a breeze—practically unnoticeable—has picked up. He moves quickly again, slowing only to light cigarettes, to yell, *You following Yip!* and as he walks the throngs of pedestrians part for him, or at least that's how it seems to us. We reach the south end of Mott, where it dead-ends into Chatham Square, and then we bear east, making our way onto East Broadway. We honestly try our best to keep up with Yip—or, at the very least, to follow his smoke. He says hi to people; he randomly shouts out their names and gives a single frantic wave. He looks back over his shoulder to make sure we haven't fallen too far behind.

We stop on East Broadway, maybe fifty or seventy-five yards after it crosses Catherine. There, just across from the Q Q Bakery, is a white garage that looks as if it's constructed from cinder blocks of different sizes.

"Here," Yip says.

With a single muscular heave, he lifts the door. And as it flings up and slams against the garage's roof it rings loudly, too loudly, and he shouts and shakes his head. He motions into the darkness, to the down ramp that leads into the structure. He looks at us, waiting for us to make our first moves down the slope, and when we don't he says, "It's not far, it's just dark."

His steps echo like stones dropping in water as he descends into the garage, and as we feel our way after him, Randal whispers, *Jesus Christ, I can't see a thing*. Yip is right, though—it's not far to the car: after maybe twenty-five yards or so the claustrophobia of the skinny ramp seems to fade. Or it seems to open up in the dark so that we can at least breathe. He tells us to hold tight, and then we hear him mumbling to himself, his heavy footsteps becoming quick shuffles—not stones plunging, but more like pebbles skipping along the surface—and after he lets out a happy yelp there is a loud buzzing and the room fills with bright white light.

He stands near Lucy, resting his head on her hood. He's smiling. "I told you she's beautiful."

But she's not beautiful—I know this already. Or maybe she is, but not in the conventional sense. Not in the way a person who hasn't driven her would really understand. Here, in the light of the garage for instance, her gold coat registers more as wet hay that's browned along its edges. Her headlights are dusted: they are covered in this thick grey film, sediment that looks like it's been gathering for centuries. I don't know if my granddad ever saw her when her front grille was perfect, when it had its original sheen—I know that I never have. I run my hand over the silver piping. I feel every scratch, every nick, every groove.

Randal opens the driver's side door and the rusted hinges creak as they swing. He pokes two fingers into a deep tear in the seat's white leather, pushing them into the stuffing until his knuckles disappear. He sits and grips the steering wheel at ten and two o'clock.

I stay crouched near the front bumper, following the uneven lines of her front hood, of her broad windshield, of her wind-torn canvas roof. I put both hands on the grille.

There's a sound, then—Yip's mobile rings deep within his apron. He apologizes profusely, more than he probably should, but I guess there's this general feeling that A Moment is occurring and that his phone has killed it.

When the solemn quiet has been restored, Yip reaches into the bottomless pockets of his apron and promptly throws me a set of keys. I stand, and as I catch them he says, "The little key is for the glove compartment." He adds, "You know where you're going? Where you're taking your *ye ye*'s life?"

"Yes," I answer. "Yes, we've got his map."

Randal steps out of the car, rounding to the shotgun side. He watches us, his hands stuffed into the back pockets of his shorts.

"And you'll go fast?"

"We'll go fast."

"And Mrs. Dalloway?"

"She'll be safe."

"That's not what I meant."

Yip looks at me for a moment, his eyes glazing over from the other side of Lucy's hood, and when I think he's going to totally erupt in tears, he races over to me. He squeezes me.

He says: "So tiny! So tiny and dancing!"

Then adds: "And when you see him, tell him he still owes me fifty bucks."

What I Remember

1956–1957: Locked Away

By Colin A. McPhee

When my father and I returned from the Avalon on the last Friday in November, I could still taste my own blood from when I'd punched the boy. Additionally—while we were gone, my mother had locked herself in the bathroom at the top of the stairs.

Neither my father nor I had any way of knowing how long she'd been hiding in there, but as he knocked on the door and as I knelt at its base, peeking into the slant of light that snuck out from under it, she made it clear that she had no intentions of coming out any time soon.

"Luce," he said. "Come out of there. You've got to eat something."

"How do you know I haven't?"

He pressed his forehead to the white wood. Closed his eyes, licked his upper lip.

"Mom." I imagined how my voice must've looked as it snaked its way underneath the door, as it flopped across the floor and curled around her ankles. "What're you doing in there?"

"Painting my toes," she told me.

"Damn it, Lucy."

"Language."

My father slowly banged the door with his forehead until from within she sighed, "Oh, Ali, knock that off."

"We saw a good one tonight, Mom," I continued, my face still pressed to the space at the bottom of the door.

"Oh yeah?"

"Invasion of the Body Snatchers."

"Tell me about it."

I recounted the entire picture for her, starting with the newsreel that played before the opening credits. I painted Santa Mira in seamless detail, the way the hills that framed it ridged and folded. The houses, I said, looked as though they'd been pulled from a train set. I laid out my theories: how Kevin McCarthy was good enough, but how I thought, personally, King Donovan was the star. Then, once I began on the pod people, my father walked downstairs.

That evening she stayed in the bathroom until well after midnight, and when she did finally emerge her toenails were painted a glossy red.

During the ensuing weeks, locking herself away became something of a pattern for my mother. She started doing it only on Friday evenings, but before too long it transformed into a ritual that was practiced at any point of the day, on any day of the week, and no matter who was in the house.

In early January of 1957, exactly a year after the Avalon had opened, I lay on my stomach in our home's front room, my chin propped up by fists as I watched the television, *Howdy Doody.* I don't recall exactly what time it was, though it must've been relatively early, as my father hadn't returned to Westchester from the city, where he had a job engineering bridges. Behind me, my mother read a women's magazine, pausing occasionally to run her toes—still painted red at that point, always red— along a sheepskin rug.

Looking back, I wouldn't recall the sound of her turning the magazine's slick pages, or the quiet hum she composed whenever she wasn't thinking about anything in particular; instead, it'd be the faint clicking of her nails as she drummed them along the coffee table. A series of heavy sighs. The creak of her neck as she looked out the window. The strain of her voice as she stood abruptly and said, *Will you please excuse me?*

I'd never been asked that question before. I was nine—my permission in our house hadn't been needed for much of anything. As such, I stared. I folded my legs beneath me, stretched my spine as far upward as it would go, and I stared.

"Well?" she said, this time with greater urgency.

"Yes?"

It wasn't any mystery where she'd disappeared to—during those months, whenever my mother was lost, it was safe to assume that she'd locked herself in the bathroom, that she was singing to herself as she painted her toes, her fingers, her lips. Still, though, on that evening I followed her. I crept stealthily on my hands and knees; I hid behind the staircase's wooden baluster, its curves splashed in dusk's purple light. I pressed my ear to the bathroom door and I peered underneath it, like I'd done on that first night. I was only able to catch glimpses of her calves, her bare feet.

I considered providing other, extensive recaps of films I had recently seen. *Godzilla: King of the Monsters!* or *Bus Stop*, which I knew she would've enjoyed because she'd always had a fondness for Don Murray. But then there was that thing she'd said—how she'd asked my permission to be excused—and this gave me pause. I sat and listened instead.

When she did emerge on that night in January, I was still crouched on the staircase, but dusk had turned to night and in that darkness I barely recognized her. She'd put curlers in her hair and she'd painted her lips red. Under each eye were heavy patches of blue shadow. My mother was at once a plain and striking woman: her beauty wasn't the sort that was thrust upon her, but rather pooled in her imperfections and then radiated outward. On someone like her, makeup looked cartoonish and wrong.

She walked with resolve and blind purpose, tripping over my shoulder as she marched down the stairs.

"What do you think?" my mother asked, when she'd regained her composure and steadied herself. She framed her face with both hands. "Marilyn Monroe?"

"Lana Turner," I told her.

"Even better."

. . .

On Wednesday of that week there was a heavy snowstorm and my mother escaped from the bathroom long enough to take me sledding, though I don't remember having asked to go. She appeared in the family room early in the evening, the makeup still on, her shoulders draped with a thick knitted shawl.

"Come on," she said. In one hand she held my jacket; she reached the other one out to me.

We trudged through knee-deep powder to a series of three hills located about a half mile from our home. Traversing their pitches, we made our way to the top of the second-tallest slope, where we waited as she caught her breath.

"You go," she told me. "And I'll watch from here."

I knew immediately that I had picked a hill that was too high and too steep. I knew it the instant I felt the wind whip too harshly against my face. The way it pulled too tightly at the corners of my eyes. I don't remember whether I fell from the sled before its runners slicked across the ice patch, or if it was vice versa: if the ice patch was the reason I fell. Either way, I rolled some fifty yards. I tumbled the way you do in crashing waves, when directions such as up or down become interchangeable. The only concrete knowledge I had was the biting cold of the snow that was worming its way into my sweater and was melting along the soft spaces on my spine. Eventually I stopped by a row of low evergreens, my head thudding dully when it collided with one of the trunks.

My mother, wheezing, rushed to me. While my eyes were shut, locked down by ice, I heard the sound of her boots shushing in the snow. She wrapped her arms under mine and pulled me from the debris of branches. Awkwardly she took me in her lap and began quickly, nervously stoking my snow-slicked hair.

"Don't cry," she whispered as she rocked.

And the thing was, at that point I hadn't started crying—and I don't remember giving any indication that I'd start. The pain from the accident seeped from my skull through the veins in my neck, and it throbbed, but as it did so it also warmed. The sort of pain that's comforting despite itself.

But still, she said it again. *Don't cry.* She repeated it until it became a calm, placid plea, until I felt the weight of her tears mix with the absolute lightness of the melted snow on my neck.

Two days later, when my father and I drove to the Avalon to see *Dance with Me, Henry,* I began my search for the boy.

I hadn't seen him since November, when both our noses had bled in the theater's bathroom. At first his absence was pleasing; for weeks after our confrontation I slunk behind my father's legs as we made our way through the cinema, a brick in my throat as I anticipated what it'd be like to catch sight of him. I insisted Friday after Friday that we sit in the balcony's back row and leave before the credits had ended. Finally, as we tripped through the dark toward the theater's exit during one of those visits, the reality enveloped me like a lukewarm bath: I hadn't seen him, or him me. I'd slipped into hiding and so, inevitably, had he. Yet, once the comfort of his absence had taken root, I became acutely aware of how much I needed him, how fiercely I yearned for his answers. The solutions that I believed he possessed.

I began my search slowly but precisely. While my father purchased popcorn and spoke with the ushers, I lingered near the giant urn at the bottom of the stairs. I circled its base and ran a hand along its engraved side, searching for any sign of him. Before the film started, I took to the steps on the grand staircase so I could peer down into the urn's belly. I leaned in as close as I could. Whispered, *Hello,* only to hear an echo of my own voice.

At home, meanwhile, my mother was locking herself away for longer stretches of time. She'd slip out briefly, accidentally, her lips a darker shade of red, her skin a paler shade of white, her hair curled and teased out in unskillful flares. As February turned over into March, the house fell into disrepair. In the sink, dishes piled up in malconstructed skyscrapers, threatening to topple whenever the faucet was turned on. My father did what he could: washed, scraped, scrubbed, burned. But he'd exhaust himself easily; while my mother reconstructed herself upstairs, he'd collapse into the sofa and come up with different endings.

I intensified my quest for the boy. I clambered between the theater's rows before the audience filled them. I sat in every seat I'd seen him use, waiting for him to materialize next to me. On the Friday my father and I purchased tickets for *Funny Face,* I pulled Earl, the lobby manager, aside.

"Earl," I said, my hands shoved into my pockets in tight fists. "I've got a question."

He slipped an arm around my shoulder: "Talk to me, Colin."

Over the past year my father and I had come to know Earl quite well. First as a sort of informant—someone who would provide us with the calendar for the Avalon's releases before it was printed in the paper; then, as a kind of saint—a free box of chocolates on some weeks, a bottle of soda on others; and finally as a friend. A greying companion who'd shake your hand, slap your back. Ask about your mother.

"That boy," I said to him in a half whisper. "Have you seen him?"

"What boy?"

"*That boy,* the one who snuck in on opening night."

He looked down at me for a moment, his hand still draped across my shoulder. His face fractured into a puzzle and then re-collected itself.

Earl lifted his hand from my shoulder and set it on top of my head. He ruffled my red hair till it stood on its ends.

He laughed. "You're killing me, Colin."

Thus I continued my search alone. The first Friday of April, I stood in the same bathroom where I'd last seen him. Under the same buzzing lights, I scanned the sink for spots of his blood, my blood. Stains that had been overlooked that might—somehow—congeal into his form.

I left him notes. They were handwritten scrawls on the back of ticket stubs that I hid between seats, wedging them into the spaces between cushions. They started off as reconciliatory and apologetic: *Hi, where have you been? My dad says this is the worst winter in twenty-seven years. Sorry about your nose.* The next week I returned to find my notes still there, unanswered and passed over by the theater's custodial crew. I took the ticket stubs and crossed out what I'd previously written. Over it, I composed new notes, lacing the missives with explicit demands:

We need to talk.

I don't know what happens to her.
Tell me, please, if she's dying.
And then, six weeks later when she did, a final one: *You were right.*
Happy?

I put the pieces together, but only many years later; I came to understand why she hid away. Why she started to use makeup, however clumsily, to mask her decaying form. How she swore off movies because the predictable melodrama of her own death was enough. I imagined my mother as she thumbed at the problem she discovered on that first night: a sinuous lump of skin and tissue underneath her left breast. How she pressed herself in various states of concentration: hyperfocused, concerned, half-hearted, distracted. How she'd withdraw her hand. She'd use it to examine other pieces of her awkward frame—fragile hips, new creases along the corners of her eyes, useless flaps of skin hanging from the undersides of her arms, and how, in fits of desperation, she'd try to cover them up. But inevitably she'd return to the lump: she would move it up, down, in, out, left, right. She'd play marbles under a layer of her flesh.

She'd prod and poke and become better acquainted with the bulb, the thing that'd taken refuge in her chest. She'd tell herself it was shrinking, maybe, that it was smoothing into the soft folds of her body. She'd tell herself that it was growing, that in intervals of expanding centimeters it was overtaking her breast.

I remember now that there were fights, too. During the slight moments when she'd step out from the bathroom, there would be arguments between her and my father in the family room. I'd listen to them as I lay in my room. My father insisted that she see a doctor, though my mother always refused. Toward the end, when she finally did agree, they were told that the cancer—as my father had feared and as my mother well knew—had become metastatic and had hit stage 4. It had reached its desperate arms outward, taking hold of her lymph nodes and the surrounding tissues. This was in 1957 before chemotherapy and radiation and commonplace lumpectomies and five-kilometer fundraising walks. They were told by doctors in New York, Connecticut, New Jersey—by at least one man in Boston—that the only option was a radical mastectomy, which was then a gruesome procedure that would not only remove her breasts, but the surrounding lymph nodes and muscles, and likely a chunk of her ribs. There was no telling if it would work, and when it was finished, she would be left looking like—for lack of a better comparison—a question mark: hunched, deformed, depleted of significance or certainty.

From the family room my mother shouted, "I won't let them carve me away," and the floor of my bedroom trembled.

The service was on a Saturday in June that was hot, and happy, and bright. The night before, my father and I had gone to the Avalon to see *The Incredible Shrinking Man* with Grant Williams, and as we'd done at the theater, we left a vacant seat between us in the front row of the church. And also as he'd done in the theater, my father tried to reach across to me, though only once, but he stopped before he fully took hold. There was a slight brushing of skin as he grazed my shoulder. I remember very clearly that I wanted to feel him for longer. I wanted my hand to be smaller. I wanted to hold on to one of his thick knuckles with my five tiny fingers.

After that, my father stopped accompanying me to the Avalon entirely. It didn't matter if the theater was showing *Peyton Place* or *Sayonara*, he stoutly and stubbornly refused. In the preceding weeks, his problem with any given picture had grown beyond the unsatisfying endings. Increasingly he took issue with how stories began. Likewise, he said their middles—their guts—weren't strung together appropriately. They unraveled at the wrong times, at points of minor interest; the consequences they precipitated meant next to nothing. No one was heroic enough.

I don't know where my father went during those nights when I sat through movies with two empty seats beside me: whether he drove directly home, or whether he and the Buick wandered, itinerantly, along the soft curves carved by the roads of the Lower Hudson. There were other women, I knew: there were dates, flings, affairs, fleeting flirtations, but they never amounted to much. In retrospect, I don't know how I would've reacted if they had—whether I would've slipped into some new sort of arrangement or simply rescripted a version of my life in which this person didn't exist. It doesn't particularly matter, though: my father would never truly get over my mother. He believed—for better or worse—in the singularity of love.

In June of 1958, my father left me at the Avalon to see a movie alone. The picture slotted for the week was *From Hell to Texas*—the first Don Murray film the Avalon was premiering since *Bus Stop,* and a movie my mother would've liked. I was still trying to convince him to accompany me to films at that point, and so I brought it to his attention when he pulled up to the curb alongside the cinema's entrance in the old Buick.

"It's supposed to be good," I told him. "The best, even."

"Yeah?" He didn't bother putting the car in park as we idled. He unlocked the doors and pressed a nickel into my palm, saying, "Call me when it's through."

He gave me a weak smile, a quick tilt of his lips' corners. He told me that if I didn't hurry I'd miss the preview reel—which, two years earlier, we'd designated as a film's best part.

"Really," he told me, shooing me out of the car, "you're going to be late."

Incidentally, the movie wasn't all that good. It wasn't horrible, but it wasn't all that good. Don Murray was wonderful—I still think my mother would've liked that—but I'd argue that the rest of the cast wasn't as compelling as it could have been. Dennis Hopper seemed stiff, and as much as I wanted to, I couldn't buy Diane Varsi as Juanita Bradley. Something to do with her hair.

When I phoned my father and he arrived to pick me up, I told him he'd really missed out.

Also, I asked, "Where's the Buick?"

He was leaning against a parked car that wasn't ours: a used '56 Bel Air. It was yellow, the color of wet straw, and it was laced with scratches. The side-view mirrors winged out in awkward, unhelpful angles; there was a gash in the paint along the passenger's side door that looked like some sort of flesh wound. One of the rear windows was missing.

"This is the new Buick," my father said. He had seen it in Kingston, New York, he explained—he'd driven by it accidentally in a lot, when he took a wrong turn—weeks earlier when he was scouting a site for a new bridge he'd be constructing. He'd traded in our old car and paid an additional two thousand dollars for the Bel Air. He told me he'd decided to call it Lucy, on account of the paint job matching the color of my mother's hair.

"So?" He raised both his palms upward, as if preparing to accept my praise.

"I think I liked the Buick better."

HOW TO BUILD A HOUSE

Finn

The road is relentless, but so are we. After we leave the garage on East Broadway, Randal and I press on valiantly, skidding out of New York and past New Jersey's grey industrial fields, its bucket-sized lakes that pool at the base of its warehouses. There's U.S. Route 22 and U.S. Route 9 and U.S. Route 1 and New Jersey Route 21 and exits 57 and 58 and 52 and the Garden State Parkway. There are sixteen-wheel semis that, despite their size, seem to spawn, then vanish, then be next to us again, running in herds like buffalo. Hay trucks that I think are driving faster than they should be—faster than we are, at least—that'll disappear into the black space of the encroaching night.

"Maybe she's dead," Randal says. Since hitting the road, Mrs. Dalloway has been corpse quiet. No scratching, no gasped meows. Just the gentle shifting of her loose skin and bones whenever we hit a bump.

"Stop that," I tell him.

"New Jersey could kill anything." He sets his ear against his pack, which is shoved between his feet. "No luck. She just hacked."

Next—Pennsylvania. We merge onto I-81 and the highway stretches in front of us, cutting through the land's fat. Lucy's headlights illuminate the sides of the road in wide arcs, projecting images of the uneven grass and the dead split trees and the truck bays that make up the state's jumbled insides. There's that airy sense you get when you're driving that maybe you're flying; that you're floating on nothing toward a vanishing point, out where the road gets swallowed up by the sky, or maybe the sky funnels down to the road.

Everything is black by the time we reach Blue Mountain. We're beginning the slow, gradual climb through the foothills, barreling through the countless tunnels, when Randal asks, finally, what my granddad did in Pittsburgh.

I say: "He saved this guy from getting crushed into a million bits."

"Really," he said. *"Really."*

"True story."

My eyes are tired from staring at the same four colors that make up the western stretches of Pennsylvania. I stretch my arm out the window and I make a wing with my hand, diving it up and down into the wind, feeling the current push my palm skyward, then—with just a tiny shift—my knuckles down.

A minute later: "How did he do that?"

"You're not going to believe me. It's the honest-to-God truth, but you're not going to believe me."

"Try me."

So I tell him.

The first time my granddad went to Pittsburgh, it was for the bridges.

He designed them for a living, great reaching things that spanned rivers and abysses and all other species of bottomless chasms. You've seen his work, undoubtedly. You've driven across it, or strolled on its footpaths, or spit from its slick railings into the infinity below, and each time, the whole time, you've never known it's his. No one's known, probably, unless No One was the sort of person who researched these things. Because while my granddad was a great man, he was also greatly humble. He was always content to let other folks take the credit, to let them slap their names onto square bronze plaques while from a distance he observed his work, connecting two worlds for the first time.

He told me that in 1963, when he and Lucy slipped into Allegheny County, Pittsburgh was laced with more than four hundred bridges, more than any city in the entire world. He'd been driving through the night and when he entered the city, it was from the south. In the waning dark he slipped through Dormont and Green Tree and so many other sleepy, leafy suburbs. It was as he climbed the back side of Mount Washington to overlook the city center, its steely innards, that dawn—pink and miraculous and explosive—broke.

It tossed its eastern light onto the Liberty Bridge's curved spine and across the Smithfield Street Bridge's famed trusses; it weaved between the Three Sisters and tickled their matching backsides; it bent the Fort Pitt Bridge's bowstring arch till the whole thing glowed red; it hit the West End Bridge last, naturally, plucking its suspensions like guitar stings till the hum of it all finally woke the city.

Or at least that's what he'd expected to see. The Pittsburgh he'd *dreamt* he'd see; the Pittsburgh that, twenty years earlier, during the height of World War II, had been the nation's number one producer of steel. The Pittsburgh that cranked out the materials necessary to make the tanks and the planes and the guns that'd squash Hitler and *zee Germans. A million tons of it in one year alone,* my granddad would say. *Try to imagine that, Finn.* I'd tell him I couldn't imagine seeing a million tons of much of anything. *Oh,* he'd say. *Oh, sure you can.*

But this wasn't twenty years ago—this was 1963—and Pittsburgh had turned into a stinking shithole. The industry that had once bellied the city was now shriveled; the government contracts long expired, Big Steel was now racked with labor strikes and infighting. And there were other problems, too. For starters, the region was in the throes of one of its worst droughts on record. The waters of the Allegheny, of the Monongahela and the Ohio—they all ran uncertain and anemic. The currents would mill in shallow puddles around the pilings of the bridges, they'd cling to the grooves in the concrete and rusted steel, collecting dust, waiting to dry up. My granddad told me that the streets were so baked and dry that the asphalt would crack if you managed to stand in one place for too long. (And he would know—it happened to him. Right there on top of Mount Washington. There was a snapping sound, then a plume of black dust—and *bam,* his left foot was four feet under.) He told me how there were ladies who had no water for their gardens, so they fed their roses milk; how there was a man who'd trained his dog to lick dirt off his car, because there wasn't any water to wash it.

And also, he said, there were the fires. They'd started in January, when twenty five-alarm blazes leveled seven city blocks on Pittsburgh's Northside. Then, in April, when my granddad arrived and the embers in the sad empty lots were just beginning to cool, there was a new batch, set by a never-to-be-found arsonist. New rooms bubbling with ash, new flames licking singed shingles. Ignited roofs that, from where my granddad stood on Mount Washington, looked like torches in a mob.

The fire department did what it could, of course. It erected its ladders against the buildings' half-burnt walls; it pulled folks out of burning doorways. But remember, there was this drought—there was only so much water the rivers could afford to give—so the men didn't have enough juice to run their hoses. Instead, they used squirt guns. Honest to God. The colored plastic sort you'd find at a five-and-dime store. They had a whole arsenal of them, I swear. My granddad saw the whole thing go down.

From where he parked Lucy he watched the smoke as it wafted upward, bleeding into a sky that was already blanketed with a mix of smog and soot. Fires or not, the pollution in Pittsburgh was some of the worst in the country, my granddad said. While the steel industry was on the outs, its factories still managed to cough up toxic clouds daily. The city's residents did what they could: insisting that the street lights be turned on at noon; stumbling to the grocery store with a flashlight; smoking cigarettes for a reprieve of fresh air. Still, not much of it worked. It was for this reason, I think, that the old man wasn't able to see the bridges. He wasn't able to see a goddamned thing at all.

It was midmorning when he finally decided to leave his perch at the top of the incline. My granddad began winding down Mount Washington's north face toward the city, flicking on Lucy's headlights to see the road in front of him, to cut a path through the smog and soot. More than once he had to stop in order to wipe her clean; he used a white handkerchief to clear peepholes in her windshield. He told me it was a ghost town on that day: a city with four hundred bridges that led into it, which—then—were only being used as escape routes out.

He didn't know where he was going. I guess that's something I should get across now. He'd come to see the bridges, of course, to admire their mechanical beauty, but my granddad was the kind of guy who felt that beauty was only allowed to be beautiful if it was found accidentally. His plan was to traverse the city streets fortuitously, to hike through the buildings' ashy canyons that snaked between the rivers until he stumbled upon the next way out, the next way in.

It was in this way that he and Lucy wound through downtown Pittsburgh, past the squat headquarters of the *Post-Gazette* and the skyscrapers on Grant Street. He drove straight when he could see, and when he couldn't he'd turn. Through the Strip District and East Allegheny, Bloomfield and Oakwood and Friendship and Shadyside. His blind traipsing took him over the Ohio at Sixteenth Street, at Thirty-First Street, at Fortieth Street. And then, over the Monongahela at Tenth, at the Birmingham, at the Hot Metal. My granddad managed to cross 273 of the city's bridges before he stumbled—awfully and serendipitously— upon the Hill District.

It was a pocket of the city due east of downtown, on the other side of Crosstown Boulevard. He told me how it was spectacularly bad over there, in the Hill, how if Pittsburgh was hell and its residents were sinners, then this must've been the place they were sent when they'd done something incredibly atrocious. Eighth circle bad. Malebolge bad. But it hadn't always been like this, he'd learn days later, when he was back in Westchester researching the places he'd just seen. (He was like this, my granddad. A great humble genius, but also a constant learner. A real polymath. Each time a new encyclopedia was issued, he'd read the latest edition from A to Z. He'd highlight the fresh entries. That's a true story. The man's mind didn't just remember things—facts, stories, myths—it took them apart and reconstructed them again; it built newer, better versions of things he already knew.)

In any event, the Hill District. At one point—particularly during the 1930s and '40s—the neighborhood had been a cultural cornerstone for not only Pittsburgh, but the entire country. People called it "the crossroads of the world," or sometimes "Fun City"—it was, as my granddad explained it to me, the most happening spot for music and nightlife between Chicago and New York.

At the center of it all was Wylie Avenue—and at the center of Wylie Avenue was jazz. Great jazz. Soul-lifting, spirit-crushing, boozy and bone-wrenching jazz. Famous musicians—people like Lena Horne and Dizzy Gillespie and John Coltrane and Duke Ellington; names that exist in my mind, that existed in his, as these smoky cocktails of riffs and sighs—they all played the Hill. They packed places like Crawford Grill and the Flamingo Club and the Granada Theater. People who were there to live through it said that each night the velvet notes from the players' horns would slip softly, seductively through the neighborhood's side streets, down alleys, and past cracks of open windows.

But then, as the city slumped during the postwar era, its mayor— a man named Lawrence—instituted this massive urban renewal plan. Phase three of the project focused on the Hill—which, like the rest of the city, had fallen into soggy disrepair. The projections were hubristic: ninety-five acres of commercial and residential property were to be razed to make room for new office spaces, a public arena, and additional housing. At the end of the day, none of these developments ever materialized. The music stopped: the clubs' windows were boarded up before being demolished by wrecking balls; upward of eight thousand Hill residents were displaced with only crumbs of assistance from the city. There was only one new structure that was ever built, some tenement with a roof that leaked in a drizzle.

So, that was the scene when my granddad passed from Watt onto Wylie in April of 1963. A real bonfire of the vanities, he said. Dried-up lawns that served as graveyards for half-remembered houses; chained-up bikes with no tires; deflated tires with no bikes; countless vestiges of lives forgotten.

He eased Lucy slowly, cautiously down the avenue. So few of the streetlamps were illuminated, and her faint headlights flickered with exhaustion. There hadn't been a soul in sight, he told me, until he passed Soho Street and then there was—quite suddenly—a crowd. A mob of onlookers that spilled from the empty lots, from the weeded sidewalks into the road. Their million arms were linked together in solidarity, forming an infinite chain that barricaded his path. Their gazes were turned away from him, their eyes set westward. He told me how from where he parked Lucy, on the corner of Wylie and Soho, he watched as members of the mob would throw their heads skyward at unspecified intervals, how they'd wail and shout their grievances to the clouds, how he'd cringe as their words got tangled in the smoke.

No one turned when he closed Lucy's door, or as he approached the tail end of the mob, which he now saw stretched onward, in increasing density, toward Lawson Street. He still couldn't see what was causing the commotion—the grey air was thick, he said, and the few times a gust parted it enough for him to get a visual, his view would be blocked by one of the onlookers' heads, a crown in midmourn, neck tilted back, skin bunched in thick rows atop two shoulders.

On more than one occasion, he tried to push through the crowd. He'd give a slight *Excuse me, ma'am,* or maybe a *Sir, if you could just . . .* But the strangers were impervious to his attempts. Their arms remained linked as they stood in their inflexible ranks. So he did the only thing he could do—or, the only thing a bridge maker could imagine doing: he climbed over them.

Their half-pitched heads would work as the bridge's towers, he figured, while the line formed by their sloping shoulders would stand in for the main cable. The linked arms, the suspension cables; their fisted hands, the structure's deck. He found his balance and then pardoned himself as he went. When he came across a face that was twisted in midwail, he'd offer up his handkerchief; he'd clean the tears and soot from a pair of dirtied cheeks.

Like I said, the front of the throng was at Wylie and Lawson, and when he got there, when he finally emerged from between a set of knobby elbows, this is what he saw: a record store—a place called The Rev's—with a rusted tin roof and ash-streaked walls. It was the only structure still standing on the block, though its windows were boarded and poised above it was a wrecking ball, swaying happily, dumbly.

"You're animals!" a man standing next to my granddad on the front line shouted. "Doing this while he's still in there! Animals!"

The wrecking ball swung in wider arcs, tracing smiles in the smoke.

"While who's in there?" my granddad asked.

"The Rev!" The man unlinked his arms from the two women who flanked him and he brought his hands to his face. "Oh, the Rev!"

"How long has he been in there?"

"Days!" the man shouted. One of the two women followed up with "Weeks! Ever since they went and told him they'd be taking his shop! Hasn't seen the light of day since!" She added, "Animals!"

My granddad looked up at the wrecking ball; he made a visor with his hand even though there was no sun. And because my granddad was coolheaded and direct—or, great and humble and a polymath and coolheaded and direct—he said, "Well then, somebody better get him out."

We exit a fourth tunnel and Lucy's headlights burn parallelograms along the road's shoulders. Blue beams come toward us, blinding us. The car passes and we see a million little stars that move and fade. The interstate begins a shallow decline, and ahead of us one of the foothills is capped with an electric halo of Pittsburgh's grey light.

"You'll stop me if you've heard this before," I say.

"Keep going," Randal says. "You're on a roll."

He found a way in around the back side of the shop: a place where the boards on the windows were moist and rotted and could be easily pried off. He shimmied in through the gap he'd made and fumbled while he found his footing. Because even though it was daytime, the store's interior was dark, with smoke from outside trailing along the ceiling. He told me it smelled like dirty towels—that's exactly what he said. Not dirty clothes, or dirty shoes, but dirty towels. My granddad stumbled more as he made his way through the blackness, tripping over a desk, a cash register. He called out *hello* four times but no one answered him.

He ran his hand along the wall until he found a light switch. He flipped it, but nothing happened. So he walked farther, his fingers still trailing the wall, until he found another switch. This one worked. The fluorescents took a while as they warmed up, but eventually the shop illuminated well enough for him to see the Rev, sitting alone and despondent, atop a pile of records.

The man was only about ten years my granddad's senior, but he looked older, fossilized, the dust from the decaying shop settling on his mustache and eyebrows. His skin sagged from his jowls and ears—the two lobes, my granddad said, grazed his shoulders—and his face had the look of a man who'd been unlucky enough to see the end and drive right on past it. The ground around him was littered with all sorts of things—vinyl, old posters advertising shows at the Flamingo Club, a half-finished chicken leg beset by flies. In his left hand he held a cup that was filled with gin because there wasn't any water to drink.

My granddad took the sight in quietly and respectfully; he allowed the man's eyes to adjust to the light. But then, from outside, there was the whispered creak of the chain and the mewing wails of the onlookers, the subtle *whoosh* of a wrecking ball in motion, and he said, "Friend, it's time to get you out of here."

"I ain't moving," the Rev said back.

"They're going to tear this place down, whether you're in it or not."

The Rev wiped soot from the corners of his eyes. "So go ahead and let them whether I'm in it or not."

Whenever my granddad recounted this story for me—which was often, very often—he'd always say how he wished the Rev's response, this man's desire to die, puzzled him.

"I even waited for it to, Finn," he'd say. "But the cold truth is I had no questions to ask; I understood."

I suppose my granddad learned the hard way that when someone, something made the irrevocable decision to go, there wasn't a damned thing you could do to change its mind. He'd say, "I've seen it happen everywhere. From dogs who dig their own graves to your own blessed grandmother. Only thing to be done in a situation like that is to protect the person from himself. To build up walls high enough to keep out whatever's eating him in hopes that when the sun starts shining again, he'll be there to take a better look around."

Which I'll say is precisely what he did.

While the *whoosh* from the wrecking ball grew louder, my granddad zigzagged through the store's racks, emptying them of their records, creating stacks that were three, four, five feet high on the linoleum floor. Seven separate times the Rev demanded to know what he was doing, but my granddad kept his plans hushed; he knew that if he let on in the slightest, the old man would object. He'd press himself up against one of the store's walls until that dull steel globe came crashing into his gut. And my granddad—who was above all things heroic—wasn't about to let that happen.

He knew that he'd need something with girth to start: a bass that could resonate along a scale's deepest notes, while still having a bit of flexibility. He went with Louis Armstrong. He stacked his arms with *Struttin'*, with LPs of *Black and Blue* and *All of Me* and *Basin Street Blues*. He arranged them around the Rev as he would if he were setting down the foundations for a house: great thick beams of vinyl, set squarely atop the dusty floor.

Again, the Rev shouted, "Boy, what in the hell are you doing!"

The walls were a different matter entirely. With them, he needed range. Materials that were comfortable at the bottom but could also support themselves up top. A baritone, he figured. Or a mezzo-soprano. A low tenor in a pinch. He shuffled through the records he'd emptied onto the linoleum, his feet kicking aside Rose Murphy and Blossom Dearie albums, their high-pitched trills ricocheting off the shop's walls. The shadow of the wrecking ball crept in through the window from which he entered, and it grazed his bristled neck. My granddad made a game-time decision: Mildred Bailey for the north side, Al Bowlly for the east and west faces. And for the south end, where he'd leave room for a door: the big band standards of Cab Calloway.

"I already got a house." The Rev was still sitting as my granddad secured *Minnie the Moocher* to the top of the south wall.

"You may have a house out there," he said. "But you don't have a house in here."

The Rev thought this over, turning it around on his eyes and his lips as he sipped from his gin. "I never figured you could build a house from records," he said, finally.

"You can build a house from anything."

The biggest problem, as my granddad explained it to me, was the roof. They couldn't use something heavy—your standard bass, for example—due to fear that the weight would cause the whole thing to come crashing down. The other option was something light and airy—a soprano—but then, as the Rev pointed out, what sort of protection would that offer? A third dilemma as they scanned the rummaged aisles: there wasn't much material left. My granddad had emptied the shelves to construct the foundations, the floors, the high walls—and now, the pickings were devastatingly slim. A Bing Crosby here, a Jimmy Rushing there—nothing, though, that contained the heft he knew they needed.

He turned, then, to the Rev. To the pile of records on which he sat. "What about those?"

The Rev paused at this. He bit his lower lip, wiped another clump of soot from a bone-dry eye. As he stood, ash fell from his shoulders, from the slender tips of his fingers, floating down to the floor in airy feathers.

He handed the first of the records to my granddad, who fixed it in place, the first of the countless shingles that would save them.

" 'Song for a Lonely Woman' by Art Blakey," the Rev said as he watched my granddad work. "That's the first time I saw my wife. She was sitting alone on a bench on the north side of Bigelow wearing a big old hat that covered her face. Could've been the ugliest woman on earth for all I knew. Only thing I was sure of was that woman would end up mine and this would be the song that'd come to mind each time I thought of her."

The Rev passed my granddad record after record, the pile below him shrinking as the shadow surrounding them grew.

" 'Summertime' is the first time I tasted an apricot."

" 'Georgia on My Mind' is when I got whacked for falling asleep and snoring in church."

" 'The Best Is Yet to Come' is when I realized that if the sky was blue enough you could see the moon on a clear day."

" 'Day by Day' is riding the Duquesne Incline with my old man."

" 'Stella by Starlight' is kissing girls I shouldn't have been kissing."

" 'Mood Indigo' is watching my mother dance as she dries dishes."

" 'Tuxedo Junction' is drinking too much and smoking too much and having one hell of a time either way."

" 'In a Sentimental Mood' is when I learned that love doesn't last much longer than a spider bite."

The halo over the hills grows wider until it isn't a halo at all, but instead an industrial sunrise, and at four minutes after midnight I-76 drops onto a lower section of the Allegheny Plateau and Randal and I begin to see the first buildings along the city's eastern outskirts.

No one could stand to watch once the onslaught began. Arms no longer linked, they left the place, embarking on a million different death walks to a million different homes.

The thing is, though, my granddad and the Rev didn't even hear the wrecking ball when it took out the shop's north wall. Before my granddad had sealed up the record home's door, he'd dragged in an old phonograph he'd uncovered in one of the store's abandoned corners. As chunks of the shop tumbled off the vinyl roof to the earth around them, they drank from the cup of gin and listened to the last record they had, the only one they didn't use, Stan Getz's *Here's That Rainy Day*.

When the song stopped and the wrecking ball had ceased its silent banging, the Rev emerged into a vacant lot. He kicked at the broken pieces of everything that used to be, and he looked up at the sun, which through the smoke looked like a cotton ball, all pulled and frayed and roughed up along its edges.

He turned to my granddad and said, "The sky! I haven't seen the sky in weeks."

WHAT I REMEMBER

1958–1963: Used Cars

By Colin A. McPhee

In the beginning, the Bel Air sat in the driveway unused.

After my father arrived at the Avalon to pick me up on that evening in June, the car began to make dreadful sounds—the crash of cannonballs shattering glass—and I remember halfway believing that it was protesting my presence, boorishly rejecting my father's introduction of me. But then on a Saturday morning in June he brought it to the city, to some man in Chinatown who tightened a few screws and replaced the missing rear window, and after that my father began driving away.

Initially the drives were short, and only on weekends. He'd leave for two, three, rarely four hours. If the weather allowed it, he'd remove the car's canvas top. Always during these excursions he wore a tweed hat—a ratty thing with a wide brim that he bought in the city, and which wasn't meant for driving, though I suspect he thought it was. On three separate occasions he complained of almost losing it; the car's top would be down and the wind would steal it from his head, carrying it to the corner of some old dirt road. He didn't stop wearing it, though: instead, he bobby-pinned the damned thing to his head.

Early on, he'd sometimes ask me to join him. He'd pick me up after a matinee at the Avalon, and he'd say, "How about we go someplace?"

"Where?"

He'd shrug. "Anywhere?"

I'd look at him for a moment, at how he'd pinned the hat impossibly high on his head, how he looked like a cockeyed version of James Stewart in *Vertigo* but with lighter hair and more worn cheeks.

I'd say, "Sure. Yeah, okay."

Though inevitably, each time we pulled on to the highway—448 or 9 or 117—the car would begin its abominable screaming again. The incessant booming and snapping that caused the floorboards to shake and the windows to rattle.

"It wasn't doing this earlier," he'd explain as he pulled over to the shoulder. As he popped the hood and began inexpertly examining the car's guts.

I'd be hanging out the passenger's side window and I'd yell to him, "Maybe it's me?"

He'd push the cap up higher on his head. He'd laugh meekly. "Of course it's not you."

But soon afterward he stopped inviting me entirely.

The first time my father drove away and didn't come back was in the fall of that year, of 1958.

It was October seventeenth. Sixteen months after my mother passed away. Eighty thirty in the evening. The sun had set, but the night was clear, and there were still traces of light. To the west, primarily. But also on the steel of the car: it reflected in shards off the fenders.

I watched my father from where I was sitting, on his bed. It was the only location from which, if I sat on my knees, I could see the driveway. My view was obstructed by a sycamore in the front yard, but it was enough to see him in the negative spaces left by the curves of the leaves: half of him was him, and the other half was orange, yellow, red, engulfed. It was enough to know that he wasn't looking back at me.

He placed a hand on each tire to check its pressure. He knelt at each one and ran his palm in half circles over the rubber. I laced my fingers together. Once he finished with the tires, he opened the car's hood. The creak and snap of the rust cracking against the metal hinges.

He was hidden by a branch when he leaned over the car. But over the course of the week I'd seen him do this ten, twenty, one hundred times. I'd watched him as he examined each hose; I'd heard him whisper as he checked the oil.

My father sat on the curb and lit a cigarette once he'd shut the hood. The leaves were just shadows then—any light had faded—and he sat beyond them. He held the cigarette down low, between two knuckles. Its embers grew bright each time he inhaled and then faded as his hand fell from his mouth to his side. My legs, bent beneath my body, ached as I watched him.

He sat on the curb for nearly twenty minutes. I don't remember seeing him get into the car, but I heard the door slam shut. I held my breath as he started the engine—I waited for one thousand cannonballs followed by the screams and wails of falling glass, but instead there was nothing. It just thumped as he reversed down the driveway, and then lurched as he shifted into first and plodded to the end of the street, where it intersected with the main road. But I'd lost sight of him before this. The leaves, then black, hid him once he'd cleared the curb.

I slept in my father's bed that night. I didn't leave his room once he'd driven away. I listened to the clock and I stayed on top of the sheets, wrapping myself in an unfinished blanket my mother had tried to knit. I slept restlessly. Each hour, I'd sit on my knees and watch the driveway, silver underneath the sycamore. When I fell back asleep, I didn't dream.

The next day—it was Saturday—I stayed on his bed, my own private island. I was afraid to leave. I was afraid to get water when I was thirsty, or to make toast when I was hungry. I was afraid that in the brief moments of my absence, he'd end up returning and leaving again. I was afraid, I think, that I'd miss my opportunity to convince him to stay.

I only ventured out once I had to. Once the stench of myself became too nauseating, and the emptiness sloshing about my stomach became too gnawing, I washed and dressed and rode my bike to the Avalon, where Earl allowed me to watch *The Big Country* three times for free.

After the end credits were rolling the second time around he asked me, "Had enough Gregory Peck yet?" I sat in the balcony's front row, and he took the seat next to me.

"Never."

"What about Charles Bickford?"

"I think they should've cast Don Murray."

Earl nodded slowly. He was an unusually tall man—he had to duck when he crossed through a number of the theater's doors—but the rest of his body hadn't caught up proportionally to his height. His head was a cap size too small and his shoulders were too thin and sloped steeply inward. The sleeves of the uniform he wore (a grey usher's jacket with gold piping as the trim) fully concealed his ten fingers, which stopped just below his waist when his arms were resting against his sides. His legs, though: they were long and flimsy with a grasshopper's sense of hurried mobility; his pants reached the middle of his calf.

The house lights rose and the sparse audience filed out of the theater, allowing the Avalon's ushers to sweep the aisles between the seats. I watched as they traversed the rows, picking up discarded chocolate boxes and lone soggy kernels.

Earl placed a hand on my knee. "Well then," he said. "Enjoy."

That week I watched *The Big Country* fourteen times. I memorized not only the picture's dialogue, but also the cuts, the different sorts of fade-ins and dissolves that bookmark its scenes. I ditched school entirely, spending vast stretches of my day at the Avalon. At night, when the lobby lights were finally shut off and Earl had locked the theater's front doors, I'd ride my bike the eight minutes home. I'd sit on my father's bed, my legs always folded beneath me, and I'd write movies.

The ideas I had then, when I was ten, were flimsy and weak. They stretched clumsily beyond the infantile and raw knowledge I had of the world. And when they didn't work out (which was often), I'd crush the sheets on which they were written into neat balls that I'd throw to the bedroom floor. I littered the carpet with two entire notebooks' worth of paper until, finally, I hit upon a concept with which I was familiar. Or, one that, at least to me, seemed to make sense.

The premise was this: a boy who spends his days in a movie theater, subsisting on popcorn and candy and soda, eventually starts hiding in the films he watches.

Logistically, the conceit was simple, which means that it was impossible—much more so than anything I could imagine writing now. One Saturday, as a matinee showing of *Pal Joey* was ending and the audience had its back turned, the boy simply reached one finger, then a hand, an arm, and finally his whole torso into the screen. When the curtain fell, it just missed clipping his right heel. If you were at the theater for the later showing that evening, and if you were compelled to look hard enough, you'd be able to find him: ducking between the chorus girls' legs as they belted out "That Terrific Rainbow." Swaying his blond head while Joey and Linda crooned "I Could Write a Book."

I assumed then—or, perhaps more accurately, I so *wanted* to assume—that movies intertwined in a world that was separate and complete, that once the chorus girls from *Pal Joey* had finished their act, they'd saunter over and have a drink with Auntie Mame. That despite the obvious anachronisms, Dorothy visited Tara, where she, Scarlett, and Ilsa Lund discussed Anna Leonowens's move to Siam. So, when that evening's showing of *Pal Joey* ended, the boy didn't disappear, nor did he unfold himself from the theater's dark screen back into the house: he just moved on to the next picture.

He wore broad-rimmed cowboy hats and rode horses alongside Ethan Edwards and Captain Samuel Clayton in *The Searchers;* he broke into torrential sweats while he trained alongside Rocky Graziano in *Somebody Up There Likes Me,* jumping rope and punching dusty bags. When Gaston kissed Gigi's cheek, the boy kissed the other one. It was easy, and lovely, and perfect, until one moment during *The Vikings* when he was helping to lead a bloody raid and he decided he wanted to go home.

He'd just sliced into an enemy warrior's skull when he turned to Einar, who was Kirk Douglas, but truthfully not, and said, "Look, I'm going to miss dinner."

The Viking growled, baring his teeth, which should have been yellow, but were in fact Hollywood white.

"I mean it," the boy said, cleaning the blood from his blade. "If I'm not home by six, my mom'll let me have it." He shook Einar's polished hand. "Good luck, though. Really, I mean it."

But there was no screen to melt into. No slick white vinyl upon which to dissolve himself. He tried passing through other objects: He pushed aside the chopped-up limbs of vanquished opponents and charged full speed into giant stones. He dove headfirst into Norway's half-iced sea. He sat on a pebbled beach with a bruised nose and frozen fingers.

And thus he was left to wander. To try to poke holes into the paper-thin world he'd created. In a dragon boat with one oar, he crossed trace-less seas, landing on the shores of Oz, on the lawns of Sunset Boulevard's mansions, on Wabash Avenue. He rounded his hands around glass mugs and streetlamps and pillars; he touched every object he could, seeing if he could find something that was fleshed out with the right number of dimensions. He interrupted Brick Pollitt as he leapt over hurdles and asked if he knew the way home.

The boy's father began to worry and his mother chewed at her nails; their dinner spread on the kitchen table, steaming and untouched.

The father stood and the food stopped steaming, held its breath. "I'm going," he said.

"But where?"

"To find him."

The father drove a perfect yellow car to the cinema where he'd last seen his boy. When the car ran, it was silent: unlike other cars, it hushed its throttled chugging so it could listen to the man hum. Once inside the theater, he craned his head beneath seats and dug his slender fingers into empty popcorn boxes. He shouted out his son's name into the Technicolor dark and the people filling the seats yelled, *Quiet!*

He saw him at the end of the film's credits, the boy dodging words and names as they raced across the screen. There he was, worming through the hole in an O, and then, hanging with one hand from a J's curved hook.

He called out to the boy. He said, sternly, "Enough of this! Come home," but it was moments too late: the last credit vanished and the screen went black, taking the boy with it.

And so he drove to the theater in the next town, and then to the theaters in the city. The theaters on the coasts and in the valleys and on the peaks of mountains, snow dusting the tops of their marquees. He crisscrossed his world searching for his son, who was lost threading paths through his own.

It was a crude exercise, but I kept at it each night for six years. When a page was completed, I slipped it into a deep empty drawer in my father's desk. I watched as, over time, the sheets accumulated into a weighty stack, a messy epic that weighed down the wood in which it sat. The evenings that my father was home, I'd press my ear against his bedroom door. I'd listen for the soft, static shuffling of paper.

There were other things I did to keep my father and his car from leaving.

Three different times I siphoned out Lucy's gas; I disconnected the spark plugs; I pulled at wires and valves and filthy rubber hoses without knowing what functions they served. I heard from someone, somewhere, that if I shifted gears while the car was off, the transmission would eventually give. I'd wait well into the night for my father to sleep, and I'd sit at the wheel and shift from first to second to third, for one hour, for two, for three.

After midnight in April of 1963, when I was fifteen, I crouched next to the car's hood in the garage and released the air from all four tires. If I'm remembering correctly, I had a hell of a time with it. I suppose I thought it'd be as simple as deflating a bike tire. That once I unscrewed the valve cap and depressed the pin inside, the air would rush out quickly and seamlessly; the job would take minutes.

Not so. I scrambled between the tires in the dark, listening to them, inhaling their traces of bitter asphalt. The air wasn't being released quickly enough; despite the deflating hisses, the tires stayed solid and firm. I reached from the front of the car toward its rear, trying to touch two valves at once. My arms were too short and my legs were too long. I stumbled incessantly in the black. Bruises grew on both knees from sliding against the cement and my knuckles bled. I stared at the valves. I slapped at the tires' hides with my open palm.

I was sweating and hyperventilating, but I was afraid of slowing down. Had I not felt a loose screw press against my hand when I tripped, I'm betting I would've kept running, like a dog chasing his tail, until I passed out. It felt like gravel, but sharper, and it drew blood from the lines on my palm. It was small—a quarter of an inch—with a piercing point and a rusted thread. I felt along the front right tire's inner loop until I found the valve and I slipped the screw into place, pressing it until the pin depressed and held. The air released in a wide steady flow. I waited, counted, and it kept coming.

I found more screws, rummaging through my father's workbench, through his toolbox with the broken hinge, searching blind along the dark contours of the floor. Each time I found one that was the right size, I wedged it into one of the empty valves, and the hissing grew louder, the tires harmonizing with one another. When the air leaked from all four, I told myself it was the most beautiful sound I'd ever heard.

But then the next morning, the tires were full again.

HOW TO MAKE YOUR BABY FAMOUS!

Finn

It's closing in around one o'clock in the morning, and it's been almost an hour since Randal and I arrived in this goddamned city, but we both say it feels like we've been here for years. Like we've been driving aimlessly along thousands of vacant grey streets and staring at a thousand empty storefronts passing a thousand empty cars. And we've said a thousand times that it's fun, but a thousand more times that we're tired. So finally we agree to book a room at the Forbes Avenue Suites, which is well lit and situated on the edge of a collegiate neighborhood called Oakland, and which advertises free garage parking, free cable, and rooms to rent by the hour, day, week, and month.

"What're we supposed to do with Mrs. Dalloway?" Randal asks me when we've parked Lucy. He's got his pack unzipped an inch or two and from the black space within protrudes one of the cat's gnarled paws.

"I don't know," I say. "Take her with us?"

"Can't we just, like—"

"Like what, Randal? Leave her in the trunk?"

He doesn't say anything—he just chews the inside of his cheeks. Finally: "I think she's hungry."

"We'll buy her something to eat."

"What if she eats *us*?"

"This is ridiculous."

In the hotel room, I wait until Randal steps into the bathroom, and until I hear the shower running, and until he begins some off-key rendition of "November Rain," before I release Mrs. Dalloway from the pack. She takes in the room slowly, nonchalantly, hopping with unexpected grace between the legs of a wooden coffee table and a set of stained wool curtains. I keep trying to pet her, though she won't let me; she just sort of trots away every time I graze my fingers against her arched back. It's only once I totally lose interest that she returns, sliding her balding head against my open palm.

"All right," I tell her. "I see how it is."

I slip out into the hallway, which is partly outside—a sort of balcony that looks out over Forbes Avenue and runs along the length of the hotel. The air is so thick that you can almost see it pinned to the contours of the hills, and there are no stars, only streetlamps.

I call Karen, who's phoned me seventeen times over the past four hours. She picks up on the third ring and she sounds out of breath and Hugo is barking.

"Christ," I say. "He's so loud."

I hear her opening cupboards and then closing them. Rummaging. "He's hungry. He thinks I'm feeding him."

"It's one o'clock in the morning. You haven't fed him?"

More cupboards closing. "I think," she says, "I'm out of dog food."

To anyone else, I suppose the hour at which I'm calling would seem weird, but Karen holds shares of my insomnia and has cultivated a sleepless existence of her own. She's taught me how to appreciate empty streets caked in darkness, how three a.m. doesn't have to bring around that droopy sadness of the soul. How to have dreams with my eyes open.

We get each other on the phone around one, two, three o'clock when there's something worth watching on TV. It'll be a rerun of a competition program she especially likes. Or some social experiment shtick that interests me. We'll talk about how they've cast it. How they've cut it, how they've rearranged it. How we could always do it better.

"This dog," Karen says.

"Yes. *That dog.*"

"I love him, though." She says something to Hugo I can't make out. "You know? I really love him."

"Of course." I lean my elbows on the wet rusted iron of the balcony's railing.

"It's just—sometimes I wonder if it was best. For him. Does that make sense? He would've had such a better life there."

"In Toronto?"

"In wherever he ended up."

Hugo is still barking. Karen yells *Shutthefuckup* and then apologizes to him. I'm beginning to smell; I can smell myself. I dip my nose beneath the loose collar of my shirt. Sweat and salt and something else, something airier: pine.

She continues: "I've been trying to get hold of you all evening."

"I was in a lot of tunnels," I tell her. "I don't think my phone works in tunnels."

"Regardless, I have you now."

I wipe the water from my forearms and see orange streaks. "Yes, you do."

"After you left today I met with programming."

"Did you know that the only way to get through Blue Mountain is to drive through all these tunnels?"

Across from the hall-balcony thing is a mural, a massive piece of graffiti art that flanks the east wall of a parking lot.

"They're shuffling around some things." She's still talking. Hugo has stopped barking. Now, instead, there's that motor-boat-in-muck chomp of a dog gorging himself on kibble. "There's—how did they say this?— there's a general concern that some of the network's flagship programming is feeling a bit stale."

The mural, the one across from the balcony, has shattered skulls and derelict landscapes and upturned streets: the intricate stuff of postapocalyptic fiction.

I say, "Another question: do you know what to feed a cat? Like, aside from cat food?"

Karen says, "Jesus Christ, Finn, listen to me, they're canceling the show."

I duck my nose farther back into my shirt. I speak into my chest so it muffles my voice. "They can't do that. Can they? They can't do that."

"They can. And they're going to."

"But how? How can they do that when we're the Most Popular Reality Program they have? That anyone has?"

Karen sighs and it whistles. She speaks from her chest. "I don't think that's the case anymore. I actually don't think that's been the case for a while, Finn."

She tells me then what happened. She tells me how after I'd left she'd received a call from the head of the channel's programming department—a woman called Ms. Balthildis van der Bijl (whose Dutch name, I should probably mention, literally means "of the ax"). Karen explains to me how none of this seemed particularly strange. A little different, all right, because they usually met on the first Tuesday of every month, and this call was *after* that meeting, which incidentally had gone pretty well, etc.—so, yeah, a little different, but not strange, no definitely not *strange*.

So, right: at 5:30 Karen leaves the office on Seventh, and because she has a few extra minutes and because the only thing Karen hates more than puppy mills is the subway during the summer, she decides to walk to the network headquarters, which are in Times Square, on Broadway. But then on the way, somewhere north of Penn Station, she steps in two steaming mounds of dog shit, which she thinks is supposed to be good luck in some other city, Paris or something, but here, in New York, when you're wearing *brand-new* open-toed shoes is just fantastically repulsive.

At headquarters she heads up to programming in a glass elevator packed tightly with the sort of girls that make Karen and me happy that we work in our annex on Seventh, and she doesn't even have to explain the looks they gave her, the way they held up their tilted pierced noses, the way they threw their spiteful eyes down at her shit-caked toes.

"I went to the ladies room before I told the receptionist I was there," she says. "I tried to wash myself off the best I could. At least off my god-damned *skin*. Because, I mean, can't you get something awful from . . . that? Hepatitis or something? Cholera? I'm not a doctor. But Christ, Finn. I've never seen this much crap before in my entire life. And I was sweating. Not just sweating. But, like, *shvitzing*. If you would've seen me you would've thought it was raining outside. Raining shit and sweat."

"But what happened?" I ask. "In the office? When you got in there? What did Of the Ax say?"

"She was sitting in the glass conference room—the one that faces Broadway—with three other guys, which I suppose should've been a sign. But when I sat down I still didn't have any idea anything was wrong." Because, she explains, the Ax was still wearing that big Dutch smile she has. And she was saying these fantastic things like *Oh hello, hello hello hello, don't you look vonderful* in that big Dutch accent of hers, which is really quite calming and wonderful, probably one of the best accents out there, which is sort of weird, isn't it? Because Dutch, as a language, is especially grating on the ears.

I say, "I don't know. Maybe? But Karen. When did you know something was up? *What did they say?*"

"Frankly after van der Bijl mentioned how *vonderful* I looked they got right into it. Basically, the show's not pulling weight. The past two seasons we've been clocking in a point three in eighteen to forty-nine. They think—"

"The rating systems are fucked. Everyone knows that. They think what?"

Hugo barks again; Karen clicks her teeth. "I'm paraphrasing this, all right? Just—know I'm paraphrasing this: they don't think we're producing a relatable sort of reality anymore. These good-looking kids. This demographically perfect representation. This ridiculous house with its Swedish furniture. Its Bjorn lamps and its Blarfemfarb beds and its Klaataven chairs. The general feeling is that people—that the *audience*—no longer relates. That it's just not real."

"We'll make them get jobs."

"We already make them get jobs."

"Then we'll make them get more jobs. We'll only cast people from Detroit and Tulsa and Cleveland. We'll film there, too. Did you tell them all this? Did you tell them I can make something as real as they want?"

"Finn."

"But—but no." I claw at my thumb with my forefinger until the skin has turned red, until it's in that solid-liquid place between flesh and blood. "But no, they must just not know what they're talking about. Did they give you a reason? I bet they did, right? Ha, ha. I bet it was awful. I bet we'll just have to show them that they don't know, right?"

"Finn, I'm doing everything I can."

"No," I say, maybe I yell, but I think I just say. "No, tell me what reason they gave you."

There's that sort of silence that you wish would never be broken. The kind where you wish you could just stay, suspended, between dimensions: a sort of Bizarro world where you're allowed to reconsider asking your last question.

"They've got something else in the pipeline. Another show." Karen's voice is soft. It cracks between different keys in different octaves.

"No."

"It's true, Finn. I don't know what else to tell you. Like I said, I'm doing everything I can, but this is just the way it works. They've got something else. Something that they think fits the new demo."

I will, at this point, refrain from saying the name of the new show, because—again—it might be something you'll see, but just trust me when I say that it features a trifecta of terrific awfulness, which includes mostly dead famous people, babies, and plastic surgery. Basically, in the way of some sort of summation: you have these youngish mothers. And they have these babies who are cute, but maybe not the cutest. But that isn't the point: the babies could be the cutest babies in the universe and the youngish mothers wouldn't care because, at the end of day, they want their babies to look like famous babies. Or some of them want their babies to look like famous *adults,* and that's where production really expects things to get interesting, I guess, but most of them, most of them want infants. Which is where the wigs and the costumes and a very, very potentially unethical Fort Lauderdale–based cosmetic surgeon enter the picture, and—yes. Yes, fine, fuck it, okay. *I Want a Famous Baby.*

"It ends," Karen says, "with a pageant."

"A pageant."

"To see which baby looks the most like a famous baby. Or adult. A famous adult. There might be different categories: babies who are supposed to look like babies, and babies who are supposed to look like adults."

She pauses for a moment, then asks, "Are you liking Pittsburgh?"

"We can't let this happen."

"Hugo says hello." Then, cooing: "What will happen to us, old boy?"

"For the sake of the future of the universe and Goodness and little unfamous children everywhere, we honestly cannot let this happen."

"I'll call you when I know more," she says. "Send me a postcard, all right?"

Downstairs, in the Forbes Avenue Suites commissary, there is no cat food and so, after some deliberation, I pay $11.59 for two cans of tuna and a box of wheat crackers. But then, when I return to the room, I find Mrs. Dalloway munching on a 3 Musketeers bar.

"Jesus, Randal," I say, snatching the chocolate away from the cat's paw. She looks up at me, her eyes narrowed into this space between loathing and longing. A piece of chocolate dangles from one of her whiskers.

"What?"

"That shit will kill her." I open one of the tuna cans and drain the excess water into the bathroom sink. In the middle of the fleshy chunks I wedge two wheat crackers. I present it to Mrs. Dalloway who examines the meal with her standard look of distaste and disdain.

"Finn." Randal wears the same clothes he's sported the entire day, though now he emits the vague scent of a cheap hotel shower—hard water and Ivory soap. "That cat witnessed the fall of communism. It was there when the *Challenger* exploded and the first case of AIDS was reported. It was already a year old when Kennedy got shot. A chocolate nugget will not end its life, however unfortunate that might be."

Mrs. Dalloway nibbles at the corners of the wheat crackers, taking bites as dainty as her ill-balanced form will allow. She rolls on her back and sighs, spreading out in all directions.

"She's going to hate me," I say as I watch her.

"Probably, but I wouldn't take it personally."

I sling my camcorder over my shoulder and retrieve my granddad's map from the back pocket of my shorts. "We need to get going."

"Where to?"

I unfold the map and point to the first of my granddad's new notes, one of the three that he's written specifically for me, the letters curving through the blue space formed by the Atlantic.

I say, "To scout out this house of records."

We walk east down Forbes, where we decide there's more lights and more life and just pretty much less per-capita desertion. We walk with our hands clenched in fists and shoved in the pockets of our shorts. We walk till the street's emptiness gives way to people, to small flocks of women, to packs of men in Steelers jerseys, all huddled in globes of grey ash air that hover outside the bars. We jump in the wet gutters alongside them, inhaling the smoke from their lungs as we pass.

We walk till the street begins to empty again. We stop for directions at a pub that bows just a hundred yards away from the University of Pittsburgh's Cathedral of Learning, this opulent and overthought structure that throws a shadow even at night. Inside, we sit on red vinyl stools and look across the mahogany bar to the faces of three weathered men who have their chins turned up, their eyes reflecting a TV turned to a local sports channel, and I can tell that it is the type of place where you come to finish, as opposed to start.

I order us both Lowland scotch, which sets off brushfires in my throat when I swallow it, and I suck on ice cubes between sips. When the bartender—who has a long blond ponytail and bone-white skin and a certain softness you can tell other boys mocked when he was younger but began to silently envy as he got older—when he asks us if he can get us anything else, Randal says yeah, yeah he can, something to eat.

"The kitchen closed about five minutes ago," he says, and he begins wiping at wet spots on the counter with a black towel. "I could get you some fries, though. They've got tons of fries back there."

"All right."

"But you—you're going to need to turn that camera off first."

"It's not even on."

"It is. I can see the red light."

I suck on my upper lip. The men who have their chins turned up begin to howl at the television.

"Look at them," the bartender says. "Sitting there, yelling at the top of their lungs like someone's actually listening."

He sets both hands on the counter, spreading his fingers away from one another. "To hell with it. I'll get you some fries."

Randal says, "Thank you."

"They're good," he tells us. "They're famous. Get that. If you're going to keep that thing going, get that—get me saying they're famous."

"I got it. What makes them famous?"

He looks into the camera and waits and I expect him to say something strikingly brilliant. But then: "Fuck if I know." He stops wiping and tightens his apron and disappears into the kitchen. Across from us, all three of the men wince in unison at something on the television. One of them whispers *Jeez-o-man*.

"How are they?" He's brought back a red plastic basket lined with wax paper, heaped with French fries. Randal eats one, or half of one, and he winces as it singes his gums. "Should've given you warning—they just came out of the deep fryer."

"They're good," he says.

I suck on another piece of ice.

The bartender reaches across the bar and takes a handful. "Probably not good enough to be famous, though?"

"Probably not."

He refills our glasses, then turns around to ask the men if they need anything, and they answer him with *Dabby good* and *Hauscome you gotsa ask* and *It's cordorda two* and *We got a whole nother hour* and *Keep 'em coming downa minute,* and none of it, absolutely none of it sounds anything like English.

"What are they saying?" Randal says.

"Who knows what Yinzers are ever saying?"

He pushes his hair, which looks too soft, synthetic cotton, out of his face.

"I don't know what a Yinzer is."

"Yinzers. People who say 'yinz.' People who speak Pittsburgh English. Pittsburghese."

"That isn't English, what they're speaking."

"Ha," he says. "No? No, I guess it doesn't sound like it, does it. I guess I'd probably say the same thing if I were hearing it for the first time."

"But what is it?"

"Oh, I don't know. It's just how they talk. A lot of it comes from Scotch-Irish, I think. Or German. Maybe some Slavic." He pulls more on his hair. "Whatever the ugliest languages are. Those are them, right? Slavic, German, bastardized Irish?"

Randal watches how they move their mouths, how the words and sounds sit in the middle of their fantastic melted throats. He tries incredibly hard to copy them.

The bartender puts up his hand and there are cuts on his fingers. "No," he says. "No, don't try. You're setting yourself up to sound worse off than them."

A clock above the bar blinks 1:45 in green perforated numbers. The scotch spins in whirlpools as I make circles with my glass and when I drink it the brushfires seem smaller, or at least more contained. I ask, "Can you tell me how to get to Wylie Avenue?"

"Wylie Avenue?"

"Yeah," I say, standing.

He says: "That's over in the Hill. You don't want to go there." I watch as he drops two fresh ice cubes into Randal's glass. "You go there right now, looking like you do, putting that camera up in people's business— you're not coming back with your face intact."

"I'd like to go. There's something there that I'd like to see."

"There are other places to go."

I say, "Tell me anywhere else."

He reaches for a white square napkin from a stack of them that's 8 million inches high. Pulling a pen from behind his right ear he says, "Everywhere. There's everywhere else to go." He scribbles as he speaks. "There's a mattress factory."

"A mattress factory."

"There's a Warhol Museum. There's the Art Institute of Pittsburgh. There's the South Side and the Phipps Conservatory and the Strip District." He looks at the napkin and slides it across to me. "There's everywhere else to go."

We thank him. We finish the scotch. We eat three more hardly famous fries, and we leave.

On the street, Randal and I sit on the curb and we swat at gnats clawing at our bare ankles and thighs before finally, after twenty minutes, we flag down a cab. The driver takes Forbes to the Boulevard of the Allies. We sail down giant hills. We roll down our windows and the wind crashes around us in towering waves. To the south everything sleeps, but most of all the Monongahela, which looks inky black and is interrupted only by the city's bridges, its silver bones that stretch at uneven intervals and angles.

"They're trying to cancel the show," I say when we've reached Kirkpatrick. "I spoke with Karen tonight." There's a stoplight, and there's the first traffic we've seen and so we're forced to stop.

"Maybe that's a good thing. Maybe it's time."

"That's not what you were supposed to say."

The light changes and the cab lurches forward. I lean my head against the window and I open my mouth to catch more of the night, to eat it in great wide gulps.

North along Kirkpatrick we're stopped by another traffic light, the longest one in history. The buildings on all sides of us have shrunk into sad affairs, their warped windows sloped downward into frowns.

I say, "They're replacing it with a show about having famous babies."

"I think I've seen that show before."

"Maybe," I said. "It's about these parents—these young mothers—who want their babies to look like famous children. Famous babies. So they do all these things to make that happen. Like buy them wigs and dress them up. Find doctors who will perform plastic surgery on them."

"Oh. *Oh*. Ha. That's particularly awful."

I ask, "But would you watch it?"

"Maybe? All right, it's particularly awful, but doesn't that also mean it's particularly fascinating?" Then, after a few moments: "I suppose my biggest worry would be that there'd be just too many obvious choices."

"How do you mean?"

"Well. I'm assuming that unless they've got, like, weird cuteness-competition issues, these mothers would want their kids to look like adorable baby stars, right?"

"Right. Right, sure."

"Have you ever seen a picture of Freddie Mercury as a kid?"

"I haven't."

Randal stretches his arms out and sets them on the seat in front of him. Flexes his ten fingers. "No mother would want that. No mother would wish a baby that looked like that on anyone. But, like, Shirley Temple?"

"Sure."

"Can't you see it? Every episode would, simply by default, feature at least one Shirley Temple transformation."

"I'd say at the very least."

"By the end of the first season you'd have an army of them."

"An army of Shirley Temple babies."

"That's what I'm trying to say with obvious choices."

The driver shifts in his seat, drumming his thumbs on the steering wheel.

"But what about the moral issues?" I ask.

"The what?"

"The moral issues? Of deciding for a baby that she'd like to look like Shirley Temple? Without even asking her?"

"Oh. Ha. Oh, Finn. I think we're pretty far beyond that."

It's quiet, almost. There's some dog barking somewhere. And then that bark turns to human yelling, and then grunting, swift blunt kicks, and then crumpled whimpering, and then music, something loud, then more barking, more yelling, grunting, kicking, crumpled heart-wrenching whimpers, in that pattern a million times over. I listen, holding my breath. I try to discriminate between the different voices, human and canine. I try to decide how far away they are, counting short seconds after hearing thunder.

"Is this it?" Randal rocks on his heels. We're both drunk. So drunk. The hour-old scotch draining the wetness from our mouths.

"Shh."

"But—there's nothing here."

The plot of land where my granddad and the Rev built their house of records is now empty. The few buildings that do surround it are brick and look desolate and heavy, like hangovers. When I step from the curb to the sidewalk and then onto the earth there are weeds that are too tall, and there are gnats, making laps around my neck, my ears.

The wind's starving. It blows weakly, pushing just hard enough to move the leaves of these giant oaks overhead. Slices of light from the streetlamps above us shift, following patternless tracks. I trace the lot's perimeter with the camera. I follow the lines of its overgrown boundaries, zooming in on the blades of grass so many times until the world exists solely as spotted green pixels. I expect to be trembling, but I'm actually deathly still. The only change, I realize, is that I've quite suddenly become hot. Human-torch hot.

Randal jogs to the middle of the space and the streetlamps light up his forehead and his shoulders.

I keep filming for my granddad. I go from an extreme wide shot to a long shot; I cut away to the buildings that surround the empty lot so he'll have a sense of context and place. So he can imagine where things might've stood.

"I mean, you didn't think anything would actually be here, though, right? It's not as though you *believe* that story."

He says again: "Because there's nothing here."

WHAT I REMEMBER

1964: Unbelieving, Part 1

By Colin A. McPhee

When I turned sixteen, Earl asked me if I'd like to work at the Avalon.

It was on a Sunday afternoon, and during the previous week my father had been gone on one of his itinerant wanderings, as he so often was. I had just finished watching *The Night of the Iguana* for the second time, and I can recall leaning against the ticket booth, weighing the options of what to do with the weekend's last precious hours.

"You spend enough time here as it is," Earl said. "You might as well get paid for it."

Fittingly, Earl had aged cinematically since the theater first opened. The grooves and wrinkles that pleated his cheeks were so pronounced that they seemed to be a trick of makeup or lighting—not normal wear. The grey in his hair so suddenly thick that it had to have been painted on, dyed. When he spoke, he pulled absently at a Twainish mustache he only very rarely trimmed.

"What would you have me do?" I asked.

He shrugged, and his too-short arms fell to his stretched sides. "Whatever you'd like. You know this place better than most folks who already work here."

"Give me some options."

"Ushering. Ticket sales. The projector."

Behind me, a customer counted out $1.25 for a ticket to the evening show and the wind whistled in the waning light. On at least ten separate occasions Earl had offered to give me a tour of the theater's projection room (Earl being a man who knew very much, though very much about only one thing, that thing being how movies worked), and each time I had declined. Until that day, the closest I had ever been to the projection room was the second row of the theater's balcony, from which I would periodically turn back to stare into the machine's wraithy white light.

At that point, I was beginning to parse out why I was spending so much time at the cinema. In the films I found an escape from the realities that boiled near the back of my brain. My father's absence, my mother's death—her indirect suicide. I wanted to believe, fervently so, that movies—my refuge—lacked the mechanical, banal explanations that so accurately explained those ghosts.

"How about the concession stand," I said.

I bargained for a wage of $1.75 per hour and we set a schedule consisting primarily of nights and weekends—and our house, where I was born and where my mother died, sat mostly empty and alone. I'd return there in the evenings, after the Avalon's last showing, and after listening to the echoes of locks tumbling shut, I'd search for signs that my father had been home. Fingerprints in the dust that clothed the kitchen table. Dissected newspapers. Overturned pages of my script. His ratty hat, his smell.

More and more, though, it was becoming just me. I'd brush my teeth in the bathroom at the top of the stairs, where my mother used to lock herself away. I'd lock my bedroom door when I slept at night. I'd leave the house to itself, to its conversing sounds.

The girl who worked at the concession stand with me was named Clare Murkowski. She was a year older than me, and at first I thought I recognized her in a vague, unsure way from the high school I attended, where I had very few friends and wanted even fewer. She had shoulder-length hair the color of coffee beans and a stark face: Faith Domergue in *Vendetta*, minus a quarter of the softness in the mouth and nose. Our shifts were nearly identical, save an hour or two on Sunday, when she often had to leave to babysit an eight-year-old half sister who was a result of her mother's second marriage.

"It's strange," she told me as she loaded corn kernels into a giant steel drum. "Only sharing part of something with someone."

I said, "But isn't that exactly what sharing is?" and Clare ate a kernel raw, sucking away the oil before crunching it between her molars.

"She doesn't look a thing like me. She's supposedly my sister—"

"Half sister."

"And she doesn't look a thing like me. She looks like my stepfather."

"Well, that's not the part you share."

I was wiping dust from the menu that hung on the stand's back wall while Clare slipped behind me, her boyish hips gliding alongside the glass candy display. She began positioning boxes of Milk Duds and Junior Mints in stacks, and then in perfect rows.

"I know you from somewhere," she said. "You go to Hackley?"

"Sleepy Hollow."

"Then that's not it."

"Maybe," I said, "we have the same mother."

It was the first Friday afternoon that I had worked, and as I'd learn in coming weeks, Friday afternoons were a dismally slow time for the Avalon. No one attended matinees at the end of the workweek, and the evening show didn't start until 8:00, which meant the audience wouldn't start trickling into the theater until 7:15. And so we passed those arid hours doing precisely what we were doing then: cleaning surfaces that didn't need to be cleaned, building skyscrapers with boxes of candy that'd already been neatly arranged, popping enough popcorn to fill one of the lumbering buses that we'd watch pass on Saw Mill Road. Listening to Earl as he instructed us, *Never ask if that'll be all—always say, "Will that be a large?"*

"You smoke?" Clare had fanned out the Milk Duds in a spoked half circle, peacock's feathers. She tilted her head and chewed at the ends of her dark hair as she regarded the new design.

"Sure," I said, though the truth was that I didn't; I didn't but often I'd imagine, very vividly, that I did.

Clare gave Earl a wave as we passed through the lobby's two grand doors, the brass lions that served as their handles now a little tarnished, a little rusted. And because the theater was empty, and because Earl's white head was buried in yesterday's newspaper, he waved back. A shooing away.

"You're doing it wrong," she told me when I'd choked my way through half the cigarette.

"What do you mean I'm doing it wrong?" I shifted the cigarette from the base of my fingers to between the two middle knuckles; I brought it to a different corner of my mouth. "It's smoking. You can't do it wrong."

"You can," Clare said. She leaned against the theater's brick wall and crossed her feet at the ankles. She held one elbow and let the cigarette dangle from a drooped wrist. "And you are."

There was a popping blast from a Chevy that pulled away from the curb where we stood, and we fanned the exhaust away from our faces. Clare explained, "There are seventeen different ways to smoke."

"Seventeen."

"Rita Hayworth," she said, "will hold the cigarette at the very end of the filter, and only with the very tips of her fingers. When she's not smoking it, she'll keep it chin level." Clare demonstrated and the smoke pooled between her lips.

She continued, "Now, Bette Davis. She grips it a little higher up. And sometimes—sometimes she'll rest her thumb against the butt. Then, when she exhales, it's like she kisses the air." Clare puckered her lips and the smoke flew forward in a straight, steady stream. She added, "But none of this is helpful to you. You don't want to be smoking like Rita Hayworth or Bette Davis or Jayne Mansfield. For you we need Richard Burton or Paul Newman. People who know how to brood—which, incidentally, you can do in twelve different ways."

With a thin gold lighter she relit my cigarette, which had extinguished. She gripped both my shoulders and rotated me until my back was against the brick wall. *Tilt your head,* she told me, and I did. *No—not down, up. Lift your chin up.* She flipped the collar of the grey dinner jacket we were both required to wear, creasing the fabric until the wool lapel scratched my jaw line. *Hold it with three fingers—no, not like that. Pinch it between your thumb and middle finger. Good. Now, rest your pointer finger on the filter.*

She took my wrist, which was rigid, still like a mannequin, and she lifted the cigarette to my mouth.

"Good."

"And who is this?"

"Steve McQueen."

When we'd finished outside and had taken up our posts behind the concession stand, Clare produced a journal of white lined paper bound in red cardboard, the top half of which was missing. On the bottom half she'd written in clean block letters: HOW TO DO THINGS RIGHT. She flipped three-quarters of the way through the notebook, which was alphabetized, until she reached S—SMOKING, 17 WAYS.

"I'm sure there are more," she said, thrusting the book into my hands. "But these seventeen are the best."

There were names—the five she mentioned outside, and then twelve more. In addition, each entry included a year, a movie, and a paragraph description. So:

RITA HAYWORTH. 1946. *GILDA.* Hold it at the end and with the tips. Don't blow out smoke until you have to. Best if your hair's down. And red.

I thumbed through the journal, stopping at random intervals, while Clare shoveled popcorn into a yellow box for the first customer we'd had in hours. I leaned against a counter stacked with paper cups and napkins, and I read.

S—SMILING. 29 WAYS.
S—SLAPPING A MAN. 8 WAYS (and counting).
T—TYING SOMEONE UP. 11 WAYS.
D—DRINKING A BEER (bottled). 6 WAYS.
D—DRINKING A BEER (in a glass). 2 WAYS.

K—KISSING. 4 WAYS.
L—LAUGHING. 13 WAYS.
F—FALLING IN LOVE. 9 WAYS.
C—CRYING. 319 WAYS.

We added to Clare's list over that summer. When our shifts had ended, we'd sit in the balcony's front row, our arms hooked over the brass rail, and we'd study the movies for new ways of doing things, iterations of movements we'd already memorized, and we'd scribble them in her journal, in the dark.

"I've never seen Rex Harrison wear a hat like that," I'd lean over and whisper to her.

"Write it down."

But there were also new things we saw: whole actions that Clare had missed that we wrote on new sheets of paper that were then stapled into the journal with great care devoted to keeping the alphabetical order intact. Between S—SHAVING and S—SLEEPING:

S—SHOOTING A LOADED HANDGUN. 37 WAYS.

She had a way with the Avalon's customers. Almost without fail, she could get someone to commit to a larger soda, a bigger bucket of popcorn. She'd say, How the West Was Won *spans fifty years, you know. I think that necessitates a large.* Or: *You'll get thirsty watching Conrad Birdie do all that hip thrusting—you're going to want as much soda as you can handle.* They'd smile at her—strangely at first, but then graciously, as if they'd been let in on some secret; they'd agree to whatever she was pitching as they dug in their wallets for an extra quarter.

I don't know if Clare thought she was pretty. She was, but not very; she wasn't unpretty, either. That summer she and I had both cultivated a very distinct and schooled sense of what pretty was, on the WAYS TO BE PRETTY page, and during discreet moments when it seemed like no one was watching, when she was waiting for the customer who was digging through her purse, or when I was cleaning the candy counter, I'd catch glimpses of her fixing herself. Of her looking at a magazine spread of Tina Louise or Pamela Green and cocking her head just so. Moving her hair and tucking it back on the other side. Pushing out her lips. Pulling them back in and shaking her head *no, no*.

Increasingly, I wrote pages of my script at the concession stand, during the downtime between showings, instead of in my father's room. The paper would often be stained with butter and grease, with chocolate fingerprints—but still, each night I'd slip them into the same drawer where the rest of the endless manuscript lived, breathed, ballooned. Still trapped behind a screen, the boy grew older: his hair darkened and his voice deepened; his body stretched and his shoulders filled out. When he celebrated his sixteenth birthday, he'd sailed a dozen seas. He'd ridden into a million sunsets.

Now, instead of fleeing from battles, he started them. Instead of dancing with chorus girls, he seduced them.

In the front row of the theater, his father would perch on the edge of his seat. He'd whisper, *Kiss her now, Son. NOW.*

Clare and I rarely spoke of our homes. I suppose to a certain degree we considered them blasphemous, these lives we lived outside the Avalon. Or, if not blasphemous, then certainly fictitious—roles that we had to play when the clock wound down and our shifts were over. Often, we stayed at the theater longer than we had to. We'd ask Earl if he needed help counting ticket stubs. If all the craters of overchewed gum had been scraped from beneath the seats.

We became, I think, the last two people on our own empty earth, which is why what transpired next made perfect sense, even if actually it made no sense at all.

On a Wednesday afternoon in the middle of July the air was so thick that it hung in pockets stretched between the trees. I arrived by bike at the Avalon, sweat drenched, to find a CLOSED sign set between the two front doors.

Inside, Clare leaned against an empty concession stand. In her hand:

the last two pages of my script, which she flipped between. Reading one sheet, memorizing, moving on to the next.

"You left this here last night," she said.

"Who says it's mine?"

She cycled back to the first page. She read, this time mouthing the lines of dialogue, the transitions, the scene headings.

"What's that about?" I pointed toward the sign.

"Earl was supposed to get the reel of *Viva Las Vegas* from MGM today, but someone stole it."

"What do you mean someone stole it?"

"Someone just—stole it." She shrugged a single shoulder—Audrey Hepburn, 1961, *Breakfast at Tiffany's*—indicating it was the only answer she planned on giving. Clare hated musicals—she said they interfered with the way things were supposed to be—but more than musicals she hated the Beatles, and so she viewed their entrée into cinema apocalyptically, the convergence of two evils into a single festering point.

"So what are we supposed to do?"

"Nothing. He's closed the theater until MGM can send him a replacement reel." She stacked the two pages together and then folded them in half, handing them to me. She said, "I'd like to show you something."

Clare took my hand and I let her; we both assumed, I think, that this is what she was supposed to do. That this was the way it was done. We ascended the lobby's grand staircase, where the red pile carpet now frayed along each step's edge. Past the giant amphora vase, behind which the boy used to hide, a golf-ball-sized chunk missing from one of its two handles.

"Have you been in here before?" she asked me once we'd stopped outside the projector room.

"I don't remember," I lied. Or, I tried lying.

From her pocket she produced a silver key, and she went to unlock the door, which was unlocked already, and so she ended up locking it, and then having to unlock it again.

"Earl has been training me on the projector," she said while she fumbled.

"I didn't know that."

"Well"—she leaned into the door and it jolted open—"now you do."

The room was smaller than I wanted it to be—half the size of my bedroom at home—and it smelled, very strongly, of plastic and rust. Inside, the temperature was easily ten degrees warmer than the rest of the theater, which, without its fans whirling, still baked red and sticky. I became acutely aware of how much I'd started sweating, the moisture pooling in strange places like the space between my fingers and the undersides of my wrists.

An adjoining doorless closet contained stacks of reels in different sizes: on the floor in limp cardboard boxes, on the steel file cabinet, hanging from racks on the walls. Spilling out of themselves, onto themselves, through themselves. Clare pushed them aside with her foot. Cleared a path for the two of us.

"These are the ones Earl's got to send back to the distributors," Clare said.

"He sends them back?"

"He's only licensed to show them. What did you think happened to them?" she said. "And they're usually sent back in an awful mess. The films are waxed, you know, so they can play on these projectors. They get scratched terribly, even the first time we play them."

I squatted next to the first box I came across and I pushed through the reels, all pictures I'd watched in the last two months. I chewed on the dust that snuck into my mouth.

"It's sort of funny, actually," Clare said. "That playing a film is the thing that destroys it." She knelt next to me. Picked *Cleopatra* from the box. "Here. Come here."

While the room was smaller than I expected, the projector was larger. Or, potentially larger. I had, until that point, imagined the projector in a sort of ambiguous space in which the size of something didn't actually exist.

"Watch." Clare stood on the opposite side of the projector. She placed the reel on the machine's front arm and then, as she reminded herself of the steps, she let the film's loose end fall slack until it—the film and the reel to which it was attached—looked like the number 9.

"Okay," she said, and she wiped the wetness from her hands against her wool slacks. Slowly, almost surgically, she unwound the slack part of the film, the celluloid that was devoid of any shot frames, pictures. I stood back and licked sweat from my lips as she circled around to the projector's lens, where she unclipped two sets of hinges and sprockets.

"You just . . . feed it through." She fitted the film's guide holes into the sprockets. When it slipped from the projector, she cursed and started over again. Finally, once the guides were hooked snugly into the sprockets she shut the hinges. Two small loops of celluloid formed near each one.

"This, the looseness," Clare said, pointing to each loop, "lets the film flow easier. It shouldn't be tight." She fed the slack film into an empty reel set at the back of the projector. "And that's where it goes when it's done."

When she turned it on, there was a sound that was mechanical and regimented: gears eating one another and a small box opening. I closed my eyes.

"You can look," she said.

"I don't know," I told her. "Ha. It's sort of bright."

I don't recall how many times I'd seen *Cleopatra* by that afternoon, but I'd wager that Clare had seen it twice as many. Still, though, after Clare had loaded the film, we crept into the empty theater and took our two seats at the front of the balcony. We shifted in our seats, bringing our feet to rest on the balcony's rail. Accidentally kicking the journal that lay beneath the seats.

"Were you here the day the Avalon opened?" Clare asked me. They were crowning a new queen of Egypt.

"Yes."

"Do you remember the boy who snuck in? When all the people were waiting outside?"

"Yes."

"I've always thought you looked like him."

Neither of us spoke for another hour. Approximately every twenty minutes, we'd hear Earl in the projection room—tinkering, adjusting, fixing. And also on occasion, Clare would see something new and add entries, squinting in the dark: C—CONQUERING A KINGDOM. 3 WAYS. For the most part, though, we were silent; when our arms accidently brushed, we leaned away. When we crossed our legs and our feet touched, we mouthed noiseless apologies.

When Cleopatra held the dying Antony in her arms, she looked toward the palace's gilded roof and said, "Has there ever been such a silence?"

Clare spoke. "Do you know how to tell if an actress wasn't actually able to cry and the director had to use fake tears?"

"I don't."

"Real tears stream. You can just see them streaming down her face. In these little rivers. Fake tears roll. They don't flow, they just roll. Like marbles. At least, that's what I've noticed."

I don't remember saying anything in response.

"There are three hundred and nineteen ways for a person to cry, but none of them are equal to Elizabeth Taylor. It's so subtle, isn't it? I don't care what critics say about the film. After they kiss, and he dies, the scene is only twenty-three seconds before the cut. Still—it's the way we actually cry. Lips don't ever really quiver, you know. We make them quiver because we think they're supposed to—but on their own, they don't. I don't know. There's a sort of wretched shudder, but it's a whole-body thing. Still, though. So subtle.

"You know she could cry whenever she wanted, right? That's why her tears never roll."

"I didn't know that."

"She had this awful domineering mother as a child. This woman named Sara who forced her to practice crying on cue."

I watched as Clare stared forward. As she conjured up a million different emotions that she'd seen played out across the faces onscreen. As she bit her lip to prevent it from quivering, as her eyes welled up with tears—not out of sadness, but out of dryness.

"I haven't cried in four years. I don't know how she does it." She added, "Please don't be upset with me, Colin," and I leaned over and kissed her. She shrank her head back at first, as if she was expecting to not to expect it, but then she pressed into me: the taste of popcorn and flat soda.

"That's how Humphrey Bogart kissed Ingrid Bergman, except we're in Westchester instead of Morocco, and Roosevelt stopped the Nazis," she said once she pulled her head away for a moment. She wiped bits of me from her mouth.

By the time Cleopatra's servants had presented her with the basket filled with a dozen figs and one asp, we had kissed again, and this time she told me it was how Steve McQueen kissed Natalie Wood in *Love with the Proper Stranger*.

"Confident, but also, from a different angle, a little scared."

And then, when the credits were rolling, another kiss. Clark Gable and Sophia Loren in *It Started in Naples*. Coy—but also a little cocky.

And then another, and another, and another.

She had been leaning toward me, her stomach pinched against the armrest between the seats, but she suddenly pulled away.

"I don't love you, you know," she said.

"All right."

"That's one of the six ways you can do this. You can love somebody. But I'm telling you now that I don't."

"Your elbow's hurting my hand."

"What?"

"Your elbow—it's crushing my hand on the armrest."

She shifted.

"Do you love me?"

"I haven't given it much thought."

"I don't think you should."

"All right, then," I said. "I won't."

HOW TO TAME A LION

Finn

Mrs. Dalloway doesn't like Ohio. Fucking hates it, actually, though neither Randal nor I can figure out why.

"Maybe she's a Michigan fan," I say.

Or: "Maybe she blames it for Bush's second term."

Randal pinches the bridge of his nose, squeezing the thin bone till the skin surrounding it grows white. He says, "Mrs. Dalloway is definitely a Republican."

She was silent as we left Pennsylvania, when the interstate sloped downward and the trees in West Virginia formed impenetrable walls on either side of us. So silent we figured she was dead again. But as we trekked across the shallow hills of the Allegheny Plateau, which makes up Ohio's eastern chunk, the whining started. A strangled, muffled squawk—a seagull in a blender, we said when it started—that seeped out from Randal's backpack.

She keeps at it as we make our way down the Allegheny escarpment and as we stare at the white cotton faces of the clouds that swim above the Till Plains, the Columbus Lowlands.

"Maybe we should let her out?" I ask him. "Maybe that's the problem."

When we do, though, when we get the zipper opened enough for her to sneak out into the open, Mrs. Dalloway becomes a cat possessed. She freezes on the dash and takes in the stark ruralness of the road. She flings herself against Lucy's windows like she's some abhorrent three-legged beanbag. She jumps over seats with a nimbleness that, for a cat of fifty, is pretty fucking impressive; she bats at the windshield, moving her paw in tight circles, wax on, wax off.

"Grab her!" I yell. "Jesus Christ, Randal, grab her!"

He does, finally, as she's trying to rip the knobs off the radio with her four remaining teeth. Randal's bleeding from somewhere, his elbow or his forehead. His lips are curled, and I'm pretty positive he's going to hurl Mrs. Dalloway into the grille of the next passing sixteen-wheeler, but instead what he does is, after he gets her back into the bag, he opens the zipper again, but this time only half an inch. He sticks a finger's tip into it, up to the first knuckle. Wiggles it timidly. "Shh," he tells her.

We are passing through New Concord, and then across the Muskingum River in Zanesville. Everything is extremely pretty in a very unpretty way: interesting because there's a phenomenal lack of interest.

"*Shh*, Mrs. Dalloway."

But of course she doesn't *shh*. Not even when we arrive in Columbus, which is so clean, bleached to a frightening level of urban purity. We drive through an area of town called German Village, which boasts proud red-brick homes with intricate wrought-iron fences laced across their chests; stone streets, shaded with lines of trees.

There are other ones, other villages. There's an Italian Village, a Victorian Village, an Ohio Village—though we never make it there. We never make it to the Ohio Village.

Across the Olentangy River on East Broad Street we pass the Ohio courthouse, and then the statehouse. We turn south on South Third Street and slow to a roll near the capitol building, stopping long enough to examine its white limestone pillars, its blue roof, which is the same color as the flat midwestern sky.

"It looks fake," he says. "Everything here is so perfect it honestly looks fake." And then: "Mrs. Dalloway, if you were behaving yourself, I'd let you see it."

I tell them both, "We need to find somewhere to stay."

Standing in the lobby, we clear our throats in rapid succession, sometimes on top of each other, to mask Mrs. Dalloway's staunch protests to the Buckeye State. I'm wearing the pack, and I feel her shift and tremble, punching her paw into my spine.

The problem, we're being told, is that there's a medical supply sales representatives' expo in town this week, and that its attendees have reserved large blocks of rooms in the city's more affordable hotels.

"The rooms have been booked for weeks." The receptionist clicks her nails, which are painted bone white, against the keyboard, but she doesn't type. She has smooth chiseled skin and she smells like jasmine. "They've taken over the city."

They told us the same thing at the Best Western, we say. At the Courtyard by Marriot, the Holiday Inn, the Holiday Inn Express, the Days Inn, the Red Roof Columbus North. And now—now at the Hampton Inn, which is located across from the convention center and has air that tastes like new sofas and carpet, glue that hasn't dried. Behind us a revolving door pivots and there are two men wearing polo shirts that are tucked into beltless jeans and they wheel small black suitcases.

"There's got to be something." I turn back to the receptionist. "Those people, those men, couldn't have booked every room in the city. How many medical supply sales representatives can there possibly be?"

"It's a national conference."

"Still."

"It's a multibillion-dollar industry."

"So?"

"So there are a lot of people who make that happen." Then: "Are you two sick or something?"

Randal turns to me. "Maybe you should get a glass of water."

"I think I'm okay."

"Then maybe you should get a cup of coffee or something."

"I've had like thirty-seven cups of coffee today."

"Then maybe you should . . ." He licks his thin lips and clicks his jaw. Eyes the backpack with masked concern.

"Oh. Leave?"

"Yes," he says.

I drink cold coffee from a pot in the lobby while I wait. From a vending machine I eat purple fruit snacks and the corn syrup coats my tongue. I sit on a blue easy chair that faces the revolving door and I place the screeching, jostling backpack in my lap. I watch as more men, more women, more beltless jeans circle through its glass panes.

There is a woman, a few years older than me, name tagged, arms ringed, wrapped, stacked high with plastic leis of orange and yellow and green. A man in an oversized Hawaiian shirt follows her, carrying a sign I can't read. I look beyond them to the street where we've parked Lucy alongside the curb. It's just after three o'clock.

Randal is a spectacularly good negotiator, or a very good haggler, which I assume is due to his stint selling famous autographs that were actually his own. But the thing is, as opposed to the spiel of a used car salesman or a drug dealer, Randal's haggling takes nearly forever. So once I'm done with the fruit snacks and have finished the cold coffee and he's still fucking at it I stand up and stretch. I call Karen.

She doesn't answer so I call her again. But when I get her voice mail a second time, I buy her a postcard instead. It takes me a while to think of something to write. Because Karen—she can be peculiarly sensitive, particularly when she's stressed. So I select my words carefully. I write:

Dear Karen,
Pittsburgh blew. Columbus is clean. Please
don't let me get fired. For the kids.
Finn

"How is she?" Randal asks. He lifts the bag and gives it a gentle shake. From within, Mrs. Dalloway groans.

"Still miserable," I tell him. "Did you get us a room?"

"I did."

"But how?"

"Evidently there was a room in the block no one had checked into. I guess the guys just never showed up. A Mr. Carlisle and a Mr. Perez."

"We could be a Mr. Carlisle and a Mr. Perez."

"That's what I told her."

"Is it going to break the bank?"

"I got us the corporate rate."

"Oh?"

"A hundred, plus taxes." He winks at me and I wink back, even though neither Randal nor I are especially talented winkers.

"You're very good at this."

"I once sold a Paul Henreid for one hundred fifty-three dollars."

"Is there free parking?"

"Forty for valet; twenty if we self-park in the structure across the street."

"Self-park. We'll definitely self-park."

He nods. "One hundred fifty-three for a Paul Henreid."

"Did she say anything else?"

"Yes. She said not to let the cat piss on the carpet, and that you should shower."

The sheets on the beds are white and they crack like rice paper when we lie on them. The room is much too cold in a manufactured way, but we revel in it because we can't remember the last time we weren't hot. We pass Mrs. Dalloway between us: she waffles between hissing and purring, spitting and smiling, resisting and submitting.

Randal says, "We need a young priest and an old priest."

On the nightstand between us there are two tote bags and pens engraved with industry slogans. There are T-shirts, and Mr. Carlisle and Mr. Perez's name tags, and packets of literature with primary-colored graphs on the medical supply sales industry. There are invitations for a conference-wide luau being held at the convention center. I'm on my back with the cat, my fingers combed through her sparse wiry fur. The air-conditioning pricks and bites my skin.

Randal reads, "In 2007 the top-performing firms in the industry had an average revenue of two hundred forty-five million dollars."

"That's a lot of money," I say. Mrs. Dalloway leaps from my chest to the floor, where she starts parading in oblong circles, meowing.

I leave Randal reading and Mrs. Dalloway protesting and I retreat to the bathroom and lock the door, turn on the shower. I undress in front of the mirror as the water, scalding, runs into the tub behind me. My cheeks are patterned with the uneven growth of a red beard, and when I run my hands over them they feel like old sandpaper, the sort that should be thrown away, that's been overused. My hair hangs in clumped strands, greased ropes that I pull back from my forehead while I itch my scalp.

I realize I'm too skinny: when I put a hand on my stomach I touch ribs and count them. I try to flex my biceps, which feels ridiculous but necessary. I flex them harder when I don't see some mountainous lump, but rather a thin shadowed line on the inside of my arm, flesh pulled from bone. Fog spreads inward from the frames of the mirror and I continue to look at myself: I stare at my mucked hair, the peppered red on my white cheeks, my thin arms and waist.

I keep looking until there's no more clarity, till everything's gone opaque and I've been edited to just strokes of color on a silver wall, before I push back the curtain and step into the shower.

"I think we should go to this luau," is what I say when I emerge, dripping, from the bathroom.

"Yeah," Randal says. "All right."

He's sitting on the beige carpet with his legs crossed, the cat curled around herself in his lap. The minibar has been opened and he is nursing Mrs. Dalloway with drops of Jack Daniels that he sets like beads on the tip of his thumb. She licks at each one, catching it with her rough tongue before it rolls down the contour of his hand.

When the bourbon has been emptied, he unscrews this airplane-sized bottle of Absolut.

"I don't really imagine she's a vodka sort of girl," he says, pulling her closer to him. "But this is the only thing that seems to shut her up."

WHAT I REMEMBER

1964: Unbelieving, Part 2

By Colin A. McPhee

Four days after Clare showed me how film was projected, my father returned home. He was there for two nights, during which time he washed the dishes that'd stacked in the sink, phoned a dozen shrouded acquaintances, and paid the bills that had multiplied on the kitchen table. Then, on the third morning, he began the pattern of rituals that served as precursors to his next departure.

It began, always, with a map: an outdated guide to America's highways that he'd flatten across the kitchen table before circling the cities and towns that freckled its surface. The coffee table in the living room would become cluttered with month-old newspapers from other cities, certain articles and headlines circled in black and red and blue ink. He'd make sandwiches he wouldn't eat; he'd do a dozen loads of laundry and forget the clothes in the dryer. Each time the rituals began I would search through his desk drawer for my script; I would rub the corners of the thousand pages; I would look for signs that they'd been touched. That he'd read about the boy who was fighting and fucking and finding and losing, all behind a screen.

"Where do you go?" I asked him on that morning. I'd washed and dressed for the Avalon, and I was already sweating through the grey wool sports coat.

He stood from where he was hunched over the table. He extended a hand and tousled my hair. It was a strange gesture, I remember: I was taller than he was at that point. He had to stand on his toes to reach above my forehead.

"Why don't you just follow him," Clare said to me, once I'd arrived at work and had relayed all this to her.

"I don't have a car."

"I've seen that thing he drives. I doubt it goes too fast." She opened a box of Red Vines that she'd taken from the glass candy display. "Just do it on your bike."

Since *Cleopatra*, the conversations between Clare and me had become stilted. I stood at the other end of the concession stand, filling boxes with too much popcorn as I listened to her flirt with our male customers. When the theater was empty, she wrote in her journal alone. Whenever I alerted her to a way of doing something that was new—how to pack an attaché case with tear gas, per James Bond in *From Russia with Love*—she'd inform me that it was, in fact, old. That she'd seen it too many times before.

Still, as she chewed on the end of a Red Vine and I passed behind her, I placed a hand lightly on the small of her back.

"What?" she said, and her spine straightened.

"What do you mean, *what*?"

"You just touched my back."

"I'm sorry," I said. "It was an accident."

She said nothing; she just peeled away a second Red Vine.

I didn't think I was in love with Clare, at least not yet. I had told myself that I wasn't in love with her when we kissed four days earlier, and in the time since I'd made every effort not to fall in love with her. I was also convinced that I didn't want Clare to be in love with me. But more than all this—more than Clare not loving me—I didn't want Clare to love anyone else. And if she did, when she felt his weight upon her, I wanted her to be closing her eyes and imagining me.

The movie playing that week was *A Shot in the Dark*, with Peter Sellers, and when we'd completed our shifts Earl told Clare and me that we were welcome to stay and watch the evening showing for free. We both thanked him separately and politely declined.

"Have a good night," I told her as we passed through the Avalon's front doors, one of which was spiderwebbed with cracks from where a rock had hit it a month before.

"Same." Then, as I unhinged my bike's lock: "I still think you should follow him."

If he hadn't been halfway down our street when I rounded the corner, I'm not sure if I would have taken Clare's advice. But he was, and so I did.

When I approached the car on my bike, he slowed and rolled down the driver's side window.

"How was work?" he said.

I told him *fine*. And then, again: "Where are you going?"

The hat tilted forward and blinded him; he pushed it up higher on his head. "This hat," he said. "This damn hat."

"All right then—when will you be back?"

"Soon."

"What does soon mean this time?"

"There are clean dishes in the cupboard," he told me.

I suspect on that evening he knew that he'd be followed. Perhaps it was the way I'd asked those questions: I'd asked them at least a hundred times before, but never with such unmasked defiance. Or it was the way that I paused, straddling my bike with both feet planted solidly on the asphalt; it was him seeing me seeing him in his rearview mirror as he inched toward the first intersection. It was that contrite sense parents get when their children have caught them. Because he didn't go anywhere that night. After I hid my bike behind a hedge in our front yard, I crept to the end of our block and I watched—half curious, half bored—as my father drove in tight circles on an adjoining street.

"Try again," Clare said the next day. She paged through the journal. Found S—STALKING. "Try Sean Connery in *From Russia with Love*. The opening scene."

That night, I waited. I heated up soup and changed from my uniform and into jeans. I sprawled on the couch and busied myself with an episode of *To Tell the Truth*. When he walked behind me, I watched in the reflection on the television screen as he, again, tousled my hair. When I heard the cannonball smash of the car's ignition, I turned up the volume and slipped on my sneakers.

In 1964, Sleepy Hollow was still a place that went black at night. The population hadn't changed substantially since I was born, and the houses, which were separated by meadow-wide lawns, existed in disconnected hazes of light. There were seven traffic signals and about as many streetlamps, and the darkness was left to wreath between them intact and uncut.

I pedaled furiously. I stayed one hundred yards from the car, and I swerved around the few pools of light that did stream down to the street. When traffic approached in the opposite direction, I took to the sidewalk and dodged the oncoming beams. Twice I clipped the edge of a mailbox with my inside elbow, leaving bits of skin behind.

He took Beekman Avenue to North Broadway, and there, at one of the seven stoplights, he turned south. I thought for a brief instant that he'd spotted me; when the light turned green, he waited for a few seconds too long, the car choking as it idled in neutral. But then, a Ford that had pulled up behind him honked, and my father—and I—continued.

We followed North Broadway until it became South Broadway, below Benedict. The bike's pedals were moving so quickly, so furiously at this point that they seemed to take my legs with them, tying them and untying them into knots as they circled, requiring no effort from me, though still my knees and calves and thighs burned white. I threw on the brakes once—when the car lumbered onto the Tappan Zee Bridge—and I remember very vividly the bitter smell of rubber and the taste of salt just below my nose.

I stalked him still. Over the Hudson, which in the night looked like nothing but a ragged slash in the earth, and then into South Nyack. A mile north, directly across the river from the house where my mother died, he pulled into a lit parking lot on Remsen Street, a few yards from where it intersected with Piermont. I maneuvered my bike into the row that ran parallel to the one in which he'd parked, and I ducked behind the high hood of a Chevrolet. Crouched on my haunches, I had a direct view of the interior of my father's car through the rear windshield.

He held the newspaper clippings he'd collected—the articles from cities in other states—up to the light. I remember that. The night was still oppressively hot, and sweat stung the corners of my eyes. I swatted absently at the bugs that circled above my head. I couldn't read the papers' actual copy, but I recognized the print when the light hit it. When it created shadows where he'd circle something in thick ink. He studied each one for the better part of a minute before folding it and setting it on the shotgun seat. When he finally stepped out of the car, he kept his hat on.

I hid behind one of the Chevy's rear wheels as he passed me. Though, looking back, I hardly think that was necessary: he walked with so much resolve, so much blind purpose, that I doubt he would've noticed me had I slammed my fist across his jaw. John Wayne in *The Longest Day*. I waited until the clack of his oxfords against the pavement grew faint; I crawled toward the front of the Chevy and spotted him as he slipped behind a red and blue sign, into a restaurant and bar called the Sandpiper.

For the next twenty minutes, I wrestled with myself; I sat on the ground and held my knees, my ass fixed to the pavement. I refused to believe that such a simple explanation had existed for the past six-odd years; that this all came down to an antitwist, an anticlimax, to a *bar*. Some winged insect landed on the tip of my nose and I considered: what of the longer absences? The stretches that didn't last for a night, but rather for days, a week, the better part of a month? The long periods after which he'd saunter through the door with last Saturday's *Cleveland Plain Dealer* tucked beneath his arm? I stowed my bike behind a rusted dumpster and followed his tracks across the lot.

The Sandpiper's interior was large but intentionally suffocating; I recall it reminding me very much of the one country club I'd been to with my parents and two friends of theirs, back when my mother was still alive. The dining room's ceiling was high and painted burgundy, but

a low-hanging series of lamps darkened with stained-glass shades created a second, much more oppressive roof under which families ate at
broad square tables. All the room's fixtures—the door handles, the table
legs, the frames of chairs—had been painted a brassy gold that reflected
green, red, blue. I found an empty booth with a high quilted back from
where I could sit, undetected, and view the bar, which was mahogany
and horseshoe shaped, and in front of which my father stood. His back
toward me.

For the better part of twenty minutes, he was alone and I was alone,
save the bartender who served him a scotch, and the waitress who served
me a Coke. But then, as my father ordered a second, a third drink, the
Sandpiper's door would occasionally swing open, and there would be
the intrusion of noise from the outside—passing cars, the popping of
exhaust—and a scattering of men, and some women, would ease their
way past the tables and to the bar. They were businessmen, mostly, the
types I imagined my father cavorting with when he worked in the city.
Wool pants and starched white shirts, sleeves rolled up to their elbows.
Suit jackets hung on the hooks beneath the bar. Hair slicked back in wet
waves that lifted from their foreheads. They sat, or stood, on either side
of my father, and they greeted him with light slaps on the back, shallow jabs to his shoulder, and the only thing I can remember thinking is
wanting to quietly take the hat from his head. To comb his hair with my
fingers. To fix the fraying collar of his shirt.

I slouched in the booth. "You want another Coke?" the waitress
asked me.

"How much are they?"

"A dollar."

"I've only got a dollar on me."

She poured me a glass of water. She walked away briskly, muttering
something that I couldn't quite make out because a man at the bar was
saying, "McPhee, tell us that story again. The one about Detroit."

He winked at a man standing on the other side of my father, who
added, "Was it Detroit? Or was it Pittsburgh? It was Pittsburgh, wasn't
it, McPhee?"

There was a blond woman standing next to him who had her hair coiled on top of her head—she laughed and slid a hand over the man's shoulder.

"It was Pittsburgh!" my father said.

"Pittsburgh!" the man said. "How could we forget!"

My father motioned to the bartender for more scotch—Paul Newman in *Cat on a Hot Tin Roof;* the man who first approached him signaled for everyone else to come closer.

I drank thirteen glasses of water as my father spoke—I remember that very clearly. I'd become very hot and found it impossible to cool down. I listened first with fascination, and then with concern, and then with humiliation, dread, as he retold an unpracticed, unpolished story about a man he wished he were who visited Pittsburgh to save another man's life. He blundered dates and details, and when the crowd interrupted him—*We thought you said it was in sixty-three, McPhee, but now you're saying it was this year?* Or, *One hundred or two hundred bridges, man, get it straight!*—he'd correct himself incorrectly. My cheeks burned as he created a world that didn't exist, a world in which he didn't exist, a world from which he'd robbed relevant pieces in order to construct irrelevant shapes.

The woman with the blond hair balanced on her head said, "Tell us, McPhee, how would a person go about making a house out of old record covers?"

My father reached for a stack of napkins and, with them, tried to engineer walls, a door, a roof. The napkins slid from the bar and floated like so many leaves to the wood floor. When he tried to save the last one from falling, he knocked over his scotch. The sound of the crowd jeering masked the slap and snap of glass breaking, but I placed my dollar on the table and left anyway.

I waited three hours for my father, the liar, to emerge from the Sandpiper. I pulled my bike from behind the dumpster where I'd left it, and I leaned against the trunk of his battered car, squinting as the broad light from the streetlamp pressed against my eyes. I kicked at rocks until there were no more rocks; I counted stars until there were no more to count; I picked at my cuticles until each of my fingers bled.

When he did push through the restaurant's door—it was nearing midnight and the rest of the crowd had long since left—I stood up perfectly straight. I waited while he dropped his hat, tripped as he endeavored to pick it up, dropped it again, finally placed it, cockeyed, on his head. I waited longer when the bartender chased him down, halfway across the parking lot, to inform him that he hadn't paid his tab, not for that night or the four previous nights. And then again longer, much longer, while he shoveled through his pockets for loose bills, quarters, dimes, nickels.

When he got a good look at me, when he smiled and raised both hands and shouted, *Colin!* I mounted my bike and I left.

He didn't return home that night. I assume he slept in his car, but he didn't return home. I stayed up until dawn—not waiting up for him, but burning the pages of the script that I'd written. I removed the crisp sheets from the desk drawer where, over the past six years, I'd left them for him, and I carried them down to the kitchen sink.

At first I burned each page individually, theatrically, starting at the beginning. The boy slipping through the screen. The boy as a cowboy. The boy as a Viking. The father as a hero. I held a match till the flame singed my finger, and then I touched it to the sheet, engulfing one of its corners. I'd keep the page in the air till the rising heat burned my forearm, and then I'd drop it in the sink, where its ash would mix with the paper burned before it. Looking back—Bee Duffell in François Truffaut's 1966 adaptation of *Fahrenheit 451*.

But this became too time-consuming. Once the boy had grown up I placed the remaining sheets into the sink in hundred-page chunks and torched them, intermittently pausing to run the faucet and scoop wet soot into the trash.

HOW TO FALL IN LOVE

Finn

I meet Nancy Davenport like this:

After Randal has subdued the cat and she's been seduced by a bliss-fully drunk sleep, we buy these two Hawaiian shirts (patterns of coconuts and hula dancers, oversized, rayon, the type worn by men who watch golf on television) at a department store in downtown Columbus. We outfit ourselves with other things we consider to be very medical supply sales represenative-y, like khaki shorts with no belts and white tennis sneakers with no socks, though neither of us can remember a time we've actu-ally *met* a medical supply sales representative. We change silently in the hotel room, stepping over the cat, who lays supine on the carpet. In the welcome bag on the nightstand, we find two identification badges—Mr. Perez and Mr. Carlisle's—and we pin them to each other's shirts.

"Maybe you shouldn't be Mr. Perez," Randal says.

"I could be Perez."

"You're much more of a Carlisle. With that hair."

We switch.

Before we leave, I press a finger against a bare patch on Mrs. Dal-loway's throat, checking her furtive pulse.

"She's still with us," I say.

Randal rolls her onto her side. "In case she pukes."

The convention hall where the luau takes place is hollow and smells like a sports club. We sit at a round table and I film us as we drink free mai tais and eat sweet pulled pork with sugar glazed pineapple rings.

"Turn that thing off," Randal says. "People are staring."

Only one person sits alongside us—a man in a mossy shirt with bright yellow pineapples and white umbrellas on it. He says nothing while he shakes the ice in his glass and pulls the strings of meat apart with his fork before eating them. The tablecloth is blue and plastic, and features a beach party scene, so many cartoon women in bikinis, their legs stretching on for miles.

"I'm going to get more of this pork," Randal says.

"You're the worst Jew I know."

He looks at me for a moment, and then at his empty plate. He walks toward the long lines of buffet tables in a smaller adjoining room. I watch him as he goes, dodging two inflatable palm trees the size of skyscrapers that climb up the room's high sterile walls. He knocks on the fin of a foam surfboard propped up against one of the trees' trunks and then tries to restabilize it after realizing he's knocked it cockeyed. He gives up on it after about ten seconds and lets it fall to the ground.

Most of the conference attendees have drifted toward the center of the space, where they dance awkwardly and apprehensively to the musings of this ukulele band that performs on a stage that's covered in sand and made to look very *Gidget Goes Hawaiian*. The dancing rayon bellies, tattooed with mangoes and papayas and coconuts, crash into one another.

So I can get a better shot I move to a tiki bar that's been erected between a photo station with a blue screen that says "aloha" above it and a small, empty karaoke stage. I sit there, ordering mai tais from a man sporting a grass skirt over black wool pants, and I wait for Randal to find me. It's ten o'clock or at least somewhere around then and the people dancing are becoming more at ease with their collective awkwardness: instead of cringing and apologizing when they step on each other's feet, they laugh. They take it as an opportunity to touch each other, to make a million points of contact before they retreat in huddled pairs to empty tables and the room's darker corners.

"This thing was outside last year. They had citronella torches to keep the bugs away," a woman says. She's been standing next to me the whole time I've been at the tiki bar, though until this moment I've yet to notice her. She's older than me, I think, though then again, perhaps not: she could either be twenty-eight or twenty-three or thirty-four. Pale skin that hasn't recently seen the sun, with permanent freckles and a few dark moles. Blond hair, clipped along the shoulders in a straight, geometric plane.

"Was it?"

"It was. But it turned out Bob Thurston, from Hill-Rom, was, like, severely allergic to citronella," she says. She's wearing a dress that is black, and knee length, and has two birds of paradise blooming on the tits, which incidentally don't entirely fill the dress, and so the flowers fall in half bloom until she adjusts the thin straps on her shoulders, which she's doing now. "He got too close to one of the torches and he went into anaphylactic shock—just like *that*. It was ugly: poor Bob shaking on the ground, gasping for air, with none of us able to do a thing about it."

The woman squints at my name tag and I do my best John Carlisle impression, though I don't know what that's supposed to be, entirely.

"But sort of funny—in a dark way, at least. Though I don't think anyone here would admit that. You've got a group of people who spend most hours of every day in hospitals proclaiming to be experts on what doctors need in order to be better at their jobs. And then, when Bob Thurston gets too close to a citronella tiki torch and stops breathing, no one's got a clue about what needs to be done. The only thing we can do is hug each other and bite our nails until the paramedics show up."

She points to her name tag. "I'm Nancy Davenport." Then, pointing to the camera that hangs from my right shoulder, "Is that thing on?"

I tell her no and I shut it off. I set down my mai tai and I push the piece of ice I'm chewing to the pocket of one cheek, and I tell her, "I'm John Carlisle."

"Oh." Nancy pulls at her dress, readjusts the long, fingering petals. "I mean, you know he died two months ago, right?"

I look across the room to Randal, who is shaking hands with a group of young men. Telling jokes, laughing cartoonishly. Pointing to his name tag and introducing himself.

I say, "That I did not know."

"Yeah," Nancy nods. "Selling medical supplies—not for the faint of heart. It was something bizarre. Not citronella-reaction bizarre. But I remember thinking it was weird." Then, once the band has shifted to ukulele renditions of big-band standards: "I remember now. A staph infection. MRSA. After cutting his finger while slicing oranges for his son's soccer team. He was able to make it to the kid's final game, but he died twelve hours later."

"That's a rough twist."

"No kidding."

"But a fantastic story."

"Right?"

"I'm Finn McPhee."

She shakes my outstretched, teriyaki-glazed hand. After some moments she says, a quarter jokingly, "Do you dance, Finn McPhee?"

"No," I tell her. "I mean, not really."

"It's fine—they don't either."

Nancy Davenport favors the same perfume used by my mother's sister and she wears too much of it; that's the first thing I notice when I'm pressed up close to her. I forget what it's called. It starts off smelling holiday spicy: oranges and cloves. But then when it leaves you—when the person walks away—you're hit with sandalwood and cedarwood and, I think, mothballs. My aunt, when I knew her, wore it mostly on her neck and when she hugged me it was stifling, murdering the more submissive scents around it. Nancy Davenport wears it there too, on her neck, and also on her lithe wrists and underneath her arms and in the tiny ravine of flesh between her breasts.

She sways her hips in figure eights, almost off the beat, clinging to it by a precious few milliseconds. Occasionally, she'll pluck up her sagging dress.

On dancing, a note: I meant it when I told her *not really*. The last time I did it was at a company holiday party a year earlier—and then, even then, it was a rather spastic jump-flail-spin combination that, when asked, I lied and said was Bulgarian. In any event maybe part of me is a bit timid, but I think more so I'm hung up on disappointing Nancy Davenport and her perfume and her eyes, which I'm just noticing are green and hungry and almond shaped.

A song ends and we, and everyone else, become suddenly embarrassed by what we were doing in the moments that preceded the silence. Nancy says, "That shirt you're wearing is particularly offensive."

I will say, though, that I do get better. Three songs later I'm no longer stepping on her fragile feet and I'm drunk enough from the mai tais to forget that I don't know how to dance, maybe even convincing myself that I'm good. And Nancy! While her vim isn't necessarily interminable, she does put up a good show, shaking and leaping and corkscrewing and hollering.

When the ukulele band twangs through its rendition of "Shout," she slips off her shoes. She holds them in one hand and tells me she's in desperate need of some air.

I follow her through the convention center's glass front door, out to a long, tightly mowed emerald lawn. Nancy Davenport half reclines on the grass, her legs stretched out in front of her, crossed loosely at the ankles. It's humid, so humid, and the night moves around us in long ribbons that smear the light from the yellow streetlamps. Nancy adjusts her birds of paradise.

I ask her, "Where are you from?"

"Here," she tells me. "Right here."

"As in, Columbus?"

She props herself up on one elbow. "As in, about two hundred yards up North High Street."

"I see." I pull at the blades of grass. "And how long have you lived there?"

"About two years."

"And before that?"

"Before that, Victorian Village, which is about six blocks west. And before that, OSU, but the south campus, which is about a mile down the road."

She falls flat against the lawn and her blond hair spills out around her head. Her dress inches higher, exposing white thighs that seem to stay thin, the same width, as they reach higher, higher, higher.

I ask, "How long, exactly, have you lived here?"

"For as long as I can possibly remember, and probably then some," Nancy says. "I think I was likely living in Columbus before I was even born in Columbus."

Two people, a salesman and saleswoman from the luau, stumble out of the convention center, down the concrete path to the sidewalk that runs in front of it.

"It seems like a nice place to live," I say, and I pull my knees to my chest.

"Nowhere is a nice place to live if you've been there forever."

She folds her hands behind her head, which make the birds of paradise flatten themselves even more.

"When you move around I imagine it's easy to catalog your life, you know?" Nancy continues. "'When I was five, I lived in this house, in this town. When I was fifteen, we moved to Detroit.' That sort of thing. But when you stay in one place you don't have that—that sort of reference. You can't figure out if you're getting older or younger. The place changes, Columbus changes, sure. But you get used to the change—the change becomes predictable. You say, 'Oh, they're finally doing something with that empty lot.' Then, three months later, there'll be a new glass building—something with steel beams—and you'll find yourself asking if there was ever an empty lot in the first place. The city builds up around you, and you stay exactly the same."

Nancy stretches her arms. She pushes her palms upward, slicing through the gelatin air. "Anyway."

After the better part of a minute I say to her, "So, get out. Leave."

She fixes her hands behind her head again, her hair clumping between her fingers. "You don't think I've tried? That's why I took this job. I figured I'd get to travel, right? Visit different hospitals in different cities. I even thought, Hey, maybe Cyanta would give me some great region. The West Coast, even. I'd get to see California."

"But—"

"But I got Columbus." Absently, she runs a finger along the edge of her name tag, which is pinned, at an angle, between her breasts. "There are worse places to be, I know. It's actually a lovely city. There are a million ways to distract yourself. But I suppose the problem with the distractions here is the problem with distractions everywhere: after a while they become so monotonous that you find yourself actually going back to boredom to distract you from the boringness of the distractions.

"I went through this phase where I took up new hobbies. About one every two months." Nancy removes something from her eye—an errant insect, some piece of the night. "I rock climbed at this indoor gym. I grew miniature bonsai trees on my windowsill."

"And . . ."

"They'd hold my interest in the beginning, they'd be something new. I gave them all up, though. I guess I could never shake knowing what they actually were." And then, very suddenly, as if she's just remembering me: "Where are you from?"

"New York City."

"That," she says, "must be nice."

"It's all right," I tell her. "It smells a little too much like people and nuts."

She half nods, strangely. "And you're not John Carlisle."

"No, because he's—"

"Dead. So then why are you here?"

I say, "I'm a circus performer."

She pinches the bare skin on the back of my arm and I jolt the camera. "Knock it off."

I rub the reddening skin. "For real. I swing from trapezes. I'm a trapeze artist. You wouldn't believe how dangerous it is—swinging from the tops of poles and flying into midair. But then, I guess it's not for everyone."

"Tell me something true."

"Who says that's not?"

"I do." She leans back into the grass again, dissolving into the green, closing her eyes.

"Something true," I repeat. "Okay. All right." And this is what I tell her:

The *Spirit of Columbus* was a 1953 model Cessna 180 with an apple-red nose and broad white wings. On March 19, 1964, an Ohio girl named Geraldine Mock took off in the *Spirit* from the Port Columbus Airport. Twenty-nine days, twenty-two stopovers, and 23,103 miles later, she became the first woman ever to complete a solo flight around the world. She flew east, across the Atlantic to Morocco, dipping over the Arabian Peninsula to India—Calcutta—finally bulldozing the Pacific's blue until she reached America, until she reached home. It wasn't an easy trip: Mock flew through blinding sandstorms as she crossed the Sahara. The plane was slammed with lightning and severe weather, both freezing and scalding. Still, she persevered, skating into the record books, stamping her inky thumbprint on history.

All of this is true and totally verifiable. What's truer, though: if it hadn't been for my granddad, she wouldn't have been the one to do it. There was someone else—another woman—who was poised and ready before her.

She was a pilot and her name was Charlotte Sparrow—honest to God, that was her name. When my granddad first saw her, she was thirty-two years old. They met almost accidentally at the end of February in 1964, the first time he sailed into Columbus, about a year after he engineered his house of records in Pittsburgh. The sky the evening he arrived was elastic—stretching between red and violet and blue and black—and Lucy was all in. She'd been choking on fumes evaporating in her belly over the past ten miles. He'd been driving her on 161, past New Albany, and then south down 270 when she finally gave up ten miles northeast of the city, outside a box-shaped hangar a stone's throw from the airport.

The relationship between my granddad and Lucy wasn't always an easy ride. Mostly he found her quirks at least amusing, maybe endearing: the way she got ornery on certain dirt roads; the way she griped and bitched on hills that were too steep. There were times, though, when she wasn't just a handful, but a bona fide pain in the ass. She'd come unglued on a back road in Minnesota, a hundred miles from anything, in the middle of the decade's worst snowstorm. Every time they crossed Death Valley, her windows would jam. He'd watch the pavement evaporate in underwater waves from behind the melting glass. *Damn it, Luce!* he'd cry. *Of all times!*

But that's just the way it goes, he'd always tell me. Half of loving someone is being okay with hating her—at least some of the time.

It wasn't sleeting and it wasn't snowing, but they—both my grand-dad and Lucy—had fallen victim to this particular disposition when she called it quits near that hollow white hangar.

"This is the way it's going to be, is it?" he said once she'd stopped, once gravel no longer crunched beneath her tires. They'd been driving for more than seventy-two hours. "You're something else, Luce. A real piece of work." And her headlights blinked off. He stepped out onto the road and into the chilled Ohio night. To the southwest, Columbus's abridged skyline shot up like a set of blunted fingers. He'd never dream of hitting Lucy—neither the wife nor the car—but if there was ever a moment when he wanted to club a tire with his heel, to put a dent in her hood, by God, he said, that was it.

And so to stop himself from doing something he might regret, he busied his hands. He shoved them into his pockets. Went about digging out a bent pack of Lucky Strikes from the sports coat he was wearing. He had a cigarette pinched between his lips and was poised to light it when he heard a woman say, "What's the problem?"

She'd emerged from the hangar without my granddad seeing her, and she wiped her hands with a grease-spotted cloth, cleaning each fin-ger like she was turning a screw. He said she wore a brown bomber jacket with the sleeves pushed up above her elbows; blue jeans with stains cup-ping the knees. Blond hair clipped at the shoulders. But it was her skin, he said, that got him. The moon that night was the brightest Ohio and the world had seen in sixty years; it had orbited so close to the earth that when you gazed up at it, you'd swear it was a hole that had been punched out of the sky. Cities turned streetlamps off and cars drove with no head-lights—there was just no need for them.

He told me how she was the only thing that was brighter. He told me how she glowed. How she threw out shadows at night. My granddad tipped his hat to her. Chivalry had already started in on its long death by 1964, but my granddad, he was still a man who tipped his hat.

"It's this car," he called out to her. "She's fed up with me."

When Charlotte Sparrow walked toward him, my granddad had to reach for his sunglasses. She popped Lucy's hood and my granddad combed the hair that snuck out from underneath his hat with three wet fingers.

"My parents were around for that moon," Nancy Davenport tells me.

"So you know what I'm talking about."

"I don't remember them saying anything about streetlamps."

Charlotte Sparrow told my granddad that the problem was the ring gear on the flywheel was damaged. When he asked if he'd be able to get a mechanic to fix Lucy that night, she looked up at the moon and shielded her eyes from its blaze.

"Not at this hour," is what she told him.

She did, though, let him stow the car in the hangar where she kept her plane, another Cessna 180 that she called the *Red Lady*, after the famous sixteenth-century pirate. They pushed Lucy from the road's shoulder and across the building's pebbled lot; they both leaned their shoulders into her thick trunk. Twice she resisted, he told me: she dug her tires into the gravel and pressed her back bumper against their bent knees. So they pushed harder. Once they had her inside, Charlotte cov-ered her with a thick canvas tarp.

"It'll be fine here," she said to my granddad.

"That your plane?" My granddad pointed to the *Red Lady*, which wasn't red, but blue with yellow stripes.

"It is."

"Where is it you fly her?"

"Everywhere."

"Everywhere?"

"That's the idea."

In Charlotte's Chrysler they drove into the city, where they ate dinner, and ordered coffee, and ambled along the trails of Whetstone Park in Clintonville. At midnight, they watched two men play an infinite game of tennis and listened to the ball ponging off the blue-green grass. They briefly joined a picnicking family, who offered them each quarters of a squashed ham sandwich. They walked to a jelly-bean-shaped pond where they fed it to ducks that swam happy and confused in the moon's daylight. As a mallard gorged himself on a bit of white bread, Charlotte Sparrow explained her around-the-world plans to my granddad.

"All the way?" he asked her.

"I'll be the first woman ever."

"That's really something. When do you leave?"

"In two days."

The mallard swallowed the soggy chunk of sandwich with violent twitches of his head. He fluffed his feathers and shook his beak; he dove beneath the pond's silver surface.

"Really something," my granddad said again.

Charlotte Sparrow rolled down the sleeves of her bomber jacket. After far too many moments, she said, "Yes. Yes, I suppose it is."

Nancy Davenport rests her blond head against my shoulder and says, "I don't think I like where this is going."

He was a criminally easy man to fall in love with, and he loved to fall in love. This was, as he explained it to me, a very real problem. Once, in Memphis, a set of Siamese twins who were connected by their pinkies tied him to their bedposts and showered him with kisses till his skin blistered. When he finally managed to escape (it was while the two girls were showering), they were so desperate to find him that they severed themselves with a paring knife so as to double their search efforts. Another time, in the Florida Everglades, a spurned alligator wrangler of disproportionate strength threw my granddad into the pit that held her most ferocious beast when he politely declined her advances. It would've ended terribly had he not managed to charm the gator—a thousand-pound mother of forty-seven dubbed Debbie—as well. That night, when the wrangler refused to grant him use of her telephone to call a tow truck (Lucy, keen to act up at inopportune moments, had come undone again), he pocketed himself between Debbie and her babies, his head rising and falling in time with their scaled paunches as they slept beneath the strange Floridian sky.

With Charlotte Sparrow it happened as it always did, which was quickly, and with very little warning: a clear sky suddenly darkened, and before he could blink he was up to his knees in love's slough, wading through it in slow mired steps. He was that sort of person: humble, and a polymath, and above all a hero, but also—also amorous. My granddad loved facilely and adeptly and with fantastic longing. Always, though, there was a feeling—a barely noticeable squeezing near the base of his spine—that reminded him that while his women were dancing and somersaulting through love's thick muck, he was incapable of giving all of himself. Because all of himself had been reserved for—and had expired with—someone else.

Whenever he was telling the story and he reached this part, he'd take off his hat and hold it against his chest. "I hope you never have to do that."

"Sleep with a family of alligators?"

"Give all of yourself to someone," he'd say.

The day that Charlotte Sparrow was scheduled to fly around the world, she woke up early and poached two eggs for my granddad. He'd stayed there—in her one-bedroom apartment on McKee Street—for the past two evenings. The sun hadn't fully risen yet, but as he speared one of the yolks and watched as the yellow mess wetted a piece of toast, there wasn't any need to turn on the kitchen's lamps: Charlotte sat across from him and the luminescence of her skin was enough to eat by. It was enough by which to read the headlines of the *Dispatch* to her, to wash his plate and stack it in the cupboard, to kiss the spot where her neck curved into her radiant shoulder.

He spun her till she faced him. He squinted his eyes and he said to her, "We'd better get you to the airport."

And her smile became tarnished, falling at the corners of her mouth. "Yes," she said. "We better."

Instead, though, they watched the sun rise from a small oval window above the bathroom sink—the only one that faced east. It painted the bathtub tangerine and Charlotte Sparrow told my granddad she'd be the first woman to fly around the world tomorrow.

"It's not as though it's going anywhere," she said while the dawn fought to be brighter than she. "The world I mean."

But she didn't become the first woman to fly around the world the next day, because on the next day there was always the next day. Each morning she would cook my granddad eggs—fried, poached, scrambled, sunny-side up. Each morning he would bring the *Dispatch* close to her skin and read the headlines aloud; each morning he kissed the same soft groove in her neck, where eventually he left a darkened tattoo of his lips. And after they had crowded into her bathroom to watch the world wake up, there was always this: there was always tomorrow. Until two and a half weeks later, on March 19, when Geraldine Mock guided the *Spirit of Columbus* out from the hangar next to Charlotte's—and suddenly, there wasn't.

They'd read about Jerrie's pending departure (she was known in certain high-flying circles as Jerrie) the morning before, and they drove to Port Columbus to watch her lift her wheels from the earth. While the previous nineteen mornings my granddad had been in Columbus had been cloudless—the sky so clear it looked breakable—dawn on the nineteenth was particularly overcast. The fog formed a low ceiling that suffocated the light, and without the competition, Charlotte's skin dulled.

Small crowds had gathered near the runway from which Jerrie Mock took off. They grouped together in shapeless clumps of hats and knit sweaters and gloves, and when the red and white plane spun and vanished up into the fog, they cheered and they stretched their hands toward the sky. They waved signs and banners bearing slogans painted in stark letters.

Messages like: GOD SPEED, JERRIE. Or YOU'RE FLYING HIGH, MOCK! And, YOU'RE MY HERO, ~~CHARLOTTE!~~ JERRIE!

Charlotte watched the spectacle from the open entrance of the hangar while my granddad waited inside. He tripped about in the half dark and listened to the echo of his footsteps say things to one another in the empty space. When he came upon Lucy and slipped a hand under the canvas tarp that covered her, her hood was cold and lifeless and sticky with a wet coat of dust. The fresh mud that'd been caked on her wheels when he first arrived in the city had crusted over and fallen off; it lay like ash at the base of the tires.

"Well," Charlotte said to him from behind. "That's that."

He turned to face her and even though he could hardly see her through the fog and the dark and the dullness of her skin, he was 99 percent certain their expressions mirrored each other. Because he knew that while loving someone means hating them part of the time, it also means quietly resenting them for keeping you from all the things you were supposed to do.

That afternoon he found a mechanic who'd fix the ring gear on Lucy's flywheel, and the next morning he told Charlotte, sweetly and absolutely, that he was leaving.

They stood on the bank of the same pond where they'd fed ducks ham sandwiches in Whetstone Park. They'd rolled their pants up so the cuffs pinched just below their knees; their toes sank into the silt as they tossed pieces of crust to the mallard. From across the pond another younger duck made a move for a slice of bread and the mallard squawked and flapped and lunged for the intruder's neck.

"I'm sorry," he said.

"I understand."

"You do?"

"Yes," she said. "Or, maybe not. I suppose the problem is I understand, but I also don't." Then: "But what will I do?" She'd just begun crying when she asked my granddad this.

He tore the heel of a loaf in two and hurled both pieces to the birds. "You'll fly. You'll go around the world twice."

"Will I?" Then: "No. No, I don't think I will."

She continued to cry and the tears turned from streams to tributaries to full-blown rivers. They fell from her cheeks to the crooks of her arms to her knees, where they splashed—rapids hitting boulders—waterfalling into the green pond. The torrent persisted. My granddad held Charlotte while the ducks fled the scene. The pond's surface rose, bubbling and spilling over the park's trails and lawns, over its eleven thousand rose bushes. She cried until the Olentangy River flooded, swallowing the bridge that crossed it along West Broad Street. And the residents of Columbus bailed Charlotte Sparrow's tears out of their homes with plastic buckets as she said to my granddad, "If I can't grow old with you, I don't want to grow old."

So, she didn't.

Nancy Davenport adjusts her dress, and when she speaks it's directly into my neck and it gives me chills. "She didn't what?"

"Grow old."

Over the years, my granddad made a habit of swinging into Columbus to pay visits to Charlotte Sparrow, and each time she looked exactly the same, with the exception of her skin, which would never glow again. In the 1970s, while the flesh on my granddad's hands began to loosen around the knuckles, her fingers stayed smooth, uncallused, porcelain. In the 1980s, when the first streaks of grey found their way into his auburn hair, hers stayed blond, ungrown, unchanged. In the 1990s: no new freckles and no new spots.

The last time my granddad was in Columbus was in the spring of 2002, from what he's told me. His bones had become dry and weak, and six weeks earlier he'd snapped his ankle during a nasty fall—an injury that left him walking with a steel cane for half a year. Charlotte held his arm as they made their way to the pond, the taut young muscles of her bicep flexing each time he tripped. When the ducks—who were not the ducks of 1964, but rather the duck children's children's children, who'd been told stories by their predecessors—saw Charlotte and my granddad approaching, they took to the sky.

"You've got to stop this," he said to her when they reached the pond's edge. "You've got to get older. You've got to change."

She told him, "I think I've forgotten how."

There's more to the story. There's the part about how every time my granddad would leave Columbus, Charlotte Sparrow would flood the Olentangy with her tears—because while my granddad was humble and a polymath and amorous, he was also incredibly tear inducing, particularly for the women who loved him.

I stop, though, here. At this part I've just recounted. Instead of continuing, I look at Nancy Davenport, who has pulled her blond hair away from her forehead and has tucked it behind her left ear.

"What?" she asks, once the silence has become uncomfortable.

I switch the camera on and train it on her: "It's just—you could be her, you know."

As she considers this, she begins to sweat. From where we're sitting we can still hear the ukulele band each time one of the convention attendees opens the glass door.

Nancy Davenport kisses my cheek. "Stop," she says.

OH SHIT

Colin

I yell, "Dad?"

Then, when there's no answer, "Where the hell have you gone?"

He was just here. Minutes ago, I swear, he was here. I was hunched over my desk in the office upstairs, writing down whatever I could remember from our past and—he was here. His throttled voice shouted, *Colin!* and he'd punctuated it with a wet cough. I pressed my mouth to the floor, like I do every day, and I inhaled the bits of dust, musk, a chewed-off fingernail. I yelled that we still had time, that we wouldn't miss Derby Death Match 2000. And then I returned to the keyboard. But now, as I stand alone in the dark den, studying the impression that his loose body has made on the sofa—*Dad, where have you gone?*

In the kitchen, I lower myself to my hands and knees and search beneath the small white table. When he doesn't materialize, I pull open half-closed cupboards. I push aside stacked plates and used forks and glasses with a quarter inch of water in them. I peer behind cookbooks that I don't remember buying, into the mouths of dirty mugs, as if I'm looking for a set of lost keys instead of a dying man, and still I shout, again, *Dad?*

As I push through the house's old, crowded back hallways, the passages connecting the kitchen to Finn's old room, I become overconscious of my left hand, which is trembling at twice the speed of my right. I slip it into the pocket of my khakis and grip my left thigh in some attempt to stop the tremors. I tighten my fingers around the flesh until my nails push through the cotton and leave crescent-shaped incisions in my quads. I say, *Funny, Dad. Really, really funny. Come out now. Come out, we're going to miss it.*

When the wind from the bay sends the front door swinging on its hinges, colliding with a cheap ceramic vase, I jump. I lose my footing and knock my forehead against an empty bookshelf. I place a hand on reddening flesh, feeling the early stages of the bruise that will sprout along its surface. At the end of the hallway is the open door, the door he's opened, framing Vallejo Street and a cerulean Pacific sky and the places, the so many fucking places for my father to lose himself.

My palms begin to moisten and I say, "Shit."

I lost Finn once, too, when he was four years old at a beach in Santa Monica. He was ten yards from me, building sand castles—a speck of white against the blue. I turned away for ten seconds, it couldn't have been any longer, so I could slather sunscreen on the backs of my knees— and I lost him. Too terrified for tears, I leapt and tripped over a hundred angry sunbathers, screaming his name at a volume that never seemed loud enough. Ten minutes later, a lifeguard discovered him—happy, laughing, oblivious—near the snack stand.

Now, standing in the driveway, shielding my eyes from the tempered San Franciscan sun, I realize, too quickly, how similar losing a father and losing a son can feel. There's the same gripping of the stomach, the familiar weakening of the knees. The cramping of the toes into slipknots. That peculiar emotional proportion: four parts panicked dread to one part humiliation. The knowledge that—despite myself—I won't be able to stop shouting his name until I find him, though each time I hear my voice echo off the surrounding homes, I'll wince. I'll be hyperaware of other people spying on me through their half-cracked windows. I'll hear the faint traces of their judgments—the way they scold me, to one another. *What a father,* they'll say. *What a son.*

I start walking west down Vallejo, but then, rethinking the decision, I turn east, then west, then east again. How could he have possibly gone so far with his walker? Had he developed some warp-speed option that

he's been hiding from me? Some switch I've yet to find, yet to flip? The
times I need him to move quickly—when we're late for one of his countless appointments, when Finn is waiting to be picked up at the airport—
he's devastatingly slow. He bungles each step, he stumbles over himself.
When I tell him to hurry, he looks at me, raising a single eyebrow as if to
say, *Of all the inconceivable options, Colin. Of all of them.*

"Colin?"

I jerk my head up to find our next-door neighbor. I know her name.
I know I do. For the past fifteen years, we've shared a side yard—a spit of
concrete that's vanquished annually by the spring weeds. We've endured
the same tedious homeowners association board meetings, often sharing
quiet complaints about the weak coffee, the stale cookies. But why, as I
count the grey streaks in her blond hair, as I watch her slip her fingers
into two leather gardening gloves—why can't I remember her name?

"Oh," I say. "Oh, hi. Hello."

"Beautiful, isn't it?"

"Pardon?"

"The sky."

With a gloved finger, she pushes hair from her cheek. She holds a
basket with a trowel and rusted pruning sheers. We both turn our chins
upward as a plane soars overhead, slicing a single white cloud.

"Not a lot of days like this one," she says.

"No. Not a lot of days like this one."

She smiles weakly and pulls each glove higher up on her wrist; she
flexes her fingers.

Before she turns away, I say, "Hey, you didn't happen to see my dad,
did you?" And I hope, almost instantly, that she failed to hear me.

"Your father?"

"Yes. Yes, my father." I lock my knees and ankles, preventing my toes
from turning inward, the magnetism of disgrace. "He went for a walk."

"He's walking on his own now?"

"I—yes. Sometimes."

Her lips pull together. *You've lost him, haven't you.*

These things happen.

"That's fabulous."

"If you see him, would you mind telling him—"

"To come home."

On the corner of Broderick and Union I find him curved over his walker, his spine articulated by a series of sharp juts that protrude against the blue fabric of his oxford. When other pedestrians—joggers, mothers with strollers—pass him, they do so in wide curves.

"Dad!" I call out to him, and when he doesn't turn, when he continues shuffling away from me, I break from a jog to a run, a sprint. I yell again, "DAD!"

I take his shoulders as I reach him, leaving wet handprints against the worn fabric. At first I'm too forceful; I take hold of him too suddenly. He releases the walker and takes four small steps backward; I pull him into me and wrap three fingers around the guard belt to prevent him from spilling to the concrete.

"My God, Dad," I say. I circle my other arm around him to get a better grip on the belt. An approximation of a hug. "What the hell were you thinking? Don't ever do that. Don't ever walk alone." I repeat, then, "What the hell were you thinking?"

After a brief moment, I feel his hands grip the handles of the walker, which still rests between us. His head, which is bowed into my torso, begins to nudge gently, then with the intimation of aggression, against my shoulder.

"Dad," I say. "What?"

He says, "I've got to go," but the words are slurred: they bleed into one another, the spaces between them snipped, colors all running into a shade of black.

I ask him to repeat himself, and when the words blur again, I say, "Dad—please just slow down."

I can sense him becoming frustrated. He presses his head into me harder, more impatiently. He lifts his arms so they're level with his ribs, and then, exhausted, he drops them to his sides.

"I'm going to be late," he says, in the same half English.

"You haven't got anywhere to be."

"Your mother's waiting for me at the train station."

He wavers on his feet again, this time swinging to the left; I brace him. A car passes, the driver playing its radio much too loudly.

I close my eyes as I feel him breathe against me, as I listen to the incomprehensible sounds of his struggle—the murmurs, the sighs, the tightening of his throat as he winces at the pain.

"Where are you going?"

"We're going to the city if you'll ever let me."

"But she's gone, Dad."

He presses against my shoulders again—this time with his hands, and away. He looks at my chin instead of my eyes. He smiles, but only half his mouth lifts. He's glassy, washed out, bare.

"Colin," he says. "I didn't know you were still around."

I sit in the office of a man called Dr. Salazar at UCSF's Parnassus Heights Medical Center—a tight cluster of hospitals and research facilities nestled south of Golden Gate Park. At first I brought my father to the emergency center on the Mount Zion campus, where I waited for two hours as countless chirping machines were plugged into his arms, and where I felt more and more guilty for having wished—quietly, and in some back corner of my mind—for this day to come. But then, once he'd been stabilized, they'd transferred him here, to the cardiovascular clinic at Parnassus Heights. They slipped more tubes into the folds of his skin and I was brought to this man to discuss our options.

"He's had a transient ischemic attack," Dr. Salazar tells me.

"I don't know what that is."

The office is a cramped, windowless cube. There's one picture on the wall—a black and white photo of a wave crashing over some nameless pier—but aside from that, they're blank. No certificates, plaques, diplomas, nothing. He's taken off his white coat and hung it over the back of his chair. He wears a blue shirt with a wide spread collar and a red tie, the knot loose and askew. He clicks a silver pen impatiently when I ask for an explanation.

"It's a short interruption of blood flow to the brain. Basically a mini stroke."

"I didn't realize a stroke could be mini."

"A stroke can be all sizes."

"Who knew?"

A phone on his desk rings. He leans slightly forward to glance at the number on the caller identification screen; he allows the ringing to continue.

I ask, "Is that what caused the confusion?"

"It could've been," he says. "The good news is the effects of a TIA are normally temporary. The symptoms usually clear up within twenty-four hours."

"Normally and usually."

"Yes." And then, "We'll want to keep him here for the night, at least."

"I understand."

He picks up the silver pen again and resumes clicking it. I watch the ballpoint stab out, in, out. "The concern is this: about one-third of people who have a TIA will have a larger stroke in the near future. And given your father's medical history, that percentage is likely significantly higher."

"Likely."

"It's higher, Mr. McPhee."

"Significantly?"

"Significantly." Then, "You might consider a caretaker."

"You mean a hospice?"

He says nothing.

I ask, "Can I see him now?"

The woman in the bed next to him may have to have the lower half of her leg amputated. She's elderly—about my father's age—and a week ago she tripped and had a nasty fall while retrieving the newspaper from her driveway. She bandaged the wound as best she could, but her circulation is dismally poor, and in the ensuing days it became infected, festering toward gangrene. A blue curtain has been pulled between the two beds, but I listen as a doctor—not Salazar, but another one—relays this news to the woman's daughter.

I lean over to him. I whisper in his flaky ear, "See? It could be a hell of a lot worse."

He's already started emerging from the fog, I tell myself: his eyes are still glassy, but there's a brief clarity to them, like they just need to be wiped down one more time. When he smiles, I can see the left side of his mouth struggling to lift. His hands clench, the fingers press together, and I wonder if this is from frustration or pain.

I flip through a two-month-old *AARP Magazine* while he sleeps. As the nurses arrive to change the wounded woman's bandages, I busy myself with an article about the healthiest berries instead of listening to her whimper. I consider very briefly calling Finn, but I stop myself: I tell myself that there's nothing to tell unless there's something to tell, and I dog-ear articles in the magazine that I've got no intention of reading. There are venetian blinds that have been pulled, and I watch as the light that slits through them changes.

At seven o'clock, my father wakes up. I say, "Welcome back to the world of the living," and this instantly feels wrong, but he humors me anyway. He licks his lips and creases his cheeks. I pull my chair closer to his bed, and I tell him gracious lies that neither of us believes: It was nothing. His electrolytes were just low. We need to get you drinking more fluids, that's all. No—not scotch. Water. Okay, fine, scotch *with* water.

Three minutes before eight, before visiting hours are over and I'll be asked, then forced to go home, he says, "Colin."

"Yeah, Dad?"

"Why'd you sneak into that movie theater?"

I tell him, "The same reason you lied about Pittsburgh."

HOW TO BREAK A HEART

Finn

We're awakened by Mrs. Dalloway's low baying. She's leapt atop Randal's bed and she kneads his bare chest softly, unevenly, with her lone front foot. It's a clumsy endeavor, though, and each time she lifts her paw she half collapses, her scarred and beat-up face colliding with his chin.

Randal stirs slowly at first. He opens one eye, then the other, wiping crusted bits of sleep from the reddened corners of both. But when he locks gazes with her, he yelps; he pushes himself back so his shoulders are pressed firmly against the bed's cushioned headboard. Dalloway remains calm. She continues kneading, falling, kneading, falling.

He says, panicked, "What is she doing? I mean, what the *fuck* is she doing?"

I watch this all from my bed, where I lay prone. The white synthetic down comforter kicked down just below my ass. "I think that means she likes you."

"I don't want her to like me."

"We need to buy her more tuna."

We'd forgotten to close the blackout curtains the night before, after we'd fumbled back to the hotel room through an extremely treacherous rum fog. Now, sunlight fills the room mercilessly. I close my eyes and the pain is white with streaks of orange and green.

"I shouldn't have had that many mai tais," I say.

Randal is lifting Mrs. Dalloway gingerly, trying to shift her to a pillow on the opposite side of the bed. She isn't having any of it, though: she trots back to him each time she's displaced.

"No one should have that many of anything." Then, maybe not particularly meaning it, "Why won't she just leave me alone?"

We take turns in the bathroom. We brush our teeth and splash frigid water into our bloodshot eyes, washing the dirt from our cheeks with brittle plastic-wrapped bars of hotel soap. As we stuff our few belongings into our packs, we scan the room for evidence that Mrs. Dalloway has relieved herself. A puddle of piss behind a floor lamp. A damp spot under a shallow wooden desk. A midget mountain of shit beneath the bed. But—nothing.

I squint and scratch three fingers against my right temple. "Maybe it's the tuna," I say. "Maybe it's, like, stopped her up."

"Maybe she's not actually alive."

Randal unzips his backpack and lays it flat on the floor, the wide opening facing the cat.

"Get on with it," he says.

Mrs. Dalloway looks at him and yawns. She licks her wet chops apathetically and lumbers her way in, the tip of her tail twitching as she curls herself into the shape of a fist.

After we check out we drink coffee and eat stiff cheese Danishes in a high-ceilinged lounge area called the executive level that's really just the second floor of the hotel's lobby. Small round tables and low-seated chairs are mostly filled with weary, hard-worn attendees of last night's luau. They rest their elbows on their black suitcases and they stare into the milk clouding their coffee, at their cheese Danishes, just as we do—apologetically, with a certain degree of self-reproach.

Randal has asked for my granddad's map. He shoves his fingers into his backpack and allows Mrs. Dalloway to lick the cakey glaze from their tips before he takes it from me, unfolds it, flattens it atop the table. He measures the distance between Columbus and Chicago with lengths of his thumb, counting off hundreds of miles.

"This is going to take us like six hours. Maybe more," he says. Then: "And tell me again what we're doing there?"

"We're paying a visit to a man called the Gangster."

"About?"

"A baseball."

"Of course."

I swill the dregs, the bits of ground beans, in the bottom of my cup. I consider the unpaid hotel bill.

I say, "I need to get hold of Karen."

"You can do that from the road." He adds, half of his hand still tucked inside the backpack, "Dalloway's getting feisty."

"I think you're starting to like her."

He says, "Stop insulting my character."

I push myself away from the table and snake through the other guests, their matching forgettable suitcases, until I reach an industrial-sized Mr. Coffee machine that's brewing and spitting and steaming on the other side of the room. I'm leaning over the pot's mouth so I can feel the heat and breathe in the bitter burnt smell when Nancy Davenport says hello and touches me, with just the tips of her fingers, along my right arm.

I say, "Oh."

"Oh?"

"I mean, oh, *hi*."

There's a line that's formed behind us, and so we step aside, away from the Mr. Coffee machine and toward a plastic platter where Danishes have been arranged in a flaky pyramid.

"Are you . . . staying here?" I ask.

Nancy Davenport nods.

"But don't you live just—"

"Sometimes it's nice to get away," she says. "To just sleep in a different bed."

Her skin looks slick—it carries a faint sheen. As if she slapped on some suntan lotion and neglected to rub it in. She reaches for a Danish and begins tearing off the outermost layer of crust, rolling the pieces of dough between her thumb and forefinger before placing the tiny, greasy balls onto a napkin she balances in her left hand.

I tell her, "If I'd known you were staying here, I would've walked you home last night."

"Oh, ha. It's fine. I was liking the fresh air, anyway. I mean—that's very nice of you to offer. But I was—"

"Liking the fresh air."

Across the room, Randal has his lips pressed to the backpack. They twitch as he whispers.

"Thank you for the story last night."

I say, "You don't need to thank me." Then: "It was my granddad's, anyway."

"Well. Please thank him for me, then."

I watch as the dough balls pile and multiply and I realize that I'd like very much to take the napkin from her, fold it into squares before discarding it in the trash. Hold her hand instead. That last night in the absence of knowing anything about each other that would've felt perfect and necessary, but that now—next to the Mr. Coffee machine—the action would feel edited and put-on.

"You could stay," she says then.

"Here?"

"Not for forever, ha. But another night, maybe."

Nancy Davenport smiles, but it's weak, or at the very least a bit unsure—she's trying to decide if it's the right thing to do—and then, very suddenly, she begins to cry. She sets the napkin on the table and she laughs: it's as if she's finally been surprised by herself. And this causes the tears to spill over her cheeks erratically, varying in degree between waterfalls and leaks.

I tell her, "Oh, Nancy, you'll flood the Olentangy."

And she laugh-cries harder, saying, "I won't." Then: "No. No, of course you can't stay."

When I return from the Mr. Coffee machine, Randal doesn't lift his head from the backpack, with which he is still very engaged. Instead, he speaks into it, as if he's addressing Mrs. Dalloway more than me: "Who was that?"

"No one," I say. "Somebody my granddad might've known."

. . .

The western half of Ohio, between Columbus and the border, is not flat—or, is not as flat as I suspected it was the countless times I've flown over it. But that's the difference between flying and driving, I suppose. From a plane it all looks the same: millions and millions of rectangles and squares patched in browns and reds and greens. You can't see the way the earth rolls when you're 33,000 feet in the air. You can't see the way it slopes and lifts; the way it sprouts hills when it's become bored with how things are. Lakes and rivers and a thousand tributaries when it's sad. The way it reflects light in pixilated domes instead of broad composite pillars.

We speed under a billboard that reads JESUS IS REAL in Comic Sans when we cross the border into Indiana. We pass the exits to Brooksville and Connersville and Losantville; Lewisville, Rushville, and Shelbyville. As we near Indianapolis, the slapdash intervals of isolated towns give way to more consistent urban sprawl, interchanging highways reaching out like balls of tangled concrete string. Ohio's blue-eye sky darkened when we crossed the border, and now, now rain falls softly, patiently on us. It taps against Lucy's windshield, scuffing lightly along her canvas top, two different sounds synching together in a lovely lulling melody. Randal passed out when we merged onto 465, and as he breathes against the window, mouth open, he blows circles of fog that expand then shrink then expand again.

Near Lafayette, I wake him by shaking his elbow lightly. I've pulled Lucy over to a dirt shoulder along Interstate 65 and I tell him, "I'm going to need you to drive for a while."

"What?" He rubs at his cheeks, which are shadowed with stubble. He squints out the window. Obtains a sense of his surroundings. "Why?"

"I need to see if I still have a job."

Karen picks up on the third ring and the first thing I say to her is, "You've been avoiding me."

"I haven't been, Finn." Her voice is strained, pulled like elastic at its ends. "Really, I haven't been."

"Did you get my messages yesterday?"

"I did. Both of them." Then: "I'm sorry I haven't been able to call back."

Randal has trouble shifting gears from second to third. At first I figure he's anxious, because he does it too soon, before Lucy's ready, and she shakes. She has trouble accelerating, slouching forward slowly, like we're driving through half-dried glue, until, finally, she's ready to be brought to fourth. And then, after the next stoplight, he waits for too long: Lucy's engine whinnies and clucks. At my feet, Mrs. Dalloway shifts and repositions herself within the backpack, vexed.

"What's that sound?" Karen asks.

"It's the car."

"That thing won't last for long."

"It'll last for long enough." Then: "Well?"

"Yes," she says. *"Well."*

Karen began her work on the show in 1998, a decade before I did. Whereas I've edited roughly 35 lives, she's reconstructed more than 133 of them. And this is a fact I too often forget, I think. I forget that when she first started editing lives, the program was only six years old, that it was still being considered a movement—as opposed to a relic that needed to be dusted off, retooled, reborn. She still talks about those days often—and not with some washed-up football star's sense of vacant nostalgia, but rather with confusion, like she woke up one morning and found herself wondering, quite suddenly, where those years went.

"We had some of the first openly gay characters on television," she told me the day of my first interview. "We had people—young people, real people—debating race and reproductive rights and homophobia. We had addicts and AIDS activists."

It had recently rained, and I remember how we were standing at the window in her office, looking down at the puddles that'd pooled on the roof of the T.G.I. Friday's.

"And what do you have now?" I asked.

"Drunk girls, mostly," she said. "And usually some guy from the Midwest who shaves his chest."

As Karen explained it to me on that day, the problem was that instead of the roles creating the show, the show was now creating the roles. There'd been some sort of seismic shift sometime around 2002, she said. Location scouts abandoned the gritty for the glossy: New York for Hawaii, Cancún. She didn't know who was to blame: audiences, executives, advertisers, ourselves. Across the board, we'd become greedy, she said. Too preoccupied with the present. Instead of teasing out the rawness, Karen's task was increasingly aimed at fortifying the gussied-up artificial.

"Can you help me do that?" she asked.

I told her, "I don't know. But I can tell a fucking good story."

She nodded.

And so. Over the preceding few years, Karen and I have embarked on this clandestine mission: to quietly change what so much of this has become. To reclaim what this show has forever intended to be. We've had minor successes: we've woven together some trueish moments from a transgendered man in Brooklyn, from a bisexual in D.C. More and more, though, the vision Karen inherited is being eclipsed. By bigger hot tubs and double shots of tequila. By three-way kisses and sexually promiscuous Mormons. By Las Vegas.

Randal shreds the clutch by releasing it too early and I spit: *Christ.*

"Jesus, she's touchy," he says, even though she isn't—not at all, in fact.

Into the phone I plead, "Karen, please tell me if I still have health insurance."

"I met with the Ax again yesterday," she begins. "After—"

And then—then the signal goes dead.

I'm staring at my mobile's screen, at the taunting NO SIGNAL message displayed in the upper left hand corner, and Randal says, "What happened?"

I hold the phone above my head; I press its face against the windshield. I roll down the window and hang half my body out into the open air, offering the device up to the sun.

"The signal died. The signal *fucking died.*" Then: "I hate this state. I hate Indiana. Give me your phone."

"It's out of power."

"What do you mean it's out of power?"

"It's. Out. Of. Power."

There are long flatbed trucks, hundreds and hundreds and hundreds of them. They race around one another, playing in one another's exhaust, sleek darts of fish cutting through waves. Atop their broad backs they carry white hollow cylinders the size of school buses. The sun shines through them, dazzling off their steel walls.

"I wonder what those are," Randal says.

"They're what I'm going to impale myself on if I can't find a fucking signal."

"They almost look like parts of missiles, don't they?"

There is a gust of wind, the sort of unexpected and unbridled flurry of air that can only happen on long open roads in the middle of nowhere. The white cylinders sway on the steel beds.

"We need to find a pay phone," I say. "We need to pull over."

The wind switches directions, rocking the cylinders the opposite way.

Near Rensselaer, we spot a gas station and a mini-mart that's been unfolded on the side of the road. I dig for loose change between Lucy's torn seats, in the deep pockets of my shorts, in Randal's backpack, beneath Mrs. Dalloway's bony ass. I emerge successful with a buck ninety-five, mostly in dimes and nickels, and I bolt from the car before she's rolled to a stop.

We are at the edge of the Benton County Wind Farm, a sign says, and they're everywhere, the mills. White three-bladed stalks dotting the flat green plain. They're arranged in rows, like soldiers or corn, and they spin inconsistently—one going, one stopping, one somewhere in between. I feed my fistful of coins into the pay phone's rusted slot.

I'm breathless as I say, "Karen, I'm sorry, I'm in Indiana. The signal cut out. I'm at a pay phone."

She says, "I was worried I'd miss you when you called back. I'm on my way out."

"You're leaving the office?"

"I'm leaving the city. Hugo and I are going upstate for a while. My train is in forty-five minutes."

"But—"

"They're going with the famous babies, Finn."

I notice that I've wrapped the phone's steel cord around my right wrist so tightly that my fingers have gone numb.

"Did they give you a reason?"

"Nothing more than what we talked about the other night. I suppose it's because we've become just like everything else, but only not enough."

"I don't know what that means."

"It means you're fired. We're fired."

I don't hang up the phone—I just leave it hanging, like some prisoner on a noose. One hundred yards to the left of the windmill spinning above me there is a deconstructed unit. Its three propellers lay unused, unattached in a heap; its stalk is divided into four white cylinders of equal length, the same size as the sections we just saw on the flatbed trucks. I walk to the closest piece and kick it as many times as I can before the pain begins radiating in splinters through my toes and my ankles, finally twanging behind my kneecaps. I yell *Fuck!* at the top of my lungs and over and over again and until I'm out of breath and because there's nothing—no mountains or hills—off which my voice can echo, it explodes out in each direction for miles and miles and miles. Randal and Mrs. Dalloway play in the dirt—the cat, flat on her back; the boy, rubbing her orange stomach gently with his toes. They both turn to stare at me.

WHAT I REMEMBER

1974: Los Angeles

By Colin A. McPhee

I saw her again when we'd both become adults, when she read for a role in *The Family Room* during a casting session that took place in an overlit office on Wilshire. I might not have recognized her if it hadn't been whispered—not just by me, but by many others—that she was the most terrible actress we'd seen that day, which was saying something special, because all we'd seen that day were terrible actresses.

But first:

I'd come west from Sleepy Hollow when I was twenty-seven and I was determined to write movies. I could have stayed in New York, but the city had started to drag on me: While walking along Fifth Avenue, or Park, or Madison, I'd begun to feel suffocated in the shadows of the skyscrapers—a skyline that, trapped by constant clouds, seemed like a giant inhalation itself. In Manhattan, I treaded the sidewalks nervously, overly aware of the city's brawny muscle. A person was expected to speak quickly, to get to the point; if what you had to say couldn't be said by the time a breath ran out, chances were you were saying it wrong.

I took to L.A. instantly. For the first time in years, I felt I could breathe. I often found myself making circles around the trunks of palm trees just because there was space, just because I could. On weekends, I would climb into Laurel Canyon and pick my way through the mis-

matched architecture of the homes. Long, low ranch houses set im-
probably into steep slopes. A Mediterranean villa sharing a tangle of
bougainvillea with a Japanese pagoda. A medieval castle whose towers
grazed the red tiled roof of a Spanish mission. I breathed in all of it—
all of this aggressive stab at recreating the Actual that resulted in some
monstrously beautiful Artificial. Then afterward, once the sky had turned
neon, I'd make my way to the ocean. I'd stand at the edge of piers and in
the middle of boardwalks.

I rented a five-hundred-square-foot studio apartment on Gower and
Afton that had a view of the Hollywood sign on days when the smog
had blown out across the Pacific instead of against the hills. There was a
small kitchenette with a refrigerator that the landlord said was new, but
nevertheless smelled of plastic and fish. I bought a futon, and also a small
writer's desk from a secondhand store on Fairfax after the salesman convinced me—too easily—that John Osborne had once owned the piece.
My mattress I wrapped in two sets of sheets and set it, frameless, on the
floor. I refused to close the window. I painted the room's grey walls white,
and I plastered them with posters that Earl had allowed me to take from
the Avalon. *The Graduate* and *The Sting* and *Paper Moon* and *Chinatown*.
Then, above the tub in the bathroom: *Jaws*.

For three years I had a job sorting mail at Capitol Records. Mostly
the envelopes I opened contained requests, demands, receipts. I'd pass the
note to the appropriate party; would move on to the next parcel, the next
package; would stripe my hand with another paper cut. A handful of times
each day, though, there'd be a fan letter. Some hand-scribbled note for
the Sylvers; a seventeen-year-old's gushing review of the latest Buzzcocks.
Stationery for Bob Seger—graffitied with a sloppy lipstick imprint of a
kiss. And these, sometimes, I'd steal. I'd bring them back to John Osborne's
desk in my apartment on Afton. Before I began writing each night, I'd
curve out the letters in the salutations with a felt-tip pen; I'd change "Cole"
to "Colin," "Maze" to "McPhee." I didn't know a thing about music and I'd
never played an instrument, but I don't think I particularly cared what they
were being praised for, so much as the fact that they were being praised.

My script, *The Family Room*, was sold two days before I turned thirty by an agent named Sammy who felt obligated to represent me after I'd gotten his alcoholic cousin a job in the Capitol mailroom. To celebrate, he took me to a Mexican restaurant on Beverly Boulevard called El Coyote, where we drank watered-down margaritas from glasses the size of soup bowls. There was a mariachi band that bobbled through the room, and as its members sidestepped in the thin alleys between the tables their sombreros knocked and snagged upon the low-hanging lamps. I remember having the unsettling feeling that in the wake of this good news I wasn't asking the right questions—or, that I wasn't asking any questions at all. Which was preventing Sammy from what he did best, from what I was paying him to do, which was, namely, to answer my questions.

I scooped up puddles of salsa with paper-thin chips before Sammy suggested—desperately—that we order another round of drinks.

He ran a finger along the rim of his glass, gathering salt.

"They're thrilled with it. The folks at the studio," Sammy said. "It's practically all they talk about."

"Really? That's great. That's just so great." A chip broke in half in the salsa; I used the tip of my thumb to try to fish it out without him noticing. "What are they saying about it?"

"That they're thrilled."

Our waitress, a blond midwestern-looking woman in a *quinceañera* dress, set down two plates piled with tacos set up like dominos.

Sammy picked away the things he didn't like—cilantro, red onions, fatty pieces of beef. "They love how inventive it is. How imaginative."

I said, "That's exactly what I'd want them to say."

But it wasn't inventive or imaginative. At least not in my mind. And that was intentional. For more than a decade—since Clare dissected the projector at the Avalon; since I listened to my father con his way through a series of imperfect stories—I'd swapped out the Fantastic for the Real. I no longer concerned myself with boys who slipped into movie screens, or with bloody Viking battles. Certain directors I used to idolize—Kubrick, Fritz Lang—I now dubbed as withering hacks; I've still never seen *2001: A Space Odyssey*. I wanted a world that I could see, and so I turned to realism. Cinema verité. I obsessed over Rouch, and Marker, and Jean-Luc Godard. I wrote whole scenes—whole god-damned *scripts*—about feeding a dog. About drying the dishes. About a couple taking four hours to make a single bed.

I didn't want to create any new worlds. All I wanted it to do was wipe the grime away from the window we were already looking through in the first place.

So I think that above all else, I was proud of *The Family Room*'s truthfulness. Of the basic familiarity of its subjects: a son, a daughter, and a father deciding what to do with the mother's étagère after her sudden, unanticipated death. As the objects—tiny urns, crystal sculptures of animals, a chipped piece of coral from the Indian Ocean—were removed from the case and parsed out, so were the fragile bonds that had been barely keeping the family intact.

Sammy sucked tequila from two cubes of ice. "Has anyone ever told you that you look like Dustin Hoffman?"

"No."

And as I said—she came to the casting call for *The Family Room*, which the film's producers asked me to attend. In a single day she read along with five hundred other girls for the part of the daughter, Kate. I suppose I should've recognized her when she was first called into the room, but we'd changed so much since the Avalon. I'd grown into myself and had worn my skin, while she'd learned how to piece together her beauty, I think: she took bits of it from other people and created an allure that seemed to envelop her, instead of inhabit her. Lips painted to look fuller, pushed-up breasts, and sleeveless tan arms. Legs like daggers that I couldn't stop staring at. When she looked at me, I smiled, just like how I'd been smiling at everyone else. I read the new name on the top of her résumé, and I returned to my notes.

But then she read. The side that we'd given the actresses to read was a monologue in which Kate, sitting in a darkened family room with her brother Max, recounts the day her mother came home with a small Baccarat statue of a lioness sleeping with her cub.

She said, "I remember when she showed me this." She pantomimed holding the crystal piece with two hands. "She told me, *That's you and me, baby. That's you and me.*" She bit her upper lip and brought her right hand to her chest, fluttering her fingers along the base of her neck.

The casting director removed his glasses and stopped her. "Let's start over."

"Excuse me?" she said.

"Let's try it again. And this time, try not to do that hand thing—the fingers against the neck." Then: "It's very . . . I don't know, it's very Faye Dunaway in *Network*."

"Oh," she said. "All right."

She began the scene again, but the casting director stopped her a second time—now, just fifteen seconds in.

"And that—that was very Ingrid Bergman."

She smiled nervously; she crossed her heels at her ankles and teetered to the left. "Was it?"

Twice more: too Diane Ladd, too Jane Fonda.

The casting director slipped his glasses back on, balancing the frames on his beaked nose. He said, "Thank you, Ms.—"

"Moore."

When the door had closed behind her, I leaned over to one of the producers sitting next to me and said, "I think I know that girl."

I tracked her down a second time in the parking lot outside the casting office—a squat grey building with two identical rows of square windows. We'd taken half an hour for lunch, and I found her leaning against a Honda, smoking a cigarette like Rita Hayworth.

"Clare?" I said as I approached.

"Colin? Shit, Colin, I knew that was you. Really—the second I walked in there I *knew* it was you."

"You changed your last name."

"No one wants an autograph from Clare Murkowski."

We both commented on how surprised we were to see each other—but really, there were few other places that would make more sense for us to reunite. Given how much time we'd spent in the Avalon's darkened theater, how much time we'd spent living in film frames, it was inevitable that we'd both end up here.

She stubbed out the cigarette and waved the smoke away from her face. When she hugged me she lifted herself onto her toes and pressed into me. Her neck, her cheeks smelled like lilac and smoke. When she finally released me, she still kept her hands on my arms. "Look at you! Some Hollywood big shot."

"No," I laughed. "No, nothing like that."

She straightened the lapels on my blazer and dusted ash from her cigarette that'd landed on my shoulder. "Who knew you could look so good out of that shit they made us wear at the Avalon?"

"You're awful."

"I mean it—those grey suits flattered no one. They made us all look like popcorn-wielding elephants."

I laughed and she smiled and her cheeks turned red.

She said, "But really, what are you doing here?"

Two girls with folded scripts passed by, reciting the monologue to each other. "Actually, I wrote it. I'm the writer."

"The writer!" She reached into her purse for another cigarette. "That's great, Colin. That's really something."

"It was mostly luck, I think."

She lit a match and cupped it against the wind.

"Oh, don't do that. Don't be so modest. Especially when you don't mean it." She held her cigarette at chin level and the smoke framed her face, gauzing over her green eyes, her lifted cheekbones. She'd grown into her beauty, Clare. "You want to smoke? Probably not. Ron tells me that I'm the only person in this town who smokes anymore."

"Who's Ron?"

She scratched the back of her neck with her free hand. On all sides, the sun reflecting off the windshields blinded us. "Oh—no one."

I said, "Sure. Sure, I'll smoke."

I took her book of matches. I slouched against the Honda and held the cigarette between my thumb and middle finger. I exhaled from the corners of my mouth.

"How am I doing?" I asked.

She studied me like she did when we were kids outside the theater. She moved the crook in my elbow to a different angle. Pushed against the insides of my thighs so my feet edged apart.

"Almost there. Almost Steve McQueen."

We both watched as the two girls who had been running lines fixed their makeup in the reflection of car windows, as they stapled headshots to the backs of their résumés.

I said, "So how is all this going?"

"It's great. It's fantastic." She switched her cigarette to her left hand. "God, I was horrible in there, wasn't I. I was really horrible."

"You weren't. You were wonderful," I lied. "They've been brusque with everyone."

"I always get that, you know. They're always telling me that I do things like everyone else. It's infuriating."

"Then maybe start doing them like yourself?"

"No," she said. "No, that wouldn't work, either."

"You never know. It might," I told her and she kissed my cheek.

When my lunch break was over, I asked her if she'd like to get dinner.

"You know," I said. "Just to catch up." We'd just finished our cigarettes and had tossed the butts into the gutter.

"I think that'd be nice."

"Will Ron care?"

She laughed and dipped her chin into her shoulder. She tucked her bangs behind her ears. Basically Marilyn Monroe in *Gentlemen Prefer Blondes*, even though her hair was brown.

We met at a place on Sunset called the Rainbow Bar and Grill, which Clare told me used to be called Villa Nova, where Marilyn Monroe had her first blind date with Joe DiMaggio, where Vincente Minnelli proposed to Judy Garland. The dark walls were cut up with framed pictures of famous Hollywood types, many of whom were now dead, and I took this as a sign of the restaurant's inevitable decline to kitsch—a theory that'd be rubber-stamped two years later when John Belushi would purportedly eat his last meal there. A bowl of pea soup.

"I come here all the time," she said as we slid into a red vinyl booth. She reached out and began rearranging the ketchup and mustard bottles, the salt. "I can never seem to get anyone to recognize me, though. Or even remember me."

I unfolded the menu. "I hardly recognized you." I added, "You'd been hiding those legs."

"Knock it off."

We ordered two vodkas and stabbed at the ice with our thin plastic straws.

"So how long have you been out here?" I asked her.

"Six years, I guess? Seven? I don't know. Too long, but not long enough."

She'd moved west to act when she was twenty-one, she told me.

"It was the only thing that seemed to make sense. I'd spent my life figuring out how to do things like other people did them, so I figured I might as well start getting paid for it."

In the meantime, she'd worked at one of the theaters in L.A. to make ends meet. She'd fallen in love with the pictures she'd seen of the Chinese Theatre, of the El Rey and Grauman's Egyptian and the El Capitan. The glossy images of four-story marquees and lines of limousines and red carpets unfurling like so many tongues. Of the theaters' staffs aligned out in front of them in smart, pressed uniforms. These were places that weren't like the Avalon; there were spotlights that tracked outside in great arcing swoops every weekend—not just opening night.

"Crazy, isn't it? Moving across the country to shovel popcorn and tear tickets?"

"How did you make your way out here?"

"The bus at first. But in Cleveland I got bored and bought a plane ticket."

When she arrived on an August afternoon in 1968, though, she was greeted by a rude awakening: the Hollywood Boulevard that she stepped onto wasn't the same Hollywood Boulevard from the pictures that she'd pinned to her bedroom wall in Sleepy Hollow. The dazzling glitz had somehow faded—now, everything just looked drab. Or not just drab, but dangerous. As she made her way between the different theaters along the boulevard, she was accosted by the women who worked it—girls in miniskirts and halter tops, girls with calves that'd grown too thick, too muscular from spending ten hours a night in heels, treading along an uneven and canyoned sidewalk. Girls who smelled like mouthwash and cigarettes and the leftovers of so many men. They screeched at Clare if she stood on a particular corner for too long. They stabbed their veiny fingers into her chest; they left bits of their acrylic nails in the seams of her shirt.

"I paid money to sit in one of those viewing booths at a porn store. Just so I could have a private place to cry."

She was tough, though—she always had been—and eventually, she ended up getting a job ushering four days a week at Grauman's Egyptian, but that proved to be a disappointment as well. The annoyances she'd faced at the Avalon were ever present at the Egyptian, except now on a grander scale: the smells more nauseating, the stains on the carpet in new, larger shapes. The posh premieres she'd been anticipating didn't happen as often as she thought they would, and when they did, they were a nightmare. So much running around, and yelling, and fulfilling strange demands ("There was one actress—I won't say who, but take my word that it's someone you know—who insisted that her seat be blessed by a Santeria shaman before she arrived. I'll also add this: many Santeria blessings include blood from a recently killed chicken.")

"I did get to see a lot of movies, though."

Clare flagged down the waitress and asked for a second vodka.

"And the acting?"

"I kept at it, but it wasn't panning out like I thought it would. The farthest I got was a callback for this B-horror thing. Something about people who turn into fish. I don't think it ever got made." The straw that she'd been chewing on—the one from the empty first drink—she now tied into a knot. "But then I met Ron and things started turning around."

Ron. Ron Wagner. Taller than her, than me, not as lean as he could've been, and a decade older than either of us. Hair that was then brown, but that I imagine has since gone grey, or silver, or whichever shade carries with it that cheap sense of distinction characteristic of state college professors or car salesmen or—in his case—a man who directed commercials. She said he was a frequent customer of the Egyptian; he'd been coming twice a week since long before she arrived. He'd sit quietly, alone in the back row of the theater, polishing his Coke-bottle glasses, occasionally slipping his pudgy fingers into a tub of buttered popcorn, which he never finished. For the first few weeks, he saw Clare only as she passed in the dark (after each movie began, she'd peek into the theater to count empty seats). But then, as those first few weeks turned into a month, there was an issue with the projector during the second showing on a Thursday night, and Clare was sent in by the head usher to quell the anxious audience.

"You did that like a movie star," Ron said to her as she made her way from the front of the house to the exit. The bottom half of his glasses was fogged. She had her palm pressed against one of the giant swinging doors.

"What?"

"The way you got everyone's attention. A real movie star."

"Buddy," she told him, "in this town, everyone's a goddamned movie star."

And she left.

A few days later, though, he returned. Over the next few months, his twice-a-week routine quickly became a four-a-week routine (a showing on Tuesday, a showing on Thursday, two matinees each weekend). He'd arrive early to find her, wherever she was working. He'd wait in interminable lines at the concession stands; he'd stand next to her while she swept the littered corners of the lobby.

"Ron," she'd say to him, maneuvering the broom around his feet. "I'm trying to work."

He'd crane his neck upward to inspect the ceiling's inlays. The carvings of suns, of palm trees, of a crowned, stoic pharaoh. He'd tell her, "I'm just admiring the architecture." Then he'd tell her, "The way you've got her hair today. It reminds me of Audrey Hepburn in *Charade*."

"Oh, cut it out." She'd slip the broom and the dustpan into the utility closet, taking too long with the lock. She'd pull straight the wrinkles from her uniform and tell him, again, that she wanted him to leave her alone.

But that was a lie, of course. She didn't want to be left alone by him, at least not anymore. Because what Ron had said was precisely what Clare had wanted to hear. It was, in fact, what she'd come to that god-damned town to hear; while most women want to be told that they're beautiful, Clare had come to Hollywood to hear that she was as beautiful as someone else. That she'd become expertly capable of being someone else. And so, as they're wont to do, the tables began to turn. Subtly, self-consciously, she began to seek Ron out during her shifts at the Egyptian. Then, when she found him, she'd perform for him. She'd shove her fists into the pockets of her uniform like Annie Hall; when she tore ticket stubs, she'd give him her best Faye Dunaway.

The waitress returned and we ordered two steaks.

"He ended up casting me in a shampoo commercial, which led to a bit part in a soap opera."

"Oh, I bet he did."

"Don't be coy. He's a lovely man. He really got me started." She added, "He took me to dinner first."

"What a gentleman."

She spoke of him admiringly, reverently. She praised his soft de-meanor and quiet masculinity.

I said, "We're talking about a man who directs shampoo commercials."

But she ignored me. While she buttered a triangle of bread, she de-scribed, twice, how endearing it was when his glasses fogged, how she thought it betrayed a vulnerability and innocence.

When I asked her what drew her to him most, she told me, "Cer-tainty. And unless you're an actress, you can't understand how appealing that is."

"You mean attention."

She tore the bread in half. She set both pieces on her plate but ate neither. "I think I mean certainty. I don't know. Yes—I think I mean certainty."

Our steaks arrived. As Clare cut away strips of wrinkled fat, she begged me, "But please—let's change the subject, all right? How was I today? You can be honest. In fact, please, be honest."

And because I was a man in love, and what men in love do most often is lie, I said, "You were the best."

The next morning I wrote her the first letter, and it went something like this:

> Dear Ms. Moore,
> Your performance last night at the Rainbow Bar and Grill was groundbreaking. I was moved by your beauty, your poise, and the passion with which you spoke about serving popcorn in a cinema. I wish you wouldn't end up with that Ron fellow. He seems a bit of a bore and entirely undeserving of you. I anxiously await the sequel.
>
> > Signed, with adoration,
> > Colin McPhee
>
> P.S. Marry me?

A fan letter, I told myself, as I creased the paper in half and slipped it into an envelope bearing her address. And a good one, honed from my years of reading and stealing and copying similar notes from Capitol Records. I'd typed it on my Smith Corona in the tiny studio on Gower and Afton. Even though I'd come into a not-unimpressive amount of money when I sold *The Family Room,* I was still there, and in fact very little had changed. The futon still dipped on the floor; the posters still wrapped around the walls. The only change, I think, was that I'd swapped out *Jaws* for *Jaws 2* in the bathroom.

The next day, I waited for her to call. And then when she didn't, I wrote another letter. I folded it into a second envelope, and I licked the sweet adhesive from a stamp's back. And then the next day, another, and the next day, another, and the next day, another. *Dear Ms. Moore, I—. Dear Ms. Moore, You—. Dear Ms. Moore, We—.* And always—always:

Marry me? I'd walk them to the mailbox on the far corner of Afton, and I'd slip them into the slot. I'd peek my head into the small darkness, conferring with the box: *Okay, we have a deal here. I've done my part, now it's your turn. It's your job to get it to her.*

When I'd return home, I'd stare at the phone and I'd will it to ring; I'd curse myself every time my eyes became so dry that I had to blink. I'd crack open beers before noon. I'd drink three in a row, but it wouldn't work: it'd turn me drunk and anxious, instead of just anxious. Often, I cleaned manically. I burrowed around in corners I hadn't peered into in years, sweeping away dust, and hair, and little bits of torn paper; I vacuumed the colorless wall-to-wall carpet with a handheld Dust Buster.

After two months of this, on a morning when I was foggy and gossamer brained, and when the day's light was just starting to trickle into the basin, I loaded a fresh sheet of paper into the Smith Corona. I wrote:

Dear Ms. Moore,
You're doing spectacularly in the role of my negligent childhood heartbreak. It's reminiscent, in fact, of the time you played the role of the girl who kissed me during "Cleopatra" only to tell me, immediately afterward, that you weren't in love with me. It's a good thing I didn't believe you then, either, ha ha, right?
                              Sitting, as always, on the edge of my seat,
                              Colin McPhee

My offer still stands.

This time, though, I delivered the letter myself. I waited until it was eleven in the morning, when the sun had crested the wraiths of smog, when I knew that Ron would be at work, and I drove to the house in which he and Clare lived, on the outskirts of Griffith Park. I slipped the letter beneath the welcome mat on the front porch. I rang the doorbell, and before she had time to answer, I left. I hiked into the park, on a trail that coiled under the shadow of the observatory.

That evening, half an hour before the floodlights illuminated the

Hollywood sign, the phone rang. As I leapt from my futon to reach for it, I knocked over a draft of a screenplay I'd never finish and I slammed my knee against the sharp corner of a table.

"Colin."

"A-ha!"

"What are you doing?"

"Watching *Taxi* in my underwear."

"No, Colin. With these letters, *what are you doing?*"

"So you've been getting them."

"Yes, I've been getting them. I've—"

"Are you saving them?"

I imagined shoeboxes stuffed under beds. The well-read corners of folded and unfolded paper sticking out from underneath the lids.

She said, "I—no. No, I can't. I've had to get rid of them."

"I see." Then: "But after reading them, right?"

She sighed. There was a delicate crunching sound as she shifted the phone to her shoulder. The volume of her voice slipped lower. "Yes. After reading them."

"So—there's that."

"You need to stop sending them, Colin."

"Because you love me?"

She didn't answer, and so I asked again: "Because you love me?"

"Because you're going to get me into a lot of trouble."

"So you do—you do love me."

"Colin, stop sending them."

"Is that it?"

"*Please* stop sending them?"

I respected her—at least for the most part, I'd like to think. There were moments, of course. Points of weakness during which the pang of loneliness and/or infatuation became too acute, and when its normal cures seemed not enough, leaving me still hungry, still dizzy. And during those instances I'd pull the Smith Corona from the desk to floor. I'd cradle it up to me and I'd feel its heat spread across my lap as I wrote to her. But this only happened two times, three times, four times. Six times. At the most.

And maybe those unexpected teases—"uninvited invitations" might be a better way to describe them—helped to influence what happened next, and what happened after that. Maybe she held on to those final letters—the ones she thought she hadn't wanted—and during the evenings when Ron had gone to bed, she'd creep outside into the halfhearted L.A. night. She'd read them beneath the buzzing yellow glow of a streetlamp. She'd read them over again, until she could recite the words. And then she'd look up at the observatory, with its strange curved walls and eerie protrusions. She'd think about the stars that it watched and tracked. Stars that—like love—had to be trusted on a matter of faith, especially here, in Los Angeles, where the industrial lights of the studios eclipsed them.

Or maybe that wasn't it. Maybe that wasn't it at all. Maybe it was a story that was far less romantic but far more realistic; instead of dealing in stars and observatories and timid nights, this story dealt in something else, in something banal, in traffic. Specifically: the infamous and demonic gnarl of cars that knots around the 405/101 interchange during the evening rush hour. More specifically: Let's say that Clare, a terrible driver with a notoriously bad sense of direction, could be counted on with almost-perfect certainty to become plugged into this bottleneck (thus delaying her arrival at the house in Griffith Park by two hours) each time she returned from Burbank, where she was sent on auditions approximately twice a week. For the sake of this hypothesis, though, let's also say that after one of these auditions, Clare got smart. Before she inserted the keys into the car's ignition, she said to herself, *The 405 is going to be a mess. I know it's going to be a mess. I've been stuck in that mess. I'll take Victory to the 170 instead.* And lo! She made it out of the valley in forty-five minutes. Record time. Her plan paid off. Or, it paid off, but only just barely, and only in the beginning. Because when Clare pulled into the bungalow's leafy driveway, she had to wedge her Ford next to a late-model Toyota she didn't recognize. And similarly, when she stepped into the house's foyer and called Ron's name, she tripped over a pair of heels, a blouse, a skirt into which she surely couldn't fit. Then, in the pitch-black hallway outside the bedroom: a set of lace panties, a matching brassiere, a thin ankle, her lover's too-meaty ass, a necktie, a tanned and toned arm, a fatty rib, a set of perky tits. And maybe, as her eyes adjusted and she took in the fleshy mesh, she didn't scream out quite as soon as one would expect. Maybe there was that brief moment of detached awe and objective confusion when she was left to consider just how wrong she'd been about him. That, in fact, a man with fogged glasses and a soft demeanor was just as capable of fucking a nineteen-year-old as anyone else.

There's also a substantial chance that it wasn't either of those things, that her shift in reasoning was inspired by a catalyst of which I'll never be aware, or ever understand. The important point is that she called, again, eleven months later.

"Colin? Can you hear me?"

"I can hear you."

"Okay. All right—good. I have a question. Or, not a question, necessarily. More just something to say. I guess that—"

"Just say it, Clare."

She breathed. She held her breath, then said, "Do you remember that scene at the end of *Sabrina*? When Humphrey Bogart tells Audrey Hepburn to get on the boat and never come back, but because he's fallen in love with her, he experiences this huge change of heart and he chases after her?"

"Yes."

"I think I understand that now. I think I understand what it's like to have a change of heart."

Clare's family was at our wedding, and so was my agent, Sammy, but mostly the pews were filled with extras. Friends she'd met on the set of the few commercials and soap operas she'd done, or people who served as wordless mourners in the funeral scene of *The Family Room*. There weren't too many, though: For the ceremony, we'd selected a small church in Santa Monica, on Euclid Street. It couldn't have held more than forty-five people.

Her favorite flowers were peonies—she said she liked the way they looked bashful—and so the aisles of the tiny chapel were sprouting with white and yellow blossoms that smelled like morning. They spilled out from the entrance—two propped-open wooden doors—and then onto a series of three shallow steps, where I sat waiting for my father, who was already thirty minutes late.

I'd called him every day since I'd proposed, and each time the phone rang unanswered. I sent him two invitations—one to the house in Sleepy Hollow, and one to the Sandpiper, the bar where I'd found him in Nyack. An RSVP came from neither. Still, I made sure a seat was reserved for him in the church's front row.

The sky was crowded with semidark clouds that moved east across the sky. Whenever a space opened up for the sun to break through, the sidewalk in front of the church became too bright; I'd stare at it for as long as I could before the corners of my eyes began to water and I was forced to look away. Seven months before, Sammy had taken me to a department store off Wilshire to buy a tuxedo for the Golden Globes, and I wore this suit on that day, the day of my wedding. I pulled loose threads from the jacket's cuffs and I tied the short black strings into knots, bows. Every ten minutes, Clare's mother would come and stand between the church's two open doors. At first I turned to her apologetically. But after a full hour passed, I started to ignore her; I pretended that I didn't notice her sighs. That I didn't notice her saying to Clare's father, *We don't even know if the bastard's coming.*

I heard the car before I saw it: that howl of cannonballs and broken glass. It turned north onto Euclid from Idaho Avenue and I noticed how the yellow paint had peeled off in larger sheets; how there was more rusted steel exposed around the rims of the tires, the curves of the front fender. My father parked in front of the stairs where I was sitting, and once he'd stepped out of the car I told him, "You're an hour and a half late."

"The traffic in this town!" He held both my arms. He shook me once and kissed me on the cheek. "Have you ever seen anything like it?"

"And you never wrote me back. You never responded to the invitation. How was I supposed to know that you'd actually be here?"

He brushed dust from my lapel. Straightened my boutonniere and picked a peony's petal from my shoulder.

"Did you know that the longest traffic jam in history happened two years ago, on February sixteenth?" he said. "It happened in France, between Lyon and Paris, and the cars stretched one hundred nine miles. One hundred nine miles!"

"Come on, Dad," I said. "Not today."

"It happened because of bad weather and because all of France decided to go skiing on the same day. People made fondue in the middle of the highway. I know because I was there. But the traffic in this town—"

I pushed his hands away from my shoulders, where they were still dusting, working. "I said knock it off."

He looked tired; the skin beneath his eyes pulled down in sagging crescents.

He said to me, "You're swimming in this penguin suit. You should've gone a size smaller on the jacket."

HOW TO CON A GANGSTER

Finn

My granddad arrived in Chicago on the morning of May 12, 1970—the
same day that more than a billion cisco flies descended upon the city.
They'd invaded once before, the flies, in 1895: On August 25, at about
eight o'clock in the morning, they appeared suddenly, and without warning, in furry, frenzied clumps. Mainly, the ciscoes kept to within three
or four blocks of the lake—they had a thing for water—but there were
also swarms that buzzed up Halsted Street, up Wabash. That painted the
sides of shops with their sticky toes and made dark hula hoops around
the Loop.

Back then, in 1895, entomologists at Northwestern University es-
timated the number of flies to be well over a million. The 1970 invasion, though—the backdrop for my granddad and Lucy's debut on Lake
Shore Drive—was said to be at least ten times as massive.

So: *one billion fucking flies.*

The way he tells it, the sole structure that escaped the wrath of the
ciscoes, if only partially, was the Sears Tower—and that's only because
the flies were afraid to climb so high as the skyscraper's upper floors.
("Don't be fooled, Finn," my granddad used to say. "The folks who spend
their lives in the clouds are the ones who are terrified most of falling.")
Everything else, though, was fair game, subjected to a slick, foamy coat
of cisco grime. Windows, particularly those on the first through third
floors, were covered with a dusting no less than a foot thick made up

of wings and legs and a hundred moving eyes. The old Water Tower, down on Michigan Avenue, transformed into a sort of gothic animation: its once-white stone walls and parapets now swayed and quivered, like pitch-black branches, as the flies landed, climbed over one another, changed their minds.

At Navy Pier, the USS *Silversides,* a submarine, submerged into the lake—an underwater escape.

Downtown, traffic stopped and started. Windshield wipers tossed folded fly heads into gutters. Stoplights had three colors, my granddad said: black, blacker, blackest. The ubiquitous, midvolume buzz of the flies' wings flapping was interrupted only by the crunch of their bodies being squished beneath the slow-rolling wheels of cars. Along the sidewalks, pedestrians stopped swatting at their necks, their shoulders, their cheeks: they allowed the ciscoes to perch on the edges of their noses, the ends of their eyebrows. They scratched at an itch only when they felt the absence of something, not the presence of it.

My granddad took pictures of the whole messy ordeal with a 1965 Polaroid Model 20 Swinger camera he'd picked up a few years earlier. He shook each photo until its screen fully developed into the image he'd shot: an intimation of a cityscape obscured by a thousand hair-thin legs. He sent them off to the Rev in Pittsburgh, who would die two years later; to Charlotte Sparrow in Columbus, who would always be alive.

The great-grandchildren of the Northwestern entomologists, who were now renowned bug experts themselves, gathered in their spooky Evanston labs. Huddled around pinned and preserved specimens of butterflies, of beetles, of foot-long ants, they endeavored in vain to conjure up an explanation for the Phenomenon of the Flies. The ciscoes' eggs were laid in the marshes along Lake Michigan, they knew, but the only way such a huge swarm could make its way to the city—at once—would be on the back of a robust breeze. And that day, May 12, had so far been eerily windless.

"They've just come because they wanted to," the Northwestern entomologists said in a statement released that afternoon. "Because it's an especially nice day, and because Chicago is a nice city, and because they didn't have much else to do."

The thing is, no one was particularly panicked. Because as my grand-dad put it, everyone was sure they wouldn't be around for long. It was widely known that the ciscoes, as a species, were ephemeral: after tran-sitioning from larvae into fully matured flies, they lived for less than twenty-four hours. They flew, and they fucked, and they spawned in their soggy marshes, and then they died, clogging the lake with a billion tiny black corpses. *So*, the residents of Chicago said. *So, with a life like that, why cause a fuss? Why not just let the little bastards have this—their single less-than-a-day in the sun?*

As such, the afternoon progressed like any other. The tour boats still floated along the Chicago River, stopping periodically to squeegee away insect bits from the Plexiglas windows. At the Chicago Mercantile Ex-change, commodity futures briefly spiked as industry speculators whis-pered that the flies could mean a prolonged and bountiful crop season. Outside the Art Institute, abstract painters set out teaspoons of acrylic in a thousand different shades next to long rectangular canvases: they hoped the footprints of the flies would reveal deeper truths about love, faith, humanity.

At Wrigley Field, grounds workers sported thick goggles as they tugged their nail drags along the outfield. As they drew the string line taut from home base's apex to third, to first. As they chalked out the bat-ter's box into the infield's red dirt. As they prepped the stadium for that day's game.

My granddad lived his life in New York, but he's always nurtured a special love for the Cubs. The affair started in 1938: he listened on the radio as Chicago bested Pittsburgh during a life-or-death late-season game, with Gabby Hartnett clinching the victory with a walk-off home run. When the crowds at Wrigley stormed the field to escort Hartnett around the bases, my granddad leapt on his parents' couch in New York, jumping up and down till the springs snapped. His excitement hasn't let up since.

The man—on top of being a hero, and a heartbreaker, and a poly-math, and exceedingly humble—is also a sports almanac. He can tell you what season was the Cub's best (1906, with 116 wins), and which was their worst (1962, with 103 losses). He knows who has the highest career batting average (Riggs Stephenson—.336), who has hit the most career singles (Cap Anson, who hung up his uniform in 1896, with 2,246), who's got the most doubles (also Anson), who snagged the most triples (Jimmy Ryan). Even now, he could give you the play-by-play that led to the 550-foot-long home run Dave Kingman whaled on April 14, 1976—a rocket of a shot that ricocheted off the roof of a house on Kenmore Avenue.

He loves all the players, past and present. Even the guys like Hack Wilson and Sammy Sosa—guys who fell victim to boozing, or doping, or both. He's a forgiving man, and so he loves them despite their faults, and also because of them. But he's still human, my granddad, if only barely, which is to say there are definitely members of the club whom he likes more than others. And if you were to ask for that list—that desert-island, end-of-the-world, all-time-favorite list of ballplayers—I'm certain Ernie Banks would be at the top of it.

They called him Mr. Cub, and in 1982, eleven years after he retired, he became the first of only six players to have his number retired by the franchise. He was universally loved—not only for his spectacular skill on the field (in 1955 he set a record for grand slams hit in a single season that wouldn't be broken for another thirty years), but also for his almost freakishly sunny nature: Banks had a searing love for the game, the heat of which was rivaled only by my granddad's passion for stories.

On May 12, the day the flies quilted Chicago and my granddad went to Wrigley, the Cubs were playing Atlanta at home and Ernie Banks had hit, to date, 499 career home runs. The crowd that had gathered was sparse—only five thousand spectators peppered the stadium. Still, I'd wager that the folks who filled those seats didn't care who won or who lost, but rather whether they might witness one of those rare moments when history coalesces into itself. When Ernie Banks slammed his 500th homer.

The game dragged on tediously, at that lackluster pace people bemoan when they talk about baseball being an irritatingly slow sport. Meanwhile, the day had followed suit: it had a dangerously lazy disposition. The ciscoes grew weary, resting their brittle bodies on the bills of ball caps and empty Cracker Jack boxes. The air stacked on top of itself in cakey layers.

But this windlessness wasn't necessarily a bad thing, my granddad has told me. At least not for the ballplayers. Wrigley can be a strange place, specifically when it comes to wind. Toward the end of summer the breeze comes from the west and southwest; it blows out. And that's a pitcher's nightmare: balls that should be harmless flies get an added boost and become home runs. But earlier on—say in April or May, when this game was being played—the wind comes off the lake, which is to say it blows in. It wreaks havoc on the batter. It drags down potential homers, turning them into outs. So, when Banks stepped up to the plate at the bottom of the eleventh, after the Cubs and the Braves had stalemated at 3–3, the fans silently blessed the quiet that hung in heavy sheets around them. They cooled their sweaty cheeks with flyswatters that roaming vendors were shilling in the place of hot dogs.

That stillness didn't last, though. The weather was conspiring against the Cubs. When Banks slugged a fastball fired off by Braves pitcher Pat Jarvis, the gusts from the lake suddenly picked up for the first time that day. The ciscoes lifted from their perches—a trilling black veil hovering above the field. At least three-quarters of the fans covered their eyes, and Wrigley itself held its breath; the green cheeks of the stadium turned blue.

My granddad says that everything slowed, and I believe him. Because I've seen this while I've been editing other peoples' lives. I've seen how the world decelerates its hurried rotation at moments like this: how it allows time for us to hold them, to taste them, to shoulder them. He watched as the ball inched through the taut air, slicing a blue smear through the screen of flies, which fell, one by one, into the stretched mitts of the infielders. Then, once it had soared over third, the wind began to tug at its trajectory, pulling it perilously close to the foul line, and my granddad sprang from his seat. He tackled the stadium's stairs three at a time. He crisscrossed through the fans, some of whom had uncovered their eyes and had thrown their arms into the air, where they waved in slow motion, blades of grass caught in an underwater current.

When my granddad made it to the top of the stands, the wind was just beginning to twist Banks's ball to the outside of the left-field foul line. So, he reached out toward it. He removed the flies: first by taking each one by its pair of wings and plucking it from his path. But then, as the ball slipped farther from history, he did it in great scooping handfuls: he grabbed their fleecy bodies the same way you'd shovel up popcorn, or peanuts, or sand. And finally, when he'd mowed a clear tunnel through which to stretch his arm, he did the only thing he could do, the only thing that was natural—he gave the ball a poke. He pushed it—literally—into baseball's lore.

There are two ways this story ends: the right way, and the real way. In the right way, once the world had caught up, and the fans had started cheering, squashing flies between their palms, my granddad quietly found Banks's ball and tossed it into the bull pen. He knew as well as anyone that a treasure like that would best be preserved in a museum— not on a mantelpiece. He left then. With a Braves' pennant he wiped away the ciscoes from Lucy's windshield, from her side mirrors, and he departed Chicago, content with the role he'd played in rearranging history. That's the right way.

The real way, though, goes like this: My granddad wasn't alone at the left-field foul line. Rather, a wholly despicable man whom he'd later come to know as the Gangster met him at that post. He was shaped like an underripe banana, I'm told: lean, hard, a slight rightward curve to his spine. He wore a three-piece suit, even in the stagnant heat. His hair was slicked with so much oil that when the flies landed upon it they became entrapped, their legs kneading deeper and deeper into the muck as they tried, unsuccessfully, to escape. And his hands—his hands were no palms and all fingers, these protracted claws that snatched up Banks's home run as soon as my granddad tipped it into fair play.

After pocketing the relic the Gangster disappeared immediately. And in the chaos and jubilant confusion that followed, no one seemed to notice that the game ball had gone missing. He slunk back through the crowds, making his way, eventually, to West Roscoe and North Ashland, where he ran a bookie business that swindled cash from drunks, and petty thieves, and all other species of unsavory characters. Twilight was descending on the city, and the ciscoes—who were nearing the end of their ephemeral lives—began dropping in a steady rain to the street. The Gangster slushed through the flies' lifeless corpses as he swung open the door; he wiped away their guts from the tips of his pointed shoes. And he set Banks's ball in a small glass box where it would sit, for more than four decades, waiting to be rescued.

The Gangster has died and his daughter, who also calls herself the Gangster, has turned her father's illegal bookkeeping business into an above-board pizza place that's called, appropriately, The Gangster's. She's deliberately kept the bookie's vibe, it seems: all the lights in the restaurant are banker's lamps, names and numbers and dates scratched into their green glass shades. The wood-paneled walls are tricked out with bits of nostalgia—pictures of racehorses; a greyhound chewing its tail, ribs poking through too-thin skin. In the corner, a multigenerational arcade featuring Pac-Man, Mortal Kombat, and a claw crane, the windowed box of which is filled with Cubs memorabilia. Hats. Baseballs. Tiny bats engraved with painted red C's.

Instead of booths, or banquettes, customers sit at one of five long communal tables that smell like beer and bourbon and mozzarella, their asses drooping over oak benches. Randal and I sit at the end of one of these—the one closest to the door.

"This place is weird," I say.

"So weird."

We've ordered a deep-dish pepperoni pie. We peel the tiny saucers of meat from the cheese and feed them to Mrs. Dalloway, who's got her head half poked out of Randal's bag. She belches and hiccups between bites, occasionally pausing to lick grease from her chops. Not more than five minutes ago we spotted the baseball, set in a glass case on a small shelf that's been built out above the kitchen's entrance. A gold plaque below it reads: ERNIE BANKS'S 500TH HOME RUN BALL, CAUGHT FAIRLY AND ENTIRELY SQUARELY BY MY FATHER THE GANGSTER.

"You sure you want to do this?" Randal asks.

I tell him, "I'm sure."

"It could get ugly."

"I'm a man with nothing left to lose." Then: "I just don't know how the fuck we're supposed to get it down from there."

Randal tears away the crust from an uneaten slice of pizza. He chews it slowly, thinking, pursing his lips. He drums a finger against the space between his eyebrows. He winks both eyes at the four corners of the room.

"What?" I ask, finally.

He stands. He says, "Leave the details to me."

I ask *What?* again, but he just puts a hand lightly on my shoulder. At the cashier, past a maze of men spinning pizza slicers, he exchanges a five-dollar bill for twenty quarters. Dalloway alternates between roaring and clucking anxiously as she fixes her hourglass eyes upon him; she lifts her one front paw from the pack and I reach down and shove it back in.

His pockets sagging with change, Randal crosses to the makeshift arcade—specifically to the claw crane, where he begins unloading his quarters. I haven't a clue what he's doing, but I know his first six attempts at it are unsuccessful: I watch as the claw pinches the edges of different prizes, as it loses its grip, as it returns to its starting position accompanied by a deflated electronic *Da-da-duuuuuuuum*. But then, on the seventh try, Randal strikes gold. He rustles up a baseball in plastic casing that's hidden beneath a bear in a blue jersey and pinstriped pants. He lifts the prize above his head, shakes it once triumphantly.

When he returns to the table, he asks if I've got a pen. He sticks out the tip of his tongue as he works, biting down on it so it appears as a pink triangle fixed to his upper lip.

He says, "Do you know what a pigeon drop is?"

I tell him, "No."

"Some people say it's a type of con. A type of trick."

"So it's a way of stealing."

"That's a dirty word. Let's call it reappropriating."

He presses the pen to the baseball's white skin and begins to draw slow, deliberate lines. I lean forward to see what he's writing, but he tells me to stand back. He tells me I'm blocking his light.

"So, the CliffsNotes description of the pigeon drop: you've got someone who has something you want. Money, some valuable item, memorabilia—whatever. We'll call this person the mark, all right? The goal is to get the mark to exchange whatever he—or, in this case she—has for something of lesser value while convincing her that she's actually trading up. Profiting from the deal." Then: "You get it?"

"I think so." Mrs. Dalloway peeks out from the bag and I give her my finger to lick with her rough tongue. "Did you learn all this stuff when you were selling forged autographs?"

He says, "That's not really how I see it. There was an old man whose dying wish was to have a signed photo of Celeste Holm. I sold him one for twenty dollars, when it should have gone for at least twice that."

"But you forged it."

"I made people happy, and I think that's what matters most."

He blows gently on the baseball, drying the black ink, a signature that reads:

Ernie Banks

"How many career home runs did Banks end up hitting?" Randal asks.

"Five hundred twelve."

"Then this will be that one." He cracks the ball against the table's corner, giving it a sizeable dent. He scuffs it along the soles of his dirty sneakers. "This will be the five hundred twelfth. Which we'll convince her is more valuable."

I tell him, "That's completely and utterly unbelievable. She'll never buy it."

Randal inspects his handiwork; he burnishes the ball on the underside of the table, giving it a good, filthy sheen.

"That isn't how these things go down, Finn. They don't depend on believability. Cons work because they rely on human nature. On the most basic, dependable parts of a mark's psyche. Things like greed, and dishonesty, and vanity, and naïveté."

He adds, "Sort of like reality TV."

• • •

We request an audience with the Gangster from the man behind the cash register. We're told to wait near a machine that flattens pennies into panoramic views of Chicago, where we loiter for ten minutes before being led, finally, through the kitchen and into an empty back dining room. Which is nicer than the front of the house, I'll say. The long tables and benches have been replaced with smaller individual tables draped with checkered cloths; the chairs have cushioned seats and all four of their legs intact. There are still the strange banker's lamps—under the glow of which you'd imagine men in wide-brimmed hats conducting unspecific and nefarious business—but these ones are larger, and their emerald shades aren't chipped. Their light gathers between the tables and against the walls, where framed artifacts of debatable veracity are tacked. A yellowed handkerchief that may or may not have been dropped by Al Capone. A half-used tube of lipstick allegedly used by Britt Ekland on the set of *Get Carter*. A very ordinary looking buckle that—evidently— belonged to Bugsy Siegel's favorite belt.

From the other side of the room, where she's seated at the far side of a circular table, the Gangster says, "What can I do for you?"

She's glamorous, but in a severe and frightening way. She inherited only the finest pieces of her father's looks: his lean, stretched frame; his long, ropy muscles. Her spine, though, seems to err slightly to the left, instead of the right. Her dark hair is fixed in a tight bun, yanked back so firmly that her forehead's wiped clean of creases. When she sets her hands on top of each other it's like a crane folding its wings—graceful, but a little off; calm, with an undercurrent of tension. She adjusts a ring with her thumb, the base of which is stained with specks of marinara.

The room's hot: heat from the pizza ovens slips through cracks in the kitchen door, wraps around the legs of chairs. With a napkin, the Gangster dabs at sweat that's appeared just above her lip and on her granite forehead. She wipes at her painted-on brows, her cheeks. I try my best to focus on all these minute details and subtle actions instead of staring straight into the Gangster's left eye—which looks like it's made of solid glass.

A fragile, violet replica of an iris inlaid in a milky-white globe.

A black dot's been painted on where the pupil should be. As we all situate ourselves, I watch it for longer than I should—I try to look away, but I can't—and it never blinks. While her right one twitches, and moistens, and dilates, and shrinks, the strange glass eye stays deathly still. It reflects the light of the room and the forms of our bodies too perfectly, too exactly.

Randal says, "We're here to make a deal."

But she can't actually see out of it, right? It's not as though it's functional; no, it's just a placeholder, a dog-ear.

The Gangster says, "Keep going."

Or, conversely: it's superfunctional. A Sauron/Wonder Woman hybrid. A full-body airport TSA scanner, and then some. She's not just seeing me, my naked flaccid self, but also strange and telling bits of my soul. I find myself sitting on the right edge of my chair, half my ass hanging in midair, as I try to elude the laser stare.

In the reflection of the eye, I see Randal cross his legs at the ankle. "Banks's baseball," he says.

"It's not for sale."

"Who said anything about money?"

He sets our forged specimen on the table. At our feet, in the backpack, I feel Mrs. Dalloway shift her weight in anticipation.

The Gangster balances the ball on the tips of her fingers. She rotates it in the yellow light, bringing it ever closer to her right eye, the good one.

"What's this?"

Randal leans forward on his elbows. "What you've got there is Ernie Banks's five hundred twelfth home run ball."

"And?"

"And it's the last one he ever hit. It's also signed—something I noticed your ball is not." He leans back so the chair's two front legs lift from the ground. "We're willing to make an even trade."

"Why?"

"I have my reasons."

The Gangster lifts her brow and the bun on top of her head shifts slightly. She taps a finger against the glass eye. Yells, "DOUG!"

The kitchen door swings open and there's a blast of cheesy heat.

A fat, mustachioed man with a doughy face dusted in flour lumbers over to the Gangster, wiping his hands against his apron. He leans into her and they converse in a series of hurried whispers. She hands him the ball and he scrutinizes the autograph; he turns it over so he's looking at the name upside down. He runs a finger over each of the letters, squinting as he feels the pen's etching in the ball's leather. When he returns to the Gangster's ear to relay his findings, Randal uncrosses his legs.

Doug stands up straight; he folds his arms and licks flour from the corners of his mouth.

The Gangster says, "We're not interested."

"You're making a huge mistake."

"Am I?"

The Gangster stands and Doug clears his throat. I steal a glance at Randal, who's biting at the torn edge of a cuticle and pressing his lips against his teeth. In front of us, the ball rolls back and forth on the warped table.

She stands. Says, "I'm a busy woman," and, from below, Mrs. Dalloway hisses.

I kick the bag once, but not hard enough. The hissing continues, growing into a flubbed attempt at a roar: a balloon being deflated, the edges of the rubber pulled so the air comes out in a minor-keyed moan.

Doug's halfway to the kitchen door, but the Gangster stops him, gripping his arm with one of her wingish hands. "What was that?"

"Nothing," I say too quickly. "It was nothing."

She glides back to the table. "Open the bag."

"There's nothing in the bag."

"I said *open the bag*."

For the first time, the left eye makes a move. As her face strains, the globe presses outward, turning the pink lining of the socket veiny and red. Entranced and terrified, I lift Randal's pack. I stand and pass it slowly to her.

"Finn," he says through clenched teeth. "No."

The Gangster places the pack on an empty chair and unzips it greedily. Her cheeks crease as she twitches into a smile, as she lifts the cat by the scruffy nape of her neck. As she flicks her single front paw, sending it swaying like some wind-ravaged branch.

"Fascinating," she says.

Dalloway responds with her best poker face.

The Gangster continues, "Doug, take the five hundred twelfth ball and give the kids the other one from out front. We'll need to order up a new plaque—call someone about that." Then, to us: "We'll take the ball and the cat. Those are the terms. Nonnegotiable."

Randal scoffs, feigning his lack of interest. "Why the hell would anyone want a three-legged cat?"

"You have your reasons," the Gangster says. "I have mine."

The skin on Mrs. Dalloway's neck folds over the Gangster's knuckles. She rubs her two back paws together and her threadbare tail twitches, curling into itself.

"I'll have to discuss this with my associate," Randal is saying, but it's too late. He doesn't get the words out soon enough. They dangle, suspended in his choked throat, as I hear myself say:

"Done. You've got a deal."

We're standing at the intersection of Belmont and Sheffield, where we've parked Lucy. Directly above us is the "L," and the trains passing on the tracks throw sparks that illuminate our faces like combustible fireflies.

Randal is yelling: "What the *fuck* were you thinking?"

And I'm saying, "I don't know. I mean—I wasn't. I wasn't thinking." I've got Ernie Banks's five hundredth homer palmed in my right hand and I anxiously pass it to the left. Playing catch with myself. "It was that *eye,* man. It was that fucking glass *eye.*"

Randal sits on a curb. He puts his head between his knees, balancing his brow on the ends of his thumbs. But he's too nervous: He stands as quickly as he sits, fidgets in both his pockets for a cigarette, and kicks an aluminum trashcan when he can't find one. The sound bangs off the steel beams of the "L" that encase us.

He says, very suddenly, "I'm going back."

"You're what?"

"I'm going back there. I'm going to save her."

"You're fucking nuts."

He takes a knee on the sidewalk. Tightens the shoelaces on both his sneakers. "We don't have any idea what they've got planned for her."

"It's a cat! What could possibly happen to her?"

He looks up at me from where he's crouched, and in the city's neon twilight his cheeks glow red, blue, green, orange.

I change my tone: "What I mean is that woman's probably just lonely. You know, like how cat people are lonely." I don't believe myself. "She probably just needs, like, a friend."

He stands and flexes his calves against the curb; he pulls each foot to his ass, separately, stretching his hamstrings.

"They're going to kill her." Then: "Follow up with Lucy. Park her along the curb one hundred feet west of the restaurant, and keep the engine running."

"This is crazy," I tell him. "You're fucking crazy."

He trots west toward the Gangster's, emerging out from under the "L" and into a triangle of light sliced out of the road by a streetlamp.

"There's blood on your hands, McPhee," he calls.

I get in the car, slamming the door so hard that the windows rattle in their frames. I stab the keys into the ignition, but I don't turn them. I pull at the ends of my greasy hair until there's a sharp pinch and four strands come loose. I thud my palm's heel against the steering wheel.

"He's lost it," I say to no one, to Lucy. I'm silent, then, half waiting for her to respond, for her radio to blink alive and dictate some sage wisdom.

A car passes us and the pavement crackles.

"Fine," I say, throttling the engine. Kicking her into gear. "Just *fine*."

It's nearing eleven o'clock, and all the spots along the curb are taken, so I double-park next to a Honda a stone's throw west of the restaurant, as I'd been instructed. White-knuckling the wheel, I count how many seconds I can stand between glances in the rearview mirror. The neighborhood surrounding The Gangster's has undergone some intense gentrification since the 1970s, so instead of catering to a circus of oddball crooks, its streets are now checkered with gay men and young couples who'll wait hours to get into restaurants that have outside seating.

I say, "Christ, Randal. Hurry *up*."

I watch the couples as they hold hands, lifting their looped arms over chained bikes, fire hydrants, children. To distract myself, I edit them into different pairs—place this woman with this man; make these two guys slip their fingers into each other's pockets; have this girl plant an unexpected kiss on her friend's cheek—things that I'll no longer be paid to do, but that would make their lives infinitely more interesting.

Then, finally, I see him.

Randal's sprinting, but awkwardly, his arms wrapped around his midsection. When he gets closer to the car, I see that his kneecaps are covered in flour and bits of mashed-up cheese. A brushstroke of marinara shadows his left eye. Dalloway's head peeks out from the collar of his shirt. Her chewed-up ears brush his jawline as she peers over his shoulder at Doug, who trails them by about twenty-five yards, hurling obscenities.

"Get her in gear!" Randal shouts over Doug's *fuck*s and *sons-of-bitch*es and *faggot*s. He says again, as he swings around Lucy's rear, "Get her going!"

We're rolling by the time he slides into the front seat. Doug launches a pizza saw at the car, but it bounces off the back bumper with a harmless clink, powerless. In the side mirrors, I see the gay men and the amorous couples take to the fringes of the sidewalk.

"We got those motherfuckers good."

He lifts his shirt and Mrs. Dalloway slithers out into the open air. He pulls a trapezoidal chunk of pineapple from her front paw and then, very theatrically, she shakes the experience from her, sending barely noticeable tears against our cheeks. Quickly, she bounds between us toward the car's rear. She presses her nose against the back windshield and watches Doug, who is currently shrinking into a fat, thrashing speck.

We've passed the border into Iowa and the night is beyond black: it's a vacuum that eats the stars. We are driving through the night.

The mobile phone rings once.

"Dad?"

"Finn?"

"It's me."

"You need to come home."

I tell him, "I'm halfway there."

There are no other cars in sight, and so the road exists for only as long as Lucy's headlights allow. A silence persists in which my father realizes what I've done. In which his breath shortens and then draws itself out again. In which I think we both realize that if it weren't for each other we'd be totally alone.

This time he says, "Please hurry."

WHAT I REMEMBER

1987: Finn

By Colin A. McPhee

There were two earthquakes.

The first one happened on October 1 and coincided with the exact moment of his birth.

"Well," the delivering doctor said, "that was interesting."

His surgeon's mask had gone askew and the stool he'd been sitting on had been knocked to the ground. Nurses buzzed around us—checking, measuring, snipping, stitching. One of them wiped clean Finn's tiny body. She swaddled him in a blanket and handed him to Clare, who was propped up on her elbows, the bed's pillows having been thrown to the corners of the room.

The maternity ward was on the first floor. Above us, I heard the frantic clack of feet running. Nervous, overcooked voices.

"Should we leave?" I asked. "I mean, should we evacuate?"

The doctor pulled the gloves from his hands. "What, because of a little tremor?" He rinsed his fingers in a sink and then reached down to pick up a roll of paper towels that'd fallen beneath a cabinet. He looked at Clare, at Finn. "Son," he said, "you're in for a lot more than that."

I watched from the hospital's window as Los Angeles tried to pull and patch itself back together. A car had run head-on into a fire hydrant, causing a steady stream of water to geyser twenty feet into the sky; the driver had turned on her windshield wipers. Newspaper stands turned over and spilled their printed contents out onto the sidewalks. People kicked through the separated pages, pulling them from their shins, their knees. They toed the curb wearily, with hesitation, verifying that the world had stopped its rollicking before they took their first steps. The next day, I'd read how the earthquake—it would come to be known as the Whittier Narrows—clocked in at a magnitude of 6.0. I'd read how, a few miles south in the city of Cypress, a ten-ton replica of Michelangelo's *David* now lay supine in the grass. I'd read how a falling slab of concrete killed Lupe Elias-Exposito as she crossed the parking lot with her sister at the state university in Los Angeles.

Finn was crying. I knelt down beside Clare's bed and looked into his puckered face as he gulped his first mouthfuls of air. Later, we'd speculate as to whether he was born because of the earthquake, if the ground's trembling and splitting gave him the final push he needed, or if it was actually vice versa, that Finn's eagerness to climb from his mother's belly made the whole world shake.

Clare whispered *shh, shh* while she brushed thin wet strands of hair from his forehead. He reached his arms out, up, his tiny fingers grasping at nothing, at everything.

"Isn't he so beautiful?" she asked.

I said, "Is he supposed to be that blue?"

For that first year, Finn was Clare's purview. I had just begun to encounter the writer's block that would come to characterize most of my adult life; just started to recognize its stern corners, its sharp edges, the perpetual shadows it threw. At that point, though, I was still convinced I could move it. I was still convinced that if I locked myself away for long enough, or if I let my eyes cross enough times while staring at the screen, I'd manage to burrow through the block's center, eventually hitting light on the other side. And so, during those long, futile hours, Clare was always the one who fed Finn, who bathed him, who went to him when he'd cry at night. We'd hear his piercing scream, and I'd make a show of lifting myself from the sheet, but she'd press a hand against my chest, say, "No, I've got him." I'd follow her sometimes. I'd creep down the hall behind her, past the office where I wrote, the shell-shaped nightlights along the wall throwing yellow against my toes. I'd watch through a crack in the nursery's door as she held him, as she rocked him.

It wasn't her, though, and we both knew it. Finn was growing too quickly, he was changing; the last thing a child provides is certainty, and certainty was the one thing she craved. So Clare—she was Debra Winger in *Terms of Endearment*, or Lana Turner in *Cass Timberlane*. She only took to mothering so much as those roles would allow her, and so I suppose I wasn't surprised—not honestly, at least—when she told me on our son's first birthday that she was planning on returning to acting. That she needed new sources of inspiration, new examples of life.

We were sitting in our kitchen with Finn, who was struggling to remove a paper party hat we'd fixed to his head.

"What do you mean you're going back?" I said. "And to *what* career?"

She was cutting squares of white-frosted cake, and I watched as her grip tightened on the knife's handle.

"What about staying here? What about raising your son?"

"Don't be such a chauvinist." She used the broad surface of the knife to scoop the slices onto red plastic plates. "I'm talking about some commercial work. A few auditions a week. And besides—he's your son, too."

"I'm sure Ron has found someone else to cast."

"Oh, ha ha. A clever one, aren't you."

"But what will we do?"

"*Jesus*, Colin, it's not like you're dealing with E.T. here. He's your *son*. You'll feed him. Change his diaper when he craps. Maybe take him on a walk if you both get bored."

She passed Finn a piece of cake and he promptly speared it with his thumb.

"No," she told him. "Don't do that."

The first few days we did little more than stare at each other. I'd moved my computer to the living room so I could work in sight of Finn's playpen—a subtly unnerving cage decorated with primary colors and eerie insects with Cheshire-cat grins. Two months earlier he'd taken his first step, and so his mornings were now spent standing, stepping, blinking, falling. Occasionally, he'd kick a discarded rattle, which would cause him to break into a gurgled liquid laugh. Whenever I left, it was only for a moment—to use the toilet, to fill a bowl of cereal—still, though, he'd cry instantly; I'd disappear behind the living room door, and right away the screams would start. Rushing back, I'd find him propped up against one of the playpen's mesh walls, his chubby fingers pinching the nylon frame. Sometimes he'd silence immediately, and sometimes his wails would continue. He'd gaze at me for one quiet moment and then hurl his head back farther, stretching his mouth to an even wider, more anguished angle. He'd say, *Oh, you. You're not who I was asking for.* Sometimes: *I was expecting someone else. Specifically—her.*

It was during one of these fits on the fourth day that I took him from the playpen. While his cries reverberated off the walls of the room, I brought him to my desk, to my computer, and bounced him lightly on my knee. My left arm was wrapped tightly around his fleshy midsection and I could feel his lungs fill with tiny bubbles of air. With my right hand I typed:

```
Shh.
Shhhhhhhhhhhh.
I'm your father.
You're my son.
There's not a lot I can do to change that.
```

As I typed and as he bounced, his crying slowly began to stop: his wails decreased in volume till they dissolved into soft, wet vowels. He reached out to me and touched my face.

```
Those are my cheeks.
Those are my lips.
That is my heart.
Pick your own nose.
```

• • •

"How'd it go today?" Clare would ask when she returned home in the evening. I would have just bathed Finn and we would be sitting in the kitchen with the windows flung open, the salty Pacific air clinging to our tongues, our eyelashes.

"Fine," I'd tell her. "Better."

She'd be trying to get him to eat, but he was becoming more and more difficult with her. From his high chair he'd pitch handfuls of mushed-up peas and overcooked carrots. Shredded pieces of noodles would hang from Clare's hair.

"Let me try," I'd tell her, slipping an arm around her waist.

"No. No, I've got it."

Finn would turn over a plate of sliced hot dogs, and the pink pieces would tumble down Clare's loose shirt. She'd stand, frustrated.

"He's being impossible."

Again I'd say, "Let me try," and he'd eat.

She started going on calls that were earlier in the morning and later in the evening; she'd leave us alone for vast stretches of the day and would rarely check in. When she did return home, I'd often be in bed, the blinds in our room drawn to keep out L.A.'s perpetual purple glow. In the dark I'd hear her undress—the dull thud of her shoes being kicked against the wall, the swoosh of a silk skirt floating down to her ankles. When she crawled into bed, she'd fold herself against my chest and I'd smell the smoke in her hair. I'd try to remember what I wrote in the fan letters I'd sent her, back when I was convincing her to love me, back when we weren't competing for attention from ourselves.

"Traffic on the 10 was nuts," she'd say.

"This late?" I'd keep my eyes closed.

"There was an accident at Pico."

"You're awful with directions."

Most times, she'd already be asleep.

The next morning, I'd type to Finn:

What do you think it is today?

I'd guide his doughy hand to the keyboard and I'd let him pluck at random letters.

```
Rqndavt
You think? My bet's a walk-on on some soap.
Xq436dn
You think she got it?
1ngr
Me neither.
```

When spring was tilting toward summer, we'd abandon the computer, our joint writing, and go on long, aimless walks along the Santa Monica boardwalk and pier. We'd watch surfers vanish into collapsing aqueous tunnels; we'd hold our breath until they'd reemerge from the wave's foamy backwash. We'd feed potato chips to the gulls, laughing and cringing as they wrestled for the crumbs, as they beat their filthy wings into one another's chests. If the sun wasn't too strong, and the temperature not too hot, I'd let him bury his feet in the sand.

"That's what you'll build castles with," I'd tell him.

He'd point out at the ocean, to the swimmers and the boats with their white stretched sails.

"That's what you'll swim across."

A girl would trot by, her heels kicking up small explosions of sand, her legs smooth bronzy pillars.

"That's what'll break your heart."

"You love him more than you love me."

It was September 28, 1989—almost two years after the earthquake. Finn, who now spoke (but too quickly, much too quickly, and with an inability to pronounce *r*s) had just been put to bed, and Clare and I had opened a bottle of wine in the kitchen. Her back was pressed into the white tile counter; her face was too heavily made-up from a panty-hose commercial she'd shot that afternoon—her first job since returning to acting. Milky foundation an inch thick. Pink cheeks. Lips the color of overripe apples.

"That's ridiculous." And then, "I can't take you seriously when you're wearing all that stuff on your face."

"I like it. I feel like myself in it." I handed her a glass of wine, and when she drank from it she tattooed the rim with her painted mouth. "And it's not ridiculous."

"It is."

She said, "But it's still the truth."

And it was, which I think is what made it so terrible. It was something that both she and I had come to realize, separately, over the past year: that without Clare I'd still exist as some version of myself, but that without Finn, without the opportunity to shape his world, an integral part of me would be lost. I'd sense her resentment of me, of him—the way her voice tightened whenever the three of us were in a room and the attention slipped away from her, the way she became frustrated with his speech problems, the way she'd tell him she didn't understand him. And I understood it. I understood the frustration over watching something that had once been hers—ours—gradually become mine. Still, though, I didn't know how to reverse it. Or, what's more: I wasn't willing to try.

"What would you have me do?" I asked her.

"I don't know," she said. "Love me a little more. Love him a little less."

"That's a terrible thing to say."

"I'm going to bed," she said.

"Wash that shit off your face first. It'll stain the pillows."

She finished the wine in two large swallows.

When she left, it was with a letter that wasn't even her own. She copied the note that actress-writer Jacqueline Susann wrote to her husband Irving Mansfield when he was drafted into World War II. She taped all four sides of the paper on which she wrote it to the surface of the kitchen table, as if she were afraid the thing would blow away and that she wanted to ensure, against all possible odds, that I'd find it. Which I did. After returning from a walk with Finn. I told him to empty the sand from his shoes while I read and then reread the note. She didn't even edit the sentences to make them relevant.

"She left to be someone else." I was saying it to no one, or maybe to myself, but Finn heard me anyway. I hadn't heard him pad softly back in from the garage.

"You can do that?" He was four at this point. His speech was still mud-dled, but he'd learned to slow himself, to breathe between his sentences.

And now, the second earthquake: it struck in January of 1994 when Finn was six, and it was eighty times larger than the first. It split streets and crumbled freeways; it dug up giant trees by their roots and tossed them like toothpicks across power lines. The news aired footage of en-tire houses that had been shifted into neighboring properties. When the dust cleared and the sirens stopped, sixty people would be counted dead. Thousands more would be injured, and forty thousand buildings would be destroyed—including half our house.

"Maybe it's a good thing," I told Finn as we picked through the rubble. Toeing through broken chairs, collapsed plaster walls. Pieces of his old rattle that I'd saved.

"Why?"

"We've got insurance, and I'd been thinking it was time to move anyway. This place was starting to feel small."

"There's only just the two of us though."

But it wasn't just the two of us. I didn't know how to explain to Finn that during the preceding years his mother had been appearing every-where. Not her actual flesh and blood, per se (the last time I had seen her was two winters before, when I had caught the latter half of the panty-hose commercial she filmed at the end of our marriage; I'd heard rumors that she'd run off somewhere with someone, that she was in Chicago, or Seattle, but that was never confirmed), but the essence of her, the things that made her up. On the corner of Olympic and Western: a girl smok-ing a cigarette in the same lips-out fashion practiced by Clare outside the Avalon. At the intersection of San Vicente and Pico: a boy drinking a beer, grasping the bottle by the neck like the way she'd showed me how to drink. In a theater on Melrose: two kids kissing once the house lights had dimmed. Before, all these things seemed like such derivatives, actions Clare had copied and practiced after recording them in her book. But now, they seemed to stem from her as original, as just the way she was. She'd learned to live as everyone, and because of that I could never escape her. She'd be in the car next to me on a crowded freeway; she'd be the waitress at the diner where I took Finn for burgers. She'd be so universally present in L.A. that much of the time it seemed there existed really only three kinds of people: Finn, 9 million Clares, and me.

"Where are we going to move?"

"I was thinking north. San Francisco."

"There are earthquakes there, too, Dad."

I felt a shard of glass crunch beneath the heel of my sneaker. Above us, Los Angeles' low-hanging sky was smogged over and grey.

We moved that June, once Finn had finished the first grade. I found us the house where I still live—the old Victorian on Vallejo Street in Cow Hollow. It was taller than it was wide—like a set of ill-fitting blocks stacked on top of one another, but not quite perfectly. From the bay windows, though, you could see the verdant hills of Tiburon, the way the fog pooled and clung to their broad wet bases. It'd been empty for years, the house, and during that time it'd fallen into a state of disgrace: coats of paint had been stripped away by the city's dense marine layer, revealing cracks in the home's wood paneling that formed strange shapes. I convinced myself that I'd make the repairs myself, and at first I took to the task with a cinematic sense of gusto. I'd nail, and sand, and saw each afternoon. I'd measure things when I already knew their lengths; I'd carry around odd wrenches and wear ridiculous belts.

But that faded. I got tired of the banging, the splinters, the gut knowledge that there're only so many ways to fix something that'll eventually fall apart again anyway. And so, over the course of that summer, we learned to dodge the house's hazards—or, perhaps more aptly, we learned to suit them to our lives. We determined that the broken sink in

the bathroom—the one that shot water up through a slit in the faucet—
was ideal for washing your face. We used loose kitchen tiles as coasters.
We placed plants and potted flowers beneath the leaks in the ceiling. We
communicated through the open spaces in the floorboards; we'd have
hour-long conversations from different rooms, different levels.

And then two months after we'd settled in, I received a call from a
woman in New York. She told me that her name was Helen, and that she
was the current manager of the Avalon. She said she wanted to inform
me that the theater was closing.

I was folding clothes on Finn's bed, in his new room. From a small
window next to his closet I watched cars thread through the arches in
the Golden Gate's south tower.

"Oh, God," I said, sitting, and the bed shifted. "That's terrible."

"I hate to be the bearer of bad news." In the background there was
that familiar machine-gun crack of popcorn exploding.

"No, I'm glad you called. It's better than reading about it in the papers or something."

"Oh," she laughed, but it was sad, quiet. "Oh, I doubt it'll make the
papers."

"You know what I mean."

"Yes, I do."

I fingered a hole in one of Finn's shirts, pushing through the frayed
fabric.

I asked, "Why's it closing?"

She sighed. "The same reason everyone else is closing—we just can't
keep up anymore." The popping began to slow, the individual combus-
tions more spaced out. "Two years ago they opened up that megaplex
farther down on Saw Mill, the one with nine projectors. We were struggling before, but at least getting by. Breaking even, you could say, at least
most weeks. The megaplex, though—that killed us. For about fourteen
months we tried to switch it up with a bunch of independent and art-
house films. But there are only so many people who can tolerate movies
like that. *My Life as a Geranium* or something. The audience just wasn't
there." There was a crunch, the sound of her eating, and I realized that

she hadn't prepared the popcorn for someone else, a customer, but had made it for herself. She added, "It's the same thing that's happening everywhere."

I'd pushed my finger through so the shirt hung around my second knuckle. The hole stretched.

"Anyway," she continued. "I wanted to let you know that there's going to be a final showing this Friday night. Before we shut down for good. *The Tender Trap*—that's what we'll be screening. It's the first movie the Avalon showed."

"I know."

"I'm going through all these records and trying to get hold of everyone who worked at the theater to let them know about it."

"That's nice of you."

"It's a lot harder than it sounds."

"I think it sounds pretty difficult."

"I started last Thursday, and today is Tuesday. So that means I've been at it for more than four days and I've still got about seventy-five people left to call."

"I don't envy you."

"Which actually brings me to a question."

"Yes?"

"You don't happen to have the phone numbers of anyone you worked with, do you? Or maybe even the cities they're living in? Some sort of lead?"

She began listing a series of names, people who'd slipped from my memory completely: the girl who worked four days a week in the box office; the guy who cleaned the bathrooms each weekend. *No*, I told her each time. *I haven't heard from them in years.*

"All right." She sighed again. "I mean, I figured as much. No one seems to know what happened to anyone else." Then: "What about Clare Murkowski?"

I said, "Who?"

"Clare Murkowski? It says you worked every shift with her for more than two years?"

I stood. I walked to a Spiderman trash can in a corner of the room. I balled up the shirt and tossed it into the bin. I looked down at my bare toes spread on the uneven floor. "She passed away," I said. Then, more forcefully, "She died."

"Oh, that's awful." Helen stopped eating; the muffled chewing stopped.

"I heard it was a car accident on the Ventura Freeway."

Quietly, I began to loathe myself, but still I couldn't stop from spinning the story. "A seven-car pileup, with a sixteen-wheeler at the end. She was thrown through the back windshield of the car in front of her. It wasn't instant. Thirty-six hours in the ICU. A lot of pain. That's what I heard, anyway."

"Jesus. I'm so sorry."

"It's fine," I said. I picked the shirt from the bin in which I'd thrown it. I found a hanger, hung it up instead. "I didn't really know her anymore."

I heard the front door creak three times, which meant it was opening, then creak once more, which meant it was shut. Finn's heavy heels were percussions on the stairs.

We arrived at my childhood home at midnight on the next Thursday, and even though it was mid-August everywhere else, it was still winter in Sleepy Hollow. Frigid rain bounced off ankle-deep puddles on the sidewalk; the wind ripped leaves from branches and painted them against car windows. As we stood in the crowded entryway, we shook the water from our heads.

I tightened my bag across my shoulder; Finn dropped his pack to the floor.

"Look at what you've done to the sun!"

My father took my son's face in his hands. He kissed each wet cheek, his cold forehead.

They'd met a handful of times, the last of which was a year earlier. My father had been breezing through Los Angeles during one of his drives, and Finn and I had traveled back down south to meet him for an afternoon at the Long Beach aquarium. I remember how I had walked a few paces behind the two of them, and how I'd watched as Finn reached up to take two of my father's bony fingers. He led him through the mazes of tubes and tanks, past walls of alien creatures swirling in explosive reds, yellows, blues. In a separate room, giant hammerheads swam above them and around them, their sleek, muscled bodies throwing shadows that darkened our faces. Finn coaxed my father to the glass, and they both pressed their palms against it. A shark whipped its arrowed tail, and I slipped over to an adjoining exhibit on jellyfish.

I stood with my face pressed close to the tube's wall and I watched a moon jellyfish sway in the current. As it bloomed, the surface light shined blue-white through its waxy membrane. It barely had control over its movements: as larger bodies passed it, it was carried along their course; when the current was at rest, so was it.

Jellyfish have no central nervous system. I read that on a green illustrated placard. Instead, their nerves are diffused—like a net—throughout their epidermal layer. There, sensors pick up certain stimuli—mostly touch, as I understand it—which is then translated to the rest of the net. But, again—there's no brain. There's no processing center. Stimuli aren't gathered, analyzed, categorized, remembered.

I felt a drop of rain trickle down the grooves in my neck, across the bumps on my spine.

"Only one more show," my father said, his hands still holding Finn's head.

"Only one more show."

"But the Avalon! What a run it's had!"

"What a run." I put my hands on my son's shoulders and pulled him into me. "We should get to bed," I said. "It's late."

By the next morning, the day of the showing, the storm had broken. The grass on the street's ancient lawns still sagged, and the gutters still flooded, but the clouds had ruptured and the sun dazzled in prisms. I awoke early, when the rest of the house was quiet, still. I'd given up my childhood room to my son and had slept on a couch in the living room that my mother had purchased before she died. Since then, either it had outgrown me or I had outgrown it: Throughout the night I switched between feeling as if I were being swallowed or strangled by its cushions. The whole house had that feeling. I don't know how much time had passed since I'd last been there, but in those years or decades, this place and I had become strangers to each other; we didn't know how to fit.

So—I drank half a cup of coffee. I left a note that said *Meet me at the theater.* And as the dawn skated across the Hudson, I left.

The Avalon was closed when I got there, but I snuck in the same way that I did when I was a boy. I have forgotten so many things, and I've lied about so many others, but this I remember. There was an alley on the east side of the building that separated the theater from a tailor's shop, which had since become a bank. I dragged a large steel trash can into the middle of the alley and then, bracing myself against the ancient brick walls, mounted it. There were a few precarious moments. I'd lost my childhood fearlessness, so each time my makeshift ladder wobbled or swayed I held my breath; I clenched my eyes shut and stiffened my spine, preparing for a fall. But then, somehow I'd steady myself. I'd press my palms against the wall harder, learning how to compensate for my age, my weight.

There was a small window on the theater's second floor. It opened into a darkened corner of the lobby's balcony where the staff occasionally stored old, forgotten movie posters that should've been thrown away years ago. When the Avalon was built, the latch that locked the window hadn't been secured properly; the screws that held it in place were loose and threadbare, so that even the lightest shove could send it swinging open on its hinges. There'd always been talk of having it fixed—at least when I worked there. *We've got to call someone,* Earl would say. *And this time, I mean it.* No one ever did call someone, though. The window's latch became a leaky faucet or a door that creaked; eventually, it was universally deemed easier just to accept the damn thing than to go through the minor trouble of having it repaired.

I landed on a 27-inch by 39-inch movie poster of *True Lies.* A pillar of blue light shone in from the open window, and in this half shadow I cursed my clumsiness and the blooming ache in my legs and then, when it began to subside, I stood and took stock of my surroundings.

Or, no—I didn't take stock. Rather, I stood expectantly. I stood like a man anxious to be reunited with a lover from whom he's been too long separated, whose face he's memorized and drawn and redrawn from scratch. And if that was the case, which it was, imagine this man's disappointment when—once his eyes had adjusted to the near dark—he found that his lover wasn't his lover at all, but rather someone else entirely. Someone harder, and coarser, and generally more disappointed in life.

The crimson carpet, which was just starting to fray when I left, was now almost completely torn up. Large swaths of it were either stained or missing. As I walked down the lobby's staircase, the carpet shifted beneath my feet, revealing the cold slabs of concrete beneath it. On the ground floor, I looked for the urn that I used to hide behind and watch the theater's audiences flow in and out. It wasn't there, though. There was a carved out ring in the floor where it once stood, but that was all.

So this was what had happened. The Avalon had fallen apart.

I'd wanted to sit in the balcony, but the doors were locked, so I selected a seat in the back row of the orchestra, and I stayed there all day. I counted how many tears there were on the screen's heavy curtain; I read the names that had been carved into the seat back in front of me at least a hundred times. I folded my knees into my chest, like I used to do when I was a boy, and I kept them there, even when the muscles screamed and burned. At two o'clock in the afternoon, when the custodial staff began cleaning the house, I waited for them to tell me to move, to get out, but they didn't. They nodded at me and as they swept beneath my lifted feet, they had conversations inches above my head. No one at the Avalon worried about who had snuck in anymore, because as of tomorrow there wouldn't be anything to sneak in to.

The film was scheduled to start at seven, and so the audience began arriving at six thirty. I scanned the faces as they entered the theater: there was the brief cringe of disappointment when someone saw the shape of things, the confusion while another person thought, *I remember it being so much bigger.* When I saw my father and my son pushing through the crowds, I flagged them over.

"This place is a dump," Finn said.

"Knock it off. It's just been around a long time. Now, sit."

I'd been sitting along the aisle, but I moved one seat in, expecting them to sit on either side of me. Instead, my father awkwardly slipped past my knees and Finn clambered over me. They sat next to each other and the seat to my left remained empty.

I asked, "Do either of you want anything to drink? Maybe some popcorn or something?"

"Sure," Finn said. He pulled his knees up so he was folded in the same position that I'd been in for so many hours. Then he turned to my father. "Keep going, Granddad."

My father tapped his chin. "Where was I?"

"The store was about to be knocked down, and you were inside in the house of records."

"Oh Christ, Dad," I said. "Don't get him started on all those stories." I stood and I shook my legs, charging blood back into their veins. "Or God forbid one of these days he actually starts believing you."

HOW TO LOSE TIME

Finn

In Nebraska, we can't drive fast enough. The road taunts us with its wide-open expanses and the state itself seems to stretch at its ends, its borders pulled in all directions until crossing it becomes a Sisyphean task. There's grass that looks broken and windswept: it lies scissored and flat against the earth for thousands and thousands of miles, and when we think we've reached the edge of the horizon, where the grass will stop and something else will begin, it doesn't. It just keeps going on, forever. We can see the weather coming, and the weather leaving: near noon, the sun—which has been a brilliant, bleached white—becomes shrouded by a veil of gauzy clouds that have been crawling in from the south since dawn. For an hour it rains—torrentially, biblically: the air sneaks in through Lucy's vents, and with it brings the scent of waterlogged earth and cow shit. But then it stops. The rain weans down to a trickle, leaving muddy spots on the car's windshield. We watch from Randal's window as the clouds continue their march north into Nebraska's infinity.

I say, "I wish we could go faster."

Randal says, "I spy something green."

"Did you hear me?"

"I heard you. It's the eighth time you've said it this morning. And this will be the eighth time I'll say this: we'll get there in time. I promise we'll get there in time." Then, again: "I spy something green."

He's trying to take my mind off all this, I know. He's been doing it ever since I woke him in the middle of the night, when he was cocooned with the cat in the shotgun seat. Ever since my father called to tell me that my grandfather has had two more strokes. One small ("The doctor called it a TIA. Have you ever heard of that before? The T stands for 'transient.'") and one large ("I took him home from the hospital the next morning, yesterday morning, and he seemed fine, but it happened that afternoon." "How bad?" A brief silence during which I hear the strange buzzing, the eerie electronic melodies of a hospital in the background. "He can't speak." "He couldn't speak after the first one." "He can't see." "He will, though." "He's experiencing a lot of pain." "That's why they made morphine." "He's in a coma, Finn. They've got him on life support. There's a tube down his throat." "That's ridiculous—get him off it." "They can't." The hospital's sounds fade as my father moves into a quieter hallway; they're replaced with the shuffle of fur and cotton as Dalloway stirs. I say to my father, "What's the last thing he said?" "He asked me to open the window." "Is that all he said?" "Yes." "Dad?" "What, Finn?" "I really wish you knew how to lie.").

"Maybe it's not that green." Randal pulls his feet up so his shins are pressing against the dashboard. Mrs. Dalloway, whom we've allowed out of the bag since her brush with death in Chicago, perches unbalanced on the peaks of his knees. She grips the khaki hem of his shorts with her dull claws. "Or maybe it's not green," he says. "Maybe it's only greenish." And then: "You could probably say that it's more of a brown. A brown green."

"Please stop."

"I'm trying to help, you know." Then: "Just guess."

"But who asked you? Who asked you to help?"

"Please just guess, Finn."

In the south, there are more storm clouds gathering; they pull themselves together like weak, amorphous magnets. They'll be here in three hours tops, I think. I look out across the vacuous landscape.

"It's that tree," I say.

Ahead of us, about two hundred yards, there's a gnarled twist of bark and branches—the only thing that obscures the horizon. We've passed the tree before, I think: we've watched it disappear in the rearview mirror only to rematerialize two hours later. Its constant presence has led to debates over whether we're driving in circles, whether the road has somehow curved into itself without us noticing.

"You're right."

"You should've picked something harder."

He says, "There's not a lot to work with."

In Nebraska's southwest, Interstate 80 follows the Great Platte River Road, which is a historic path that took pioneers to Oregon and Mormons to Utah and a great many other people to a Great Many Other Places. The road hugs the river; it forms a slight arc north but stays below the Sandhills, which are huge green dunes that roll like one-hundred-foot dice. And then it bows south, kissing Colorado's border but never crossing into it.

We drive for three and a half hours. We stop only when we have to: when we've run out of gas and when the trembling of Dalloway's leg convinces Randal that she's got to pee maybe, possibly, finally. He squats with the cat in the gravel, encouraging her and coaxing her, while I go to pay for the pump. Within the service station, there's coffee in machines labeled UNLEADED, LEADED, SUPER, DIESEL. I fill two cups with diesel. I purchase small boxes of cereal that we eat with no milk.

It's nearing four o'clock in the afternoon when we finally break from Nebraska's wall-less maze. The interstate leads us across the boundless arid prairies of southeastern Wyoming. Past low ranches locked in by hurdles of barbed wire, their irrigated lands patches of green in a vast quilt of dust. Past dry wheat fields and grazing cattle and flocks of shorn sheep. On three sides of us there are low flat-top mountains, steps of earth, the first we've seen in days. The plains press against them: prairies meeting foothills.

Miles outside Cheyenne the road dips down briefly. It takes some rounded corners and finally begins to pull upward along the first inclines of the Laramie Mountains. There are pegmatite walls of bright chemical colors; pinkish rocks that look like they were made of other rocks that were made of other rocks and then had been half-assedly stacked atop one another. We pass a town called Granite, and it's here that we encounter a very real problem.

At first she—Lucy—convulses violently. My foot's thrown from the gas pedal. I shift down to second and I try to brake, but this does nothing to appease her: she only thrashes harder, swerving to the sides of the road. And there is the shrieking: a terrible mourner's howl that sounds like the thunder of cannonballs shattering thin sheets of glass. My forearms flex and ache as I struggle to maintain control of her.

"Do something!" Randal screams above Lucy's wails. A frightened Mrs. Dalloway clings to his shoulder, burying her head against his neck.

"I'm trying!" I shout. "I don't know what the fuck is wrong with her!"

I shift down to first and Lucy protests even more vehemently. She throws her windows around in their frames, the glass threatening to splinter and crack. I cajole her onto a dirt shoulder along the side of the road and the sound of a million pebbles pelting her belly mixes with the wicked soprano of her cries. When I kill her engine, the sound lasts for two beats too long before dissolving into the silence.

Randal has his feet lifted from the floorboards. One hand encircles Mrs. Dalloway's thin neck and the other is pressed against the dash.

He whispers, "What the *fuck* was that?"

"Goddamn it," I say. "Please not now." Again: "God*damn* it."

My hands still clutch the steering wheel, but it has gone completely still, lifeless. I press my eyes shut and in their corners I see spools of silk unraveling, changing colors from blue to red.

The spot where Lucy has decided to have her fit is outside Buford, Wyoming—an unincorporated community in Albany County. It fills a small swath of grass and earth that's eight thousand feet above sea level: it's the highest town on Interstate 80 between New York and San Francisco. Its population consists of a single person: the mayor. We read all this on a set of plastic road signs that have been hammered into the brown-red dirt.

"One person," Randal says. "I bet he gets sick of himself."

"Come on," I tell him.

"Where are we going?"

"We're not sitting around here like a bunch of assholes." I point toward the small cluster of buildings that constitutes Buford. "I see a gas station attached to that store. There's got to be someone over there who can help us."

Dust chalks our ankles as we walk. The sky, which seems too close to us, is an atomic blue: it wraps around us, unfolding in the open spaces between particleboard clouds.

Except for a man in flip-flops refueling a two-story RV, the gas station is empty, and so we try the adjoining trading post. It's been retrofitted to look like an old hunting cabin: there are notched Lincoln Log walls and a sloping steel roof and a wood-planked porch raised on hewn pilings. Directly inside the glass front doors, there's a plaque describing Buford's long, if not entirely illustrious, history. It was founded under a different name in 1866, when it acted as a temporary home to men working on the transcontinental railroad, and at its height it boasted more than two thousand inhabitants. But then, as progress pushed the tracks' construction west, it took the laborers with it; the population's been shrinking since. Still, in 1880 they built a post office. And even though there was no one around to notice, they renamed the town after Major General John Buford, a Union cavalry officer who was actually born in Kentucky.

The store appears empty, but there is an overhead radio that is playing—of all things—Blondie, and as we push toward the direction of the cash register Randal hums off-key along to "Heart of Glass." We weave through aisles stocked with tacky and fascinating stuff—whistles made from elk antlers; functional pens carved from slivers of bark. Jerky made from animals that should never be jerkified. The front desk is hidden behind curtains of postcards that display the trading post photographed from every possible angle. Randal selects one from the rack, flips it over, and reads the back as I chime a small silver bell for an attendant.

"You only have to ring that thing once," he tells me. "This place isn't big. I'm sure whoever's supposed to hear you has heard you."

"Well, whoever is supposed to hear me isn't moving fast enough."

We wait for an unfathomably long two minutes, during which I continue to ring the bell and Randal's cheeks grow red. The man who finally emerges from an unmarked door tucked behind the cashier's desk is old and worn—the color of unpolished shoes. He wears a denim work shirt and faded jeans; his grey hair is parted and combed over to disguise a bald spot shaped like France. One of the elk-bone whistles hangs from his neck. On his head: a red ball cap sporting the words BUFORD: THE GREATEST ONE-PERSON TOWN IN THE WEST! Above his heart: a name tag reading FRED.

He's been eating sunflower seeds: when he smiles two soggy halves of shells cover a front tooth. He places a bearish paw over my hand to stop the bell from ringing.

"Welcome!" Fred says. His hand on top of mine feels older than it looks: cracked instead of creased; thin instead of callused. "Welcome to Buford—The Greatest One-Person Town in the West!" He adds, "Thank you so much for paying us a visit!"

Randal says, "But I thought there was only one of you."

"There is!" He releases my hand but then picks it up again, this time giving it a hearty shake. "And all of us love our visitors!"

Fred takes hold of Randal's fingers with his other hand, so that he's shaking both our hands. I watch as Randal struggles through the algebra of Fred's last sentence, his eyes pulled together.

I tell Fred, "Our car broke down about a hundred yards down the highway. We were wondering if there was someone over at the gas station who could help us out."

He picks a sunflower seed from his incisor and he nods; I watch the flesh that hangs from his chin shake even after his head has stopped moving. "Yes, yes. We can help with that, all right. Get you back on the road lickety-split."

The air that's been trapped in my throat since we arrived pushes through my lips as a happy whistle: I sigh, relieved.

But then: "First, though, a tour! Let me show you around, get you acquainted with the place. There's so much to see here in Buford. So very much to see."

"We really should get going."

It's useless, though. Fred has already swung around our side of the desk, his strange, laceless shoes shuffling like dull sandpaper along the floor. He's got the whistle balanced between his thin lips and he toots it lightly as he walks, like he's leading us through some labyrinth that only he can navigate.

"Sweet pepper venison jerky," he says, stopping. He throws Randal a plastic package printed with a picture of a grinning cartoon deer. "Voted the tastiest jerky by the citizens of Buford for twelve years in a row."

"So you voted it the best jerky for twelve years in a row."

"Go on," he says, "give it a try. If it's not the best thing you've ever tasted, you get your money back."

"But we haven't paid anything,"

He adjusts his belt buckle, which is large, and brass, and says BU-FORD. He's short and sinewy, Fred, but he's got this unexpected gut: the fabric between the buttons of his denim shirt pulls apart, revealing purple flesh, some freckles, a lone white hair. He watches us—waits.

Randal tears the package open with his teeth. He hands me a shriveled port-colored strip, and then takes one for himself. The meat's tough but workable; we both chew it like cows grinding cud. It's sweet but also salty—honey from a sweaty bee.

"It's actually not that bad," Randal says.

Fred claps. He stomps a foot.

I tell him, "Fred, we really need to get that car working."

"Right, yes. Right, of course." He wobbles on his heels, turns. He makes like he's heading for the exit, but when he reaches the end of the aisle he pulls a hairpin turn and leads us down the adjacent row. "But first!" he shouts. His hands are buried up to the wrists in a pail of chipped, flinty stones. "But first you'll want to take some of these! Authentic Indian arrowheads! Collected by the citizens of Buford themselves!"

I take one of the stones. It's paper thin, brittle, the size of a small frog. Across one of its surfaces, BUFORD has been written with Wite-Out in an uneven scrawl. I look into the bucket of a million rocks: each one contains the same tag.

I pocket the arrowhead and feel its thin crust split between my fingers. "Thanks, Fred," I say. "Now—"

"The car." He points his finger at me. A used-car salesman desperate for a deal.

"Yes, the car."

"I know just the fellow you should talk to."

"Thank God."

He blows the whistle once—this time louder than before—and he slips through the door behind the cash register, his back hunched over, his shoulders dropped.

"We're never going to get out of here," I say once the door's clicked shut. "We're never going to get the car fixed. This guy is nuts."

Randal rips at a second piece of venison jerky. "I don't know if he's nuts," he says. "Or just terribly lonely."

"I think it's possible to be both."

Despite the fact that we know he's the sole resident of Buford, when Fred reemerges we don't immediately recognize him. He's lost the worn jeans and the denim shirt. He's replaced them with wrinkled wool pants and a navy blazer that looks like it once fit him, before old age began to steal his height. The red ball cap's been exchanged for a turn-of-the-century top hat that says MAYOR in some regal font; the elk whistle for an oversized gold key. Beneath his nose is a fake mustache that's been too hastily attached: it slants at a forty-five degree angle.

"Welcome to Buford," he says, his voice tripping into a Kennedy-ish accent: canned, practiced, forced. The result of watching too many filmed speeches.

"Oh, Jesus."

He shakes each of our hands, again. "I'm Mayor Cornelius Buford, and it's my pleasure to welcome you to our humble town."

I say, "Fred, please. We need to *leave*."

Randal asks, "Wait. Your last name is also Buford?"

He pulls at the corners of his mustache. I keep waiting for him to fix it, to straighten it, but he doesn't; he's content with its cockeyed placement.

"All of us who've served as the mayor of Buford have been called

Buford." He taps the brim of his hat with a crooked finger. "A bow to Major General John Buford, if you will, for whom Buford is named." Then: "Now, what can I do you for?"

I place both hands on the desk. I spread my fingers, lean forward. "Look," I say. "You know what you can do for us. You know our car has broken down. You know we're in a hurry. You said you could help. So *please:* HELP."

He returns to fondling the edges of the mustache, plucking the polyester hairs as if they were guitar strings. "I believe you're confusing me with the keeper of this shop, son," he says. "A fellow named Fred. I won't hold it against you—it happens more often than I'd like to admit. He's a good man, Fred. Can be lazy. And always a little late with his property taxes—but a good man."

"This is hell."

"No, son, this is Buford." And then: "Now, what's this about a car?"

Randal steps forward; his hands are folded and held at his waist.

He says: "Mr. Mayor. What my friend is trying to say is that our car broke down and we're in quite a hurry—"

"That's actually *exactly* what I said."

"—and that someone—someone else who is an entirely different person than you—told us we might be able to find some help here."

"We're always happy to help here in Buford."

"That's wonderful to hear."

"I'll introduce you to Henry."

"Henry?"

"The town mechanic."

He leads us through the door behind the cashier's desk and into an office that doubles as a living space: a crisply made bed in one corner; a table, file cabinet, and hot plate in the other. The whole place smells like cedar and old mothballs. Along three of the walls are racks of hanging clothes, the countless uniforms this man wears to inhabit an uninhabited town. Some of the garments—a custodial uniform and a waiter's dinner jacket, for instance—appear as if they've gone through heavy use. Buttons missing and the cotton frayed. A doctor's lab coat, though. A referee's jersey and a policeman's belt—those all gather dust.

He tells us to make ourselves at home: Randal sits on the bed, and I find a fold-out chair hidden between the file cabinet and the wall. I flex my toes in my shoes; I drum my fingers impatiently on my knees. On the desk I notice a framed picture that's been recently polished. It's of a younger Fred: his hair mostly full and windblown, his cheeks smooth and fleshy and tan. His arm is coiled around the waist of a young woman whose head is wrapped in a red bandana, blond wisps sneaking out from the edges. Her head leans against his chest; they both smile. Above them is the road sign Randal and I saw and read on the outskirts of town. Except in this photograph, there is a single difference. The population reads "2."

I ask, "Who's this?"

He's busied himself with the racks of clothes, filing through the outfits in search of mechanic's overalls.

"That, son, is the first lady of Buford," he says. "Mrs. Marlene Buford!"

I look toward Randal, who is looking down.

"And where is she now?"

"She's hiking. Buford has some of the most renowned hiking trails in all the West."

"How long has she been hiking for?" I hear myself ask.

He's found the overalls. They were tucked behind a forest ranger's coat. He takes them from the hanger and clutches them to his concave chest.

"Nineteen sixty-two," he says. He wraps one of the denim straps around two fingers on his left hand. The corners of his eyes become smooth, wet. "There's no better hiker than Marlene Buford."

I lift the frame from the desk. I squint at the picture, the oldness of it, the way the color around the edges has faded to a glossy white.

Once he's changed into the overalls, we lead the man who might be Fred, but who is now called Henry, to the spot where Lucy has stopped. In a flurry of caked oil and dirt, he pops her hood and—whispering to himself—examines her insides. He tells us it won't be long—a jiffy—and insists that we explore the surrounding wilderness ("beautiful country, by God, the most beautiful country you'll ever see") to occupy ourselves while we wait.

Due west of the trading post we find a barely-there trail and follow it. It meanders past stout shrubs that prick at our calves and whose feathery needles become stuck in our socks. It climbs brief hills and then dips into thirsty dry ditches. Above us, the dying sun pulses pink against the sky.

After ten minutes of walking we come across a tree that springs from solid rock. It grows gnarled, like a rope that's been twisted too many times, and it has needles instead of leaves. We consider the tree's bark, and its roots, how it draws water and whatever else it is that trees need from unforgiving red stone. There is a wooden sign, a trail marker that promises that this specific tree has beguiled travelers since the first train steamed along the Union Pacific Railroad. We read it three times over. We read how this thing has come to be, how the men who laid the railroad intentionally diverted the tracks so this tree could live.

"I wonder how long this is going to take. It can't take long. We can't afford for it to take long."

"It won't take long."

Randal sets his pack on the ground and unzips it so Mrs. Dalloway can get some air. Wander around in the wilderness, if she likes.

"She's practically a cougar, after all," he says.

She pokes her head out into the open, but that's it: she stays crouched, her eyes wild and attentive, darting between the insects that dot the air, the shrub's dry branches.

Randal leans down and scratches the bald space between her eyes. He digs into the outside pocket of the pack for the baseball we conned from the Gangster. Tosses it into the air once, palms it before it begins to fall.

"Catch?"

I pull a needle from the rock tree and snap it in half. "Sure," I say.

I trot about ten yards from him, to a spot between a flat-topped boulder and a cluster of rabbit holes, and we begin tossing the ball back and forth, watching as it makes dull arcs in the dissolving light.

"I wonder what happened to her." Randal jogs to the left, catching one of my off-centered pitches with two hands.

"Who?"

He hurls the ball back. It grazes the tips of my fingers and then bounces against the red dirt.

"You've got to work for those, McPhee." Then: "The first lady of Buford."

"Maybe he killed her."

"He didn't kill her. She went hiking. She disappeared."

"He dumped her body near the Continental Divide."

"It's so heartbreaking—the way he's waiting for her to come back."

"He cut her body in two. He put half of her in a river that heads west, and half of her in a river that heads east."

Shadows pool around us. Fifteen minutes ago they were slight and anemic, but now they form indeterminate shapes. A lion or a butterfly at the base of a tree; two people kissing or the Empire State Building along the side of a smooth boulder.

Randal holds on to the ball—he doesn't toss it back to me. "He didn't kill her, Finn. You know he didn't kill her."

"I know that. Obviously I know that. But it makes a better story, doesn't it? Very Stephen King. Very *Shining*-esque." I lift both hands. "Here," I say. "Throw me the ball."

He pitches it to me, but this time it's harder than before. He doesn't rock back on his heels and lob it; he winds up and fires off a fastball that collides against my right palm with a dull, persistent sting.

"Do you ever consider that what we're doing might be wrong?"

"What are we doing?"

"I don't know. Changing all these stories," he says. "Lying."

RAW FOOTAGE INTERVIEW TRANSCRIPT, UNEDITED

Interviewer:	Finn McPhee
Interviewee:	Randal Baker
Dates:	6/12/2015
	6/13/2015
	6/14/2015
	6/15/2015
	6/18/2015
Address:	Tempe Corporate Suites
	2238 S. McClintock Dr.
	Tempe, AZ 85282
Project:	**DRIVER'S EDUCATION**

Interviewee:	Randal Baker
Interviewer:	Finn McPhee
Date:	June 12, 2015
Place:	Tempe, AZ
Transcriber:	Finn McPhee

RANDAL BAKER: Is it on?

FINN MCPHEE: Do you see the red light?

RB: I see it.

FM: Then it's on. (*Pause*) Try to look into the camera, not at me.

RB: But you're sitting behind the camera. When I look at it, I'm looking at you.

FM: Moving along.

RB: Okay.

FM: You've been wanting to do this for a long time. Are you excited?

RB: I guess?

FM: Try to answer in complete sentences.

RB: (*Sighs*) I've been wanting to do this for a long time and so I guess I'm excited.

FM: And what is it that you're doing?

RB: You know what it is that I'm doing.

FM: Yes, *I* know what it is that you're doing, but the people who are going to watch this, the people who are watching this DVD, *they* won't know what you're doing.

RB: Fine. Fine, okay. In a complete sentence: I'm here to set the record straight about what really happened during the road trip I took with Finn McPhee.

FM: Excellent. And why are you doing that?

RB: Because you asked me to so that these interviews could be a special feature on the DVD edition of the movie that you and your dad made. Because, according to you, audiences like to know the real story.

FM: Okay—I mean, don't say that. The audience shouldn't know that. Say something else.

RB: How about this—It was either this or sue you for making up shit about the things we did.

FM: But neither of us really has the energy to go to small claims court.

RB: Right.

FM: So here we are.

RB: So here we are.

FM: Let's move on. Why don't you bring us up to speed on what you've been up to over the past few years? Just explain how this all came about.

RB: After our little adventure, you stayed in San Francisco for another sixteen months.

FM: *Finn stayed in San Francisco for another sixteen months*: talk about me in the third person.

RB: Christ. Okay. After our little adventure, *Finn* stayed in San Francisco for another sixteen months. *He'd* just lost his job, and so I'm guessing *he* felt this overwhelming urge to get *his* shit together. (*Pauses, raises eyebrows*)

FM: Keep going.

RB: All right. I think he also stayed on the West Coast because there was the issue of his dad. I don't think either of them would ever admit this, but I really do think that Colin and Finn spent the last five years intentionally trying to misunderstand each other and distance themselves from the mistakes they'd both made. Basically, the father hated the son because he fucked with reality for a living, and the son wished that the father could learn to lie a little better. But then Finn's grandfather, who was the biggest con artist of them all, died. (*Pause*) Are you sure you're okay with this?

FM: Yes. Just keep going.

RB: So essentially I think death reintroduced the father to the son and the son to the father. It got them reacquainted with each other in that way that only death is capable of. It made them rebond. Reconnect. And then, because this is a totally normal thing for a father and a son to do, they made a movie about it.

FM: Explain how that happened.

RB: I can't believe I have to pretend that you're not you. (*Pause*) Finn wrote the book, and his dad adapted the script. Then he called one of his few existing contacts in L.A., someone who still owed him a favor, and they made a fucking movie. A multigenerational story about two kids racing across the country while a man deals with his dying, larger-than-life father. They used some of the original footage Finn shot during our drive, and then they cast two actors to play us and recreate the road trip. Guess what they named them?

FM: What?

RB: Randal and Finn.

FM: And how did it do?

RB: It only attracted a minor amount of success, and mostly at B-list film festivals in cities like Nashville and Denver. A few places wrote about it, though, including this highbrow New York magazine that's very well respected, despite the fact that it's got a very small readership. I actually memorized this one quote that was particularly egregious.

FM: Let's hear it.

RB: "With *Driver's Education*, father-son team Finn and Colin McPhee have accomplished something that other, indeed more seasoned *auteurs* have attempted, only to then fail catastrophically: the creation of a prism in which art and life simultaneously reflect each other in a contortion of myth and fact; a reality in which the narrator is at once inextricably involved and objectively detached." *A contortion of myth and fact.* I still can't decide if I love it or hate it.

FM: I think it's pretty accurate.

RB: That doesn't surprise me.

FM: Explain what you've been up to for the past year.

RB: I stuck around New York for the first few months after the film came out in 2014. Finn had moved back, and I think we were both determined to regain the footing we used to have with each other before everything else happened. And we did to a certain degree. If we didn't I don't think I'd be doing this for him.

FM: That's nice of you.

RB: But also—also there was something inherently different about the way we interacted. It was as if during those four days of the trip we'd managed to reveal too much about each other and what we were capable of.

FM: Oh.

RB: I'm sorry.

FM: If that's the truth . . . (*Pause*) Talk about when the girl approached you on the street. That's a good story.

RB: Right. Yeah, that is. Okay. So one day this past January, someone recognized me on the street. It was probably one of, like, the four people who actually saw the movie—but still, it was the thing that first got me thinking about leaving the city. Just escaping New York for good. It was this girl who looked about my age. While we both were waiting to cross Broadway at Nineteenth Street, she kept glancing over like she recognized me. Then finally, things became, like, so uncomfortable and obvious that she actually had to say something. So she spoke up, and the conversation went something like: "I'm sorry, but are you that guy? From that movie?" "What movie?" "That road trip movie. The one that just came out. You look just like him." I'll say this: they did an amazing job casting *Driver's Education*. Really, the guys were practically our twins. My only complaint is Randal could've stood to lose about ten pounds. "I'm sort of him," I said. "What do you mean, you're sort of him?" "I mean I'm actually him." "I'm confused." "The whole ordeal is rather confusing." "So were you in that movie or not?" "Only sort of. Like, I'm not him, but I'm the real him." "So you're not him." And really the only thing I could say was, "I guess not."

FM: That's brilliant. But then, also, there was the issue—

RB: There was the issue of Mrs. Dalloway. She's been living with me ever since we finished the trip, and for the most part she's been doing well— she just sort of hobbles around and licks my toes. But then in mid-February she came down with feline consumption. At first I thought it was hairballs—she'd been licking herself more than usual—but then when her coughing got worse I took her to the vet, who diagnosed her with mycobacterium tuberculosis. I asked him if she'd get better, and he told me that she was very old, and that the cold wet weather in New York didn't help. So I moved us here. To Tempe, Arizona.

FM: That's a lot to do for a cat.

RB: She's a very special cat.

FM: Right. (*Pause*) Okay, but also, after the movie came out, you tried to get back together with S—

RB: Don't say her name.

FM: Not even now?

RB: Not even now.

FM: Okay. (*Pause*) So how did things work out?

RB: (*Silence*)

FM: How did things work—

RB: I'm living in Arizona with a cat.

FM: I see. (*Pause*)

RB: Stop laughing.

FM: I'm not laughing.

RB: I was heartbroken.

FM: I know. (*Pause*) Let's move along.

RB: Perfectly fine with me.

FM: What do you do here?

RB: I work at this Greek restaurant called The Goddess Athena's that's owned by a Vietnamese couple named Mr. and Mrs. Phan.

FM: Do you like living here?

RB: I like the desert. I like all the different sort of cactuses.

FM: It's "cacti."

RB: I like how the moon hitting the sand keeps anything from getting too dark at night. I like that the dry air has been good for Mrs. Dalloway's breathing. I like that she's still got the energy to chase a lizard or two every day. So, yeah, I like it. We're happy.

FM: And what can we expect from you during these interviews?

RB: The truth?

FM: "You can expect . . ."

RB: Right. Sorry. You can expect the truth. At least how I remember it. Which may be difficult because I think I'm probably just as guilty as Finn is when it comes to tweaking reality; the difference is he just got paid to do it for a few years. But, I mean, I'm sure I was an accomplice to his lies, and in some cases I might've helped him to tell them in better ways.

FM: Don't admit that.

RB: Sorry.

FM: It's fine. We can cut it.

RB: Isn't that against what we're trying to do here?

FM: Don't say that, either. (*Pause*) Okay. So, you've just watched *Driver's Education*, and you've got some thoughts regarding its veracity. Where would you like to start?

RB: Oh, God. I don't know.

FM: Maybe you could begin with the smaller inaccuracies? And then explain how they snowballed into these alternative-universe fabrications?

RB: But I don't think lying works that way.

FM: What do you mean?

RB: I think that, if anything, the first lie someone tells is the largest. Like, it's the keystone of the arch, and the rest of them, the lies, are just the surrounding stones that make sure the thing touches the ground. At least that's how it was for us. There was a commitment to lying early on, after you—or, *he*—received that initial call from his grandfather. There was this conversation that was conveniently stricken from the film's shooting script when Finn convinced me to live for four days in a way that he deemed worthy of his grandfather's legacy. Just big, and boisterous, and loud, and in a way that no one really exists. And, if we didn't succeed—and I'll tell you right now, given the version of his grandfather that Finn had created, it was impossible to succeed—anyway, if we didn't succeed we'd just twist shit around and remanufacture it until, when we eventually told the story to people, they'd believe that we did.

FM: Explain that more.

RB: Take the Arthur Kill, for instance. He must've gotten the footage after our drive because we never went there. We read about it in the same magazine article, and we looked at pictures of it on the Internet together—but we never went there. Firstly because I never learned to swim, so the idea of sloshing around in those sinking boats was really terrifying to me; and secondly because motivating to get to Staten Island was always impossible. We did watch the ships from Hudson River Park, though. That part is correct. We'd lie with our shirts off and count sails and sometimes we'd talk about the Kill. What it might look like. And those conversations must've had some huge effect on him because I remember while we were driving somewhere in Ohio he said, "It'd be a great place to start this story." I told him, "But we never actually went there." And he said, "No one really cares about that. No one *will* really care about that." "What about just starting it where it actually started?" "Where things actually start is never all that interesting." And so I told him, all right, and then I asked him not to include the thing about me being unable to swim.

FM: I think we're almost out of time.

RB: I have to go to work, anyway.

FM: Can you be here the same time tomorrow?

RB: Yeah. Okay.

Interviewee: Randal Baker
Interviewer: Finn McPhee
Date: June 13, 2015
Place: Tempe, AZ
Transcriber: Finn McPhee

FINN MCPHEE: Okay, go.

RANDAL BAKER: Wait, I have a question first.

FM: What?

RB: How'd you find this place, anyway?

FM: Some classified ad in the *East Valley Tribune*. There's a company that rents out these suites by the hour.

RB: It's sort of dreary, isn't it? Grey chairs. That desk. The fluorescent lighting.

FM: You just think that because you've never worked in an actual office.

RB: Well, regardless, it was nice of you to come to Tempe.

FM: I was happy to. Besides, you refused to come to New York. (*Pause*) What's that fucking smell?

RB: (*Sighs*) It's me. It's garlic.

FM: Why do you smell like that much garlic?

RB: Today, after I finished up my second shift at The Goddess Athena's, I was changing out of my *foustanella* and into a pair of shorts when Mrs. Phan comes up to me and says, "You a Greek?" I tell her, "I'm a Jew." "You cook Greek food?" "No, I don't cook Greek food, because I'm a Jew." "You make good tzatziki?" "No, I don't make good tzatziki because I'm not Greek, I'm a Jew." "You saying you a Jew?" "I'm saying I'm a Jew." Then she just sort of squints at me while I'm zipping up my fly. And then she suddenly grabs my arm and drags me into the kitchen and goes, "It no matter. You all look the same anyway."

FM: You do look a little Greek.

RB: *Anyway*. On top of clocking in double shifts, I'm now also helping out in the kitchen. Where, as I learned tonight, there are no actual Greeks. There's a Mexican and an Italian and a pair of brothers from Portugal—but no Greeks. Mrs. Phan has got it in her head that she wants to unveil some new type of tzatziki for Tempe's Taste of Greece festival, which is in four days, and so she's got us all futzing around to create a new recipe. But the thing is, not a single one of these guys actually knows what he's doing. Like, they know how to cook Greek food, but only the basics: they can skewer some souvlaki or layer some moussaka. But that's it. When it comes to altering the original, everyone's lost. The Mexican suggested we add melted queso, which was a total disaster.

FM: That sounds disgusting.

RB: The Italian stirred in a tablespoon of marinara, which was okay, but it really just made it taste like sour Thousand Island dressing. One of the Portuguese brothers asked me, "What is it that you can do?" "I can spread it on some challah." The other brother said, "You will chop the garlic." So that's what I did, I chopped it for three fucking hours.

FM: That also explains why you're late.

RB: Yes, it does.

FM: How is Dalloway?

RB: She's fine. She's coughing again, but I'm sure it's just her allergies. There's a lot of dust here. (*Pause*) Last night she brought me a dead snake.

FM: Really?

RB: Really.

FM: That's *awesome*.

RB: I thought so, too.

FM: All right. So. Let's talk about Pittsburgh.

RB: Okay.

FM: Because that's where the editing really started.

RB: That's not true. Yip was actually skinny, and the weather—it rained the whole time.

FM: Then the *substantial* editing.

RB: That's true. Finding that empty lot where the house of records supposedly stood was a disaster.

FM: Talk about that.

RB: Basically, the taxi had to drive us around for hours as we looked for it. And trust me—there's not some dearth of abandoned spaces in Pittsburgh; there's plenty of them. Finn just had to find the perfect one. The one where he could fully imagine the house of records being. He'd make me jog out into the middle of each lot so he could get a sense of perspective. He'd yell, "You can see too many new condos in the background" and "That fence on the left side doesn't make a lot of sense." Then we'd get back in the cab and drive around some more.

FM: So, essentially, you were location scouting.

RB: That's one way to put it. We were finding the best iteration of a story that was a lie in the first place. Another way to say it is that we were manufacturing memories. (*Pause*) What?

FM: Nothing. Why?

RB: You were doing that thing you do when you're nervous. Where you claw at your thumb.

FM: Talk about Columbus.

RB: That wasn't my finest hour.

FM: Talk about why.

RB: Okay. But there are some other things I want to mention first.

FM: Like what?

RB: Like, for example, how that goddamned car broke down twenty miles west of Pittsburgh.

FM: That was a nonissue. The whole thing took two hours, tops.

RB: Still, though. It happened, and you edited it out of the story you told. And you asked me to tell the truth during these interviews, so . . .

FM: (*Pause*) Fine. That's fair. What else?

RB: How about how the car leaked? Which was terrible because, like I said, it rained most of the time. Both windows on the passenger side didn't seal completely when they were closed. They sagged about half an inch below where they should have been. We tried stuffing various objects in the space in order to plug the leak—empty soda cups, our T-shirts, Finn's head. Oh, come on. Don't give me that look. I'm kidding. Anyway, none of it worked, so we drove across the country with puddles at our feet. That wasn't fun.

FM: Can we get to Columbus now?

RB: There's one more thing: Mrs. Dalloway didn't just go ballistic for no reason. There was a bee in the car—a big one. And no one hates a bee like Dalloway.

FM: Noted. Now—Columbus.

RB: Columbus. Jesus Christ, Columbus. Okay. So there was an actual conference going on—but it was for pharmaceutical representatives, I think, not a medical supplies sales one. And I did score us an incredible rate on the hotel room, but it was at a Courtyard Marriott instead of a Hampton Inn. From what I understand, though, Hampton Inn was a sponsor of one of the festivals to which they were submitting *Driver's Education*, and so it makes sense that Finn would want to give the company a shout-out.

FM: Incidentally, I'm also staying at one in Tempe.

RB: One what?

FM: At the Hampton Inn and Suites, a member of the Hilton family of hotels.

RB: Do you have to say it like that?

FM: They're a sponsor. (*Pause*) Keep going.

RB: Okay. Finally, yes, there was a luau, which is where things may or may not have gone awry.

FM: Describe what happened.

RB: Well, we found Nancy Davenport in much the same way we found the lot in Pittsburgh—essentially, we cast her. We approached a dozen different girls who told us a dozen different stories. We'd spot them from across the room, wearing these pink leis and drinking mai tais. We'd ask them their names, their ages, their hometowns in a voice that was sort of interrogative, but mostly flirtatious. "What about that one?" I'd ask Finn when a girl had excused herself for a moment. "Her hair isn't blond enough." "Okay, then what about the one before her." "She was from Boston." "No one has to know that." And then I remember he said, "I like the way you're thinking, Randal. I like the way you're thinking."

FM: Talk about Nancy herself.

RB: To be honest, I can't say that much about her. I spoke to her for a minute or two, but I lost you—*them*—both when they went out on the dance floor. By this point it was about ten o'clock and I had been decidedly overserved when it came to those mai tais. I don't remember how many women my mother's age I got inappropriate with, but it was definitely more than two. Possibly more than four. I took shots with them—mostly things with awful names like Buttery Nipple. I found some younger men in the bathroom who were snorting lines of Adderall and I joined them, which is the reason I've come to believe we were, in fact, at a pharmaceutical sales representatives' conference. I took more shots. I sang something by Cat Stevens at the karaoke booth and I might've started crying. (*Pause*) I'm proud of none of this.

FM: The karaoke is my favorite part.

RB: Do audiences really need to know about all that?

FM: Absolutely.

Interviewee: **Randal Baker**
Interviewer: **Finn McPhee**
Date: **June 14, 2015**
Place: **Tempe, AZ**
Transcriber: **Finn McPhee**

RANDAL BAKER: *Kali oreski!*

FINN MCPHEE: You're an hour late.

RB: That's how you say "bon appétit" in Greek.

FM: Can you please just sit down so we can get started? We only have this room for another hour.

RB: I'm sitting, I'm sitting. *Kali oreski!* Mrs. Phan made all of us guys on the tzatziki team learn how to say it for the Taste of Greece festival.

FM: When is that again? I want to come.

RB: Tomorrow. The plan is that we'll say it to each customer after we've given them a sample, which'll give the whole affair an air of authenticity and elegance, I guess.

FM: How's that whole thing going?

RB: We still haven't come up with a recipe yet, but we're definitely getting closer. Last night, we mixed in a pinch of *piri piri,* which is this spicy pepper that they use in Portuguese cuisine, and it gave the whole thing a nice kick. Mr. and Mrs. Phan are supposed to do a taste test tonight, but I'm going to miss it.

FM: Why?

RB: Because I've got to take Mrs. Dalloway to the vet.

FM: Wait, really? Is everything okay?

RB: I think so. (*Pause*) The thing is her cough just isn't getting better, and now once in a while I'll hear a little wheeze if she's been running around.

I mean I'm sure it's nothing though, right? There are new sorts of plants out here and, like I said, there's a lot of dust, and so I'm sure it's just that. I'm sure it's just allergies. I'm almost positive I'm overreacting. But it's always better to be on the safe side, I think.

FM: Does she hate the vet?

RB: No. Actually, she loves it. There's this little stuffed mouse they let her bat around, and they always shower her with treats.

FM: Keep me updated.

RB: I will.

FM: So—Chicago.

RB: Everything you see in the Chicago scene absolutely and positively happened. In a pressure-cooker scenario, I had the brilliant idea to forge Ernie Banks's signature on that ball (and perfectly, I might add). I kept my cool, even in the treacherous presence of the Gangster. I bowled her over with my dashing charm and tall-dark-and-handsome looks. And when Dalloway's life was in danger, I didn't hesitate; I swept in like the hero I am and rescued her from the claws of inevitable doom.

FM: The whole point of this is for you to provide a truthful account of what happened.

RB: But I love that story.

FM: Tell me.

RB: Fine. The truth. There was a pizza place, and it was called The Gangster's, but we really had no way of knowing if it was The Actual Gangster's, if that makes sense. We weren't allowed to bring the camera inside. We tried, but every time we were caught. So the physical details (the color of the tables, what was on the walls, etc.) probably aren't all that accurate: I remember the place seeming a lot newer than how Finn's made it out to be.

FM: And the bombshell?

RB: The Gangster herself didn't exist—she's a fantastic character, but she didn't exist. Neither did the five hundredth home run ball. Or, of course the five hundredth home run ball existed, but certainly not there, in the middle of some pizza joint. From what I understand, when Banks cranked out that homer, the ball bounced off the foul line and fell into the bull pen—which is to say, no one ever really caught it in the first place. Not Finn's granddad, not the Gangster's father—no one. (*Pause*) But what sort of story is that?

FM: Indeed.

RB: I'd like to add that I did, though, win a baseball at the claw crane. And I did forge Ernie Banks's autograph across its surface. That part is all true. "We'll just show your granddad this," I said to Finn. "We'll rough it up a little bit, we'll tell him it's the five hundredth home run ball, the one he lost, and we'll show him this." "You think he'll buy it?" "You'd know better than me. I mean, it's not like the story actually happened, anyway. He's just convinced himself that it did. But yeah—yeah, I think he'll buy it." (*Pause*) What?

FM: You don't have to say it like that.

RB: Like what?

FM: You don't have to make him sound like some goddamned lunatic.

RB: I was just—

FM: I think we've got enough for the day.

RB: Finn—

FM: We're done.

RB: Come on. That's it?

FM: We don't have any more time. Because you were late. We'll continue tomorrow.

RB: You'll be at the Taste of Greece festival? (*Pause*) Right?

FM: Yes. I'll be there.

Interviewee: **Randal Baker**
Interviewer: **Finn McPhee**
Date: **June 15, 2015**
Place: **Tempe, AZ**
Transcriber: **Finn McPhee**

RANDAL BAKER: That was a disaster.

FINN MCPHEE: Such a fucking disaster.

RB: How is your tongue?

FM: It's burnt, but it'll be okay.

RB: I doubt the ouzo helped.

FM: It was the only thing around. Jesus Christ, my mouth is still on fire. (*Pause*) Why don't you talk about what happened.

RB: (*Sighs*) The Taste of Greece festival was this afternoon. For the first forty-five minutes, everything was going well. Our tzatziki was a hit—people were literally forming lines thirty yards long to get a sample of it. Which is sort of where the problem started. One of the Portuguese brothers asked if I could take over his role chopping up the *piri piri* so he could focus on skinning more cucumbers. I told him fine, even though I had no idea how much *piri piri* the new recipe called for. I just kept chopping and chopping and adding and mixing.

FM: Your first clue should've been that people started sweating when they looked at it. Their faces turned red without even tasting it.

RB: I heard someone say it tasted like habanero sauce on crack.

FM: That's an understatement. I still feel like there are firecrackers on my gums. And it's not like it's not hot as balls outside, anyway.

RB: People kept having to run to the Greek lemonade booth—

FM: Which is ridiculous, because Greeks didn't invent lemonade.

RB:—and then when there was no more lemonade, they had to run to the ouzo booth. (*Pause*) I saw a mother give her daughter two shots of ouzo just so she'd stop crying. I feel terrible.

FM: Do you still have your job?

RB: Surprisingly, yes. The Goddess Athena's scored third place in the tzatziki competition.

FM: But there were only five teams.

RB: Mrs. Phan doesn't really care about things like that. (*Pause*) You're still sweating.

FM: I know I am, okay? Talk about something else. Talk about Buford.

RB: Oh, Buford was weird, all right. But that guy—the one who played the mayor of Buford in the film—he wasn't anything like—

(*Mobile phone rings*)

FM: Is that your phone?

RB: Yeah. Sorry. I thought I turned it off. (*Pause*) It's the vet.

FM: Mrs. Dalloway didn't come home last night?

RB: They asked if she could stay over so they could keep an eye on her. I have to go. I have to take this.

FM: Can you do it here? Can I film it?

RB: Turn that fucking camera off.

Interviewee: Randal Baker
Interviewer: Finn McPhee
Date: June 18, 2015
Place: Tempe, AZ
Transcriber: Finn McPhee

FINN MCPHEE: I've been trying to get hold of you for two days.

RANDAL BAKER: I wasn't here.

FM: Where did you go?

RB: I was camping near Alamo Lake.

FM: Why?

RB: You know why.

FM: I need for you to explain it.

RB: Because I like it up there. (*Pause*) I needed to spread her ashes.

FM: What happened at the vet's office?

RB: They told me she was coughing because of the tuberculosis. That the tuberculosis had returned. Or that it never really cleared up. I don't know. Her breathing was getting shallow and they were concerned, so they started her on a medication. I guess she was allergic to it. (*Pause*) And that was it.

FM: Did you get there in time?

RB: No.

FM: I'm sorry. (*Pause*) Randal? Are you okay?

RB: She was just a cat.

FM: We don't have to do this right now. We can do this later.

RB: She was just a cat, I said.

FM: I'm serious.

RB: We could have flown.

FM: What?

RB: After your father called about your granddad's third stroke—we could have flown.

FM: *Finn's* granddad. Please say *Finn's* granddad.

RB: And we should have flown. You knew there wasn't a lot of time. We should've parked the car in a garage in Iowa City and booked a flight, instead of spending half a day crossing Nebraska and getting stuck in Wyoming.

FM: Do you think you're maybe projecting right now?

RB: Every time I suggested it, though, you just became more adamant about driving.

FM: I was asked to get Lucy to California.

RB: But still. Do you know how frustrating that was at the time? And also heartbreaking? It was like you had convinced yourself that so long as you could keep Lucy on the road you'd be able to keep the old man alive. That basically our driving—our reliving and recreating your granddad's stories—was keeping the reality of his death at bay.

FM: (*Silence*)

RB: And also, before I forget, a note about those stories for the audience: you know that they're mostly Finn's, right? Or, maybe not mostly, but he definitely had a hand in them. The granddad set down the foundations, sure: a house of records in Pittsburgh, a legendary baseball game in Chicago. But it was Finn who fleshed them out. You know, threw some meat on their bones. He took his granddad's minor myths and turned them into these sweeping epics. And I don't think it was all that hard for him—I mean, it was basically what he did for a living at the reality show, anyway.

FM: (*Silence*)

RB: I remember about a year and a half before all this happened. His granddad was still living in Westchester and I went with Finn to visit him on some Sunday afternoon. I sat in the background and I listened while they perfected that story about Charlotte Sparrow. The one about flying planes. "She was beautiful," the granddad said. "More beautiful than you'd ever believe." Finn leaned in. "Would you say she was so beautiful she glowed?" "Yes," he said. "Yes, I think I would."

FM: It was just more compelling that way. If she was brighter than the moon.

RB: But this is how it happens, right? A story outgrows its original owner, and eventually it has to leap into the mind of someone who can tell it better. I can see how the whole ordeal would be seductive to you—knowing that a person's past is in your hands. I mean, I can see how you got so caught up in it. Particularly here, with this story. The idea of this old man dying. The idea that he's twisted the truth so many times that he can't remember what it looked like in the first place. The idea that at the moment of his death what actually happened didn't matter so much as what was actually remembered. That the realization of that would help you to grow, to change, to complete your arc as a character. (*Pause*) But the fact of it—I mean, the cold hard fact of it—is that you're still a liar. We're both still liars.

FM: We're done here.

(*Interview ends. 1:27 of blank tape.*)

At 1:28:

RB: (*Standing; off camera*) How was that?

FM: (*Off camera*) It was perfect. Just as we discussed.

RB: (*Off camera*) It wasn't too mean? Like, I didn't get too harsh?

FM: (*Off camera*) No, no. It was great. (*Pause*) Dalloway dying—that was fantastic. I didn't see that coming.

RB: You played along really well. I was worried you were going to be too thrown.

FM: Never. (*Pause*) Ha. Ha ha. Dalloway actually dying.

RB: (*Off camera*) She's never going to die.

FM: (*Off camera*) She'll fucking outlive us all.

RB: (*Off camera*) You know the red light is still on, right?

FM: (*Off camera*) Shit.

RB: Whatever. We'll just cut it out.

The End

Right Now

By Colin A. McPhee

The hospital has sent in a bereavement nurse. She's young—maybe in her midthirties—and she carries herself softly, like there's a cushion of air between her and everything else. When she first came into the room, she pulled up a chair next to mine, and she took my hand in hers. She sat with me quietly. She didn't correct me the three times I called her Ann, even though her name tag very clearly reads AMY. She rubbed a thumb between two of my knuckles and she breathed steadily, practiced. My guess would be that these meetings usually last for fifteen minutes—maybe twenty minutes, at most—but she's been here for the past two hours; my father just won't die. Or, maybe more specifically, we just won't let him.

At first it was a matter of waiting for Finn.

"He should be here to say good-bye," I said to the attending doctor. My voice was half drowned out by the dozens of machines that he's hooked up to—things that beat his heart, and inflate his lungs, and fill his stomach.

And then eventually, more honestly, "Really, I'm just not sure I can do this alone."

But Finn arrived an hour ago. I knew it was him before I saw him, because I heard him trotting as he raced down the hall. He's done it since he was a kid—trot. While most people run at a steady pace, his gait is just noticeably uneven. A three-quarter count instead of common time. When he skidded into the room his eyes were ringed and he looked thinner. There was a backpack and a video camera slung over his shoulder; he had dirt on his elbows and he was covered in cat hair. It hung like cut threads from the sleeves of his shirt, from his shorts. He stopped me from standing and kissed the top of my head and then sat, very slowly, on the other side of the bed, nearest a window that overlooks the parking lot.

He pulled one grey strand of cat hair out of the corner of his left eye.

"Mrs. Dalloway was freaking out when we drove across the bridge," he said, moving. "She wouldn't get off me."

I asked, "Who?"

That was twenty minutes ago, and we haven't moved since. Each time a member of the hospital's staff asks if we're ready, one of us will say no—no, not quite yet. We'll say how we haven't quite decided on the person we want him to be.

The nurse is being as patient as she can be, but she's reaching the end of her rope. I can feel it. I can tell by the way she's standing—arms crossed, slippers turned in toward each other. She clears her throat. Asks Finn if he's thirsty.

"Do you have any scotch?"

The nurse smiles. "This is a hospital."

"So do you?"

Now she pulls the corners of her lips wider, tighter, before letting the grin drop. She clears her throat. She presents a clipboard and clicks open a ballpoint pen.

"Mr. McPhee." Then, again: "Mr. McPhee.

"I heard you the first time."

"I'm going to need you to sign these forms. Take your time." She shifts her watch—a black plastic Swatch—on her wrist.

Finn looks at my father. At the way his hands are folded on top of each other. He ducks his head through the wires and tubes and cords that extend like marionette strings from my father's arms, his face, his heart. He presses a wet cheek against his chest and I watch his head lift and fall as his lungs are filled and emptied.

"He's still breathing," Finn says.

"There are machines doing that."

"And I can feel his heart."

I say nothing, but the bereavement nurse adds, "There are machines doing that, too." Then she squeezes my shoulder. She points to the forms she's given me and continues, "Right there, Mr. McPhee. And your initials too."

Finn lifts his head and looks at her. "Given your job, I'm sure you're well aware of this," he says. "But someone's fucking dying here."

There are a few things I forgot to tell my father. Like:

He always burnt the toast.

He was a horrible driver.

I'll always save a seat for him at the movies.

The bereavement nurse clicks her jaw. She looks at my son, and then at me, as if to encourage me to correct him, to scold him, and when I don't she tells me that she needs to step out for a moment. That she needs to make copies of the administrative forms.

Finn walks to the other side of the bed, next to which is a small side table where I've set the stack of my memories—these hundred-odd pages that I've been writing over the past six days while listening to my father watch television from the spaces between the floorboards. He thumbs through them, flipping their corners.

"What's this?"

"It's for him," I say. "It was for him."

He keeps flipping the pages. I imagine him reading one, then five, then ten, then fifty. He bends the corners; he rests all five fingers upon them. "And now?"

I say, "And now I guess they're for you."

• • •

"I don't think this is the ending he wanted," Finn says.

"What?"

He's removed a signed baseball from his backpack, and he slowly passes it back and forth between his hands.

"I'm just saying—I don't think this is the ending he wanted. The one he envisioned for himself."

This is true: if there was one thing my father taught me, it's that endings never work out the way you want them to—that they're terrible, and this one is no different. They're like the last drops of wine, the final puffs of a cigarette. They're Sunday nights, or the last afternoon of summer. They're flat tires and wet pairs of socks and cold dinners. They're the sort of thing that—no matter the effort, no matter the discipline—no one can get right.

With endings, a person's fucked.

"No," I said to Finn. "No—it's not the ending he wanted at all."

I look around me at this blocky hospital with its white, sterile floors; this room with its single square window; this bed with its sandpaper sheet and foam pillows. And then at my father. Fading within it all. My father, *not* surrounded by a pack of lions on the broad, lush face of Kilimanjaro. My father, *not* using his walker to fight off bands of machete-wielding pirates along the Barbary Coast. My father, *not* banking Lucy around the razor turns on the cliffs above Monte Carlo.

"We'd spring him out if we could," Finn says.

And yes, yes I think we would: if the doctors and the nurses weren't huddled so closely around him, we would have extracted the tubes and wires from his arms, and lifted him onto my shoulders, and we—him, Finn, and me—would have escaped out onto the open road, where we would've done this the right way, the way he deserved, the way that—I'm sure—he'd want the story told.

The doctor returns, followed by the bereavement nurse.

They ask if we're ready and we say that we are. They begin to remove the machines.

But we ignore them as best we can. Standing on either side of my father's body we begin to conjure, to concoct:

"What about a house fire in Savannah?"

"Or maybe something tragic on a frozen lake in Michigan."

"Or, no. A violent exchange with Incan descendants in Peru. Over Tupperware."

I watch my son the editor pull at the bristled ends of his long hair. He says, "I think we can do better."

"Tell me."

"Fishing. In Baja. There was a story he told me about fishing in Baja." And then—then there's that familiar glint in his eye, which I've seen in my father's eyes so many times before.

He says, this time more confidently, "Yes, fishing."

"Okay then."

"Okay?"

"Let's give it a shot. Let's come up with something better."

The End, but Better

Right Now

By Finn McPhee

Once, in 1974, my granddad went fishing in Baja California, that skinny sliver of land that hangs on maps like a forgotten piece of Mexico. He'd been in San Diego the week before—this was in the summer, when the sun gilds the Pacific with copper-capped waves—and one afternoon he just decided to drive south. He said to himself, to Lucy, *It looks like we've reached the end of the road, old girl. Which I figure means it's about time we find a new one.*

They took Mexico Route 1 across the border, past the cardboard shantytowns of Tijuana, whose roofs appeared as rolling meadows of corrugated steel. Outside of Rosarito Lucy kicked up brick-red dirt along the highway. He rubbed the chalky flecks from the corners of his eyes as they undulated along the *vados,* the treacherous dips in the road that, in the wet season, fill with deep pools of rainwater. For the most part the highway was deserted. The only real traffic they faced was the periodic crossing of small herds of cows, who chewed on the dry, thorny brush as they labored across the pavement. Actually, that might not be true. Once, maybe, they came across a donkey. At night they'd sleep in Baja's flickering villages, in El Crucero and Mulege and Santa Rosalía, and in the morning, before the earth began to bake, they'd drive onward, south, to the point where the road might end.

He never got there, though. Afraid of what a terminus might actually mean, my granddad veered onto a thin dirt lane about a hundred miles out from where the highway ends in Cabo San Lucas. The sun burned his back while he followed the lane eastward past scorpions, and snakes, and scarlet-splashed rocks, until it eventually dumped him in Bahia de Palmas—a remote fishing village set along the Sea of Cortez. It was dark when he arrived. And the way he used to describe it to me—he said that there were so many stars, just so many of them, that it seemed like the night was filling the space between them instead of the other way around. He found a small cantina, where he ate a plateful of tortillas, and beans, and he drank a half-cold beer, and because there wasn't a hotel or anything (the village had a population of about a hundred people), the bartender offered him the back storage shack, outside of which was chained a spotted pygmy goat that stood three feet high.

"Did you sleep?" I'd always ask. "I really don't think I'd be able to sleep."

But he did. He'd become accustomed over the years to sleeping in new, strange places, of waking up to that terrified excitement of not knowing—if only for an instant—exactly where he was. He listened to the goat's baying, and the click of its heels as it moved about in a dream, and his eyes fell shut. And he slept, soundly, until light rushed in from the cracks in the wall and his ears began ringing with the shouting of men.

It was early, and they were prepping their boats before heading out to trawl for big game fish. They strapped thick poles to the sterns of the single-motor vessels, working silently but for one exception: at the end of the village's pier were two men whose voices cut sharp and loud through the dawn as they yelled at each other, back and forth, next to a boat called *El Pequeño Soldado*. My granddad slipped on his pants. He pulled his arms through the sleeves of his shirt and—because he was this sort of person—he walked toward them.

Someone had fallen ill. This is what he learned during an exchange of broken English and more-broken Spanish. It was one of the anglers. Without him, *El Pequeño Soldado* wouldn't be able to head out that day, and the men who crewed it would lose a day's pay.

"Nuestras familias," they said. *"Nuestras familias necesitan comer."*

They were trying to convince my granddad to join them. If you don't know anything about deep-sea fishing, take it from me (who heard it from my granddad)—it can be treacherous business. Reeling in a hefty marlin that puts up a substantial contest can take upward of three hours—a marathon of a struggle that no single man is cut out for. In other words, it requires teams. A group of men who take turns sitting in bolted-down chairs, white-knuckling the pole, passing it off to the next guy in line once they've exhausted themselves trying to reel the beast in.

"I've never done this before," he said. "I don't know how."

"¿Qué?"

"No se como."

The two men looked at each other and cocked their heads; this was a question so rarely asked because the answer was so blindingly obvious.

"Luchas," one of them said.

"¿Qué?"

"You fight." He pantomimed holding a fishing rod, muscling it back toward his shoulder. *"Luchas."*

"Yes." My granddad nodded. *"Sí.* I understand. *Entiendo."*

They motored away from the pier at seven o'clock in the morning—forty-five minutes after the last boat headed toward the horizon—and it took them three hours to get where they wanted to go. The crew of *El Pequeño Soldado* had had luck trawling near a spot referred to loosely as 1150 Bank, about twenty-five miles off the coast between Cabo San Lucas and San Jose. It's a place where the sea floor swallows itself into craggy underwater canyons, where the depth causes the water's surface to deepen from turquoise to glossy blue. While they cruised my granddad sat on a small chair perched near the boat's bow. He watched the shore fade behind the heat's hazy screen; he closed his eyes when the ocean sprayed salt in his face. Sometimes, when the motor quieted and when the boat's hull stopped slapping the sea's surface, he'd turn back to the men. The shorter of the two, Juan, commanded the wheel; the taller, Alejandro, wrapped strands of thick rope into coils.

"How much farther?" my granddad would shout. "*¿Cuánto mas lejos?*"

"Almost!" one of them would cry back. "So close!"

The bite came sometime right after noon, once they'd reach the 1150 Bank and the current had settled into a midday lull and the back of my granddad's neck had started to burn red. They were all three sitting in *El Pequeño Soldado*'s cockpit eating sandwiches and drinking *cervezas* when, suddenly, there was a violent jolt. One of the poles bent like a palm in gale force winds; its line tugged outward, lifting and jerking and disappearing into the blue.

"*¡Vamos!*"

Juan threw the rest of his sandwich overboard, and the bread split apart from itself and sank. He strapped the pole, and then himself, into the fighting chair. A hundred or so feet off the boat's bow, a marlin leapt from the water and thrashed about. My granddad held his breath as he caught sight of it, as it furiously tried to spear the air with its nose.

"You've never seen a blue like this, Finn," he said the first time he recounted this story for me. He was visiting my father and me in Los Angeles, and we'd decided to spend an afternoon at the Long Beach aquarium. I remember we were standing in a shark exhibit and there were these huge hammerheads that coasted in front of us, around us, above us. "The color of this fish—you've never seen anything like it. Like God and Nature had competed against each other to create the most beautiful blue there ever was. Bluer than blue. What blue wishes it could be."

"Okay, okay," I said. "I *get* it."

"No, son, you don't."

Juan worked the reel with brute force. He'd tease the marlin with a bit of slack, allowing it to exhaust itself, before he'd arch the rod back and reel in manically. My granddad watched the short muscles in the man's forearms clench; sweat wetted growing patches at the center of his chest, along his spine, beneath his arms.

A little bit closer now, the marlin exploded into the air again. Then it was my granddad's turn.

"You!" Alejandro coaxed him toward the seat, where Juan was still working the reel but was showing signs of fatigue. "You go!"

"All right!" my granddad shouted. He began wringing his hands to-gether and shifting his weight between his heels. "Yes, yes, all right!" Then: "What do I do again?"

Together they yelled, "YOU FIGHT!"

At first he thought his arms were going to be pulled from their sockets, he told me. Just ripped clean out into the Sea of Cortez where they'd become chum for the circling gulls. He lurched forward in the chair and Juan had to latch on to one of his shoulders and Alejandro the other in order to keep him from being yanked into the air. He planted both his heels on the deck of the boat as he felt the men's fingers burrow into his skin, the pole's handle begin to slip and squirm from his sweaty fingers. He felt the first streams of sweat canyon down his temples and worm into the squinted corners of his eyes, but he didn't dare wipe them away—he just let them sting. But then there was a moment of still-ness, a brief pause during which the marlin must've felt it safe to take a breather: the line, in a blinkable instant, went slack. And my granddad, being the sort of man who recognizes Opportunity when it presents itself, seized his chance. He began to fight.

He arm wrestled with the rod, like he'd seen Juan do minutes before. He ground his teeth together and he clenched down on his upper lip. The marlin darted right, then left, then back to the right in a blistering three count.

"It was the fastest goddamned waltz I've ever danced," he used to say. "And I swear it knew that's what we were doing—I swear it knew we were dancing. Because when it jumped out of the water again, it looked right at me. It didn't even blink."

"I don't think fish have eyelids, Granddad."

"You understand what I'm saying, son."

When they'd managed to get it within ten yards off the boat's star-board side, Alejandro took over, slipping his lanky body into the chair. While Juan had muscled the fish in, Alejandro worked with a sense of lyricism, a sense of poetry. He wove the rod in rounded arcs, like he was conducting an orchestra. The marlin's sharp, sinewy tail drummed along the sea's surface. Its thrashing was more subdued now—it was succumbing to fatigue, its body growing numb from exhaustion. That's not to say it didn't have any life in it—because, as my granddad tells it, when the fish was hauled up onto the deck, when its gills were gulping at nothing, it was still bucking its speared nose, causing the three men to hopscotch around it, blocking their ankles behind plastic coolers.

"What are we supposed to do?" my granddad shouted, but only half-heartedly. He was transfixed, again, by the blue, the spectacular blue, the sky-into-ocean-into-electric-acid-midnight blue of the beast. He leaned over the steering wheel behind which he was hiding and his eyes grew wide.

"*¡Lo golpeó!*" Juan yelled. "Hit it!"

Here's another thing about catching marlin: Once you get them into the boat, that isn't the end of it. Even out of the water, a one-thousand-pound marlin can do quite a bit of damage. So what you've got to do, you've got to stun them, basically beat them into submission.

Alejandro brandished a thick steel club. He shuffled to the other side of my grandfather, so that he was directly above the marlin.

"But wait—"

"*¡Ahora!*"

He said that first hit was too low—six inches down from the head—and the impact sounded fleshy and soft; the fish's body buckled, and its tale whipped a half-finished bottle of beer into the sea. Alejandro cursed.

"*¡La cabeza!*" Juan shouted.

Alejandro struck again, this time between the marlin's fear-flecked eyes. There was a crack—or probably more of a thud, like a sandbag being dropped onto cement—and then the eerie onset of stillness. The lapping of the ocean against the boat's hull. The bitter squawking of gulls as they fought over the soggy remains of Juan's sandwich.

My granddad held both hands to his chest. "Did he do it? Was that it?" he asked.

It was. He did. He must've. Because then—very quickly, like film unspooling from a reel—the life began seeping out of the fish. It began at the tips of its fins, where stripes of silver and that cosmic blue dulled to a sickly grey that the sun had no interest in reflecting. And then it spread upward, and outward, to the marlin's meaty flanks and to its rapier nose, in all directions at once—death blooming efficiently, democratically.

"What'd you do?" I asked him. We were still in the shark exhibit, watching thrashers spiral around each other.

"I cried."

"You did not."

"I did so."

I asked, "Did anyone see you cry?"

"Juan did. I told him there was salt in my eyes."

My granddad said something then—something about life being a sigh, and death being a gasp, and that's what made him cry, the sucker-punch sensation of the gasp, and he told me he never wanted to just fade out, not like that marlin did.

In fact, he actually said to me, "Finn, don't ever let that happen to me."

"I won't," I told him.

"Swear that you won't."

"Yeah, okay." Then: "What do you want me to swear on?"

He dug around in his pockets, which were empty. He looked around the strange, cavernous room. He pressed my five-year-old hand against the cool glass in front of us.

I said, "I swear on these man-eating sharks that I won't let you be like that marlin."

He laughed to himself and smiled. He took both my shoulders and directed me toward the next exhibit, where my father was waiting for us.

The chair's frame is wood, and vaguely modern in that its corners are curved instead of sharp, and its upholstery is purple with blue triangles. I sit on the edge of it, and I pull it closer to my granddad's body. I lean forward until the back legs lift from the ground, until I'm two inches away from the bed, from him, from his hands that are folded like he's getting ready to hear a good story.

The technicians roll the last of the machines away.

I pull a blue blanket over one of my granddad's toes, which is exposed and colorless, grey, in the fluorescent light. And I suddenly want to grip it, the toe, to see if it's cold, or alive; to pull myself close, to fold into him, to wrap myself in houses made of records and Charlotte Sparrow and five-hundred-home-run baseballs.

I'm passing Ernie Banks's baseball back and forth between my hands, and I notice that the sweat on my palms is causing the autograph's ink to bleed and leave traces of itself on my fingers. I think about how whenever anyone talks about hospitals the things they mention most are the sounds and the smells, but the truth is right now I don't smell anything except myself and I don't hear anything except my father's voice, which is low and throaty and warm, like it's passing through a screen of tears.

The room is divided in two by a blue curtain that's been pulled shut, even though the bed on the other side of it is empty. We're in the half of the room that's closest to the window, and through it I can see the hospital's half-empty parking lot, and beyond that Irving Street, and then the south slopes of Golden Gate Park. The city's swamped with its requisite layer of fog, which means that once we leave here, once we get back to my father's home, we won't be able to see the bay or the boats gliding across it. I think if my granddad were to ask me what the day he died was like, though, I'd tell him it was sunny. In fact, I'd tell him it was the sunniest goddamned day that San Francisco had ever seen. I'd tell him how there wasn't a single person who wasn't wearing sunglasses, and how the sea lions at Fisherman's Wharf were using their flippers to cover their eyes, and how the rust of the Golden Gate became so bright, so brilliant, that there was more than one motorist who refused to drive over it out of fear that the bridge was, actually, on fire.

Behind me, someone opens a window and I look up. I remember how my granddad told me there's no such thing as a life that's ended, there are just more stories that haven't been told.

A breeze lifts a few of my father's pages of memories from the bedside table. I reach out and stop them before they blow away. I set Ernie Banks's baseball on top of the stack to protect them from the wind.

ACKNOWLEDGMENTS

There are so many people who deserve my endless gratitude. So I'll do my best to thank some of them here.

Richard Pine, you seem to know exactly what to say and—more important—when to say it. I promise that this gamble we've made will pay off.

Sarah Knight is probably our galaxy's best editor. Thanks for believing in my words, even before they'd been written, and for reading this thing more times than anyone should ever read anything.

To the Dream Team at NYU—David Lipsky, Max Ross, Sasha Graybosch, Anelise Chen, Michelle Kim Hall, Anissa Bazari, Ayesha Attah, Kate Brittain, Sarah Willeman, Kayla Rae Whitaker, Maura Roosevelt, Jenny Blackman, Grant Munroe, and all the others—thanks for being kind enough to tell me when things had gone terribly wrong.

Darin Strauss and Irini Spanidou—I can't believe you never locked the door and shut off the lights when you saw me coming.

Peyton Burgess—you're a hero for driving halfway across the country with me, even though you nearly got us killed in Pittsburgh.

Ben Harvey, Clare O'Connor, Molly Schulman, Billy Kingsland, Maree Hamilton, and Lucy Carson—thanks for the wine when it was needed.

Lastly—thank you, Mom and Dad and Reid and Katie. Thank you, thank you, thank you.

ABOUT THE AUTHOR

Grant Ginder is the author of *This Is How it Starts,* which was published by Simon & Schuster in 2009. He received his MFA from NYU and lives in New York City.